# HOUSE PARTIES

Also by Lynn Levin

Poetry

*The Minor Virtues*

*Miss Plastique*

*Fair Creatures of an Hour*

*Imaginarium*

*A Few Questions about Paradise*

Translation

*Birds on the Kiswar Tree: Poems by Odi Gonzales*

Nonfiction

*Poems for the Writing: Prompts for Poets*

(with Valerie Fox)

# HOUSE PARTIES

stories by

*Lynn Levin*

For Karolyn,
With warm wishes -
Party on!
Lynn
June 21, 2023

SPUYTEN DUYVIL
*New York Paris*

ISBN 978-1-959556-03-9
Cover art/design: t thilleman

Library of Congress Cataloging-in-Publication Data

Names: Levin, Lynn, 1953- author.
Title: House parties : stories / Lynn Levin.
Other titles: House parties (Compilation)
Description: New York : Spuyten Duyvil, [2023]
Identifiers: LCCN 2022053649 | ISBN 9781959556039 (paperback)
Subjects: LCGFT: Short stories.
Classification: LCC PS3562.E889645 H68 2023 | DDC
813/.54--dc23/eng/20221220
LC record available at https://lccn.loc.gov/2022053649

*For my family*

## Contents

# The Path to Halfway Falls

The mountain trail was steep, and the tansy scent of bear clover wafted through the April air. Chuck, Higby, and Dean set out at first light intending to head to a lookout over a valley. About an hour and a half into their trek, the three friends met a wide-eyed man and a dark-eyed woman descending the trail. The man, his voice breathy with excitement, told the three friends that he and the woman had seen an extraordinary sight: a slender waterfall not in the guidebooks or maps. This was Halfway Falls, a secret passed from hiker to hiker. Fed by snow melt and spring rains, Halfway Falls sent off veils of mist that looked like flying angels, and the stream of water was so thin that it evaporated before it reached the ground. That was why they called it Halfway Falls.

"You can always go to the lookout," said the man, who seemed to know where the men were headed and was, for some reason, addressing Dean in particular, "but you can only see Halfway Falls now."

"See it before it disappears," urged the woman, also eyeing Dean.

A secret place. Flying angels. A sight you could only see now. Dean could sense that the couple was exceptionally, almost preternaturally eager, and their enthusiasm inspired in him an overwhelming desire to see the awe-inspiring Halfway Falls.

Over the past year, twenty-eight-year-old Dean, a wallpaper hanger, had known much of duty and little of freedom and joy. He lived with his mother, who suffered from multiple sclerosis, and he was her main caregiver.

Higby and Chuck watched Dean's face. Dean's thin moustache moved like a subtitle from which they could almost read his inner debates.

"How long a hike?" asked Dean. His sister had grudgingly agreed to check in on their mother while Dean went to Yosemite. She also commanded that he be back home in Fresno by four-thirty. If he were late, there would be all sorts of consequences. It meant that the friends would have to leave the park by two o'clock.

The strangers assured him that Halfway Falls was not much farther than the lookout, only in a different direction. As they were speaking, a raven landed before them, strutted over, and cocked its head skeptically at the man and woman.

"We should do this, guys!" exclaimed Dean. "Seize the day." Dean's face glimmered. He was slightly pudgy with hazel eyes and rosy cheeks.

"Nothing ventured," said Higby, drawing his hand

through the blue-green streak in his hair. He was a barista at a Starbucks.

"How did *you* hear about the falls?" Chuck asked. He shifted a glance at the two strangers as if to spy some in-cahoots look between them.

"From other people on the trail," said the woman.

"It takes three hours to get to the look-out," said Chuck with a keen edge in his voice. "Did you guys start hiking at four o'clock in the morning, in the darkness? And what about those others? Did they start out at midnight?"

"I don't understand what you mean," replied the man with a blank expression.

Dean took the directions from the couple. They were to follow the present path up to a rock that looked like the famous comedian Bob Hope, turn left, and hike off trail through the forest; they weren't sure how far, maybe half a mile. Then they were to listen carefully for the sound of falling water. Owing to the slender stream of the falls, the sound was faint. Nearby was a rock outcropping that looked like a mountain lion with its mouth open. To see the falls, all you had to do was climb on top of the mountain lion rock and hang over on your stomach.

"Gotta see it to believe it," said the man.

"It's almost mystic," said the woman. The couple waved as they made their way down the path.

Dean glanced at his watch; it was just past eight o'clock. One who liked to be prepared, Dean wore a khaki vest with twenty or so pockets in which he slotted maps, a compass, binoculars, his wallet, car and house keys, hand sanitizer, pens and a small spiral notebook, cell phone and charger, a bear horn, a whistle, a box cutter, hard candies, a bandana, a Swiss Army knife, some nylon rope, the phone numbers of his mother's doctors, and, in the biggest square pocket, a ham sandwich, a PB&J, some cookies, and trail mix. Slung over his shoulder was a blue canteen. He took a swig of his water.

Dean looking pleadingly to Chuck, who served as their trail boss. The manager of a health club, Chuck was the most experienced hiker in the group and the fittest. He was in the habit of frequently checking his cell phone, and he wore touch-screen gloves that allowed him to text in the early morning chill. Dean and Higby knew that Chuck was involved with a woman who was not his wife, and on the long ride from Fresno to Yosemite, Dean at the wheel, Chuck and the woman had constantly texted each other.

"I'm doing this for you, Dean," said Chuck.

Dean thanked his friend. He felt his heart grow wings. Filled with anticipation, liberated, excited to be on his way to something marvelous, Dean at first found it easy to keep up. Chuck had picked up the pace to make sure they'd be back in time.

"Gentlemen," said Chuck. "I have to tell you this Halfway Falls thing is pretty high on my hooey meter. And that off-trail stuff sounds shady."

"It means going deeper into the wild," said Higby. "Of course, we came here for the wild." He tried to sound self-assured. "But they didn't tell us how far it was to the Bob Hope rock." Higby marched second in their single-file line. In his knapsack, he carried an excellent supply of canned drinks, along with a gourmet lunch prepared by his chef wife. The men had been friends since middle school, and Dean was the only one who did not have a woman in his life. His job, hanging wallpaper by himself all day in empty rooms, made him even lonelier.

Chuck turned around. "And they didn't tell us if the Bob Hope rock was big like a boulder or little like a regular head."

"I'll know it when I see it," said Dean with perfect faith.

"You'd better," said Chuck. His comment made Dean

feel sheepish and burdensome, but then Dean wondered if he had misread Chuck's tone.

"This will be cool for everyone," said Dean. He thought of his mother home alone. He hated the injustice of her condition, and he didn't fully trust his sister to attend to their mother's needs. A Steller's Jay winged by. All three turned to admire the bird's cyan-blue plumes and black-crested head.

Ponderosa pines and a few black oaks fringed the trail along with the bear clover and some manzanita bushes. Although all three wore hiking boots, each slipped every so often on crumbly path. Bird song rang out in the morning air. They kept an ear out for a growl or a rustle in the forest that might indicate a mountain lion or a bear.

Chuck glanced at his phone. "I can't get a signal up here," he groused. "No bars."

"Better not see any bars," joked Higby.

"I brought a bear horn," said Dean. "Why don't you put your phone away and enjoy nature."

"Because Feather is nature. Besides, the old ball and chain doesn't like it when I text Feather in front of her." A smirky smile turned his face askew.

"I wonder why," said Dean.

"Feather? Her name is Feather?" said Higby.

"That's her gym name. She's a yoga instructor." He elevated his eyebrows suggestively.

Dean disapproved of Chuck's cheating. Chuck's wife was a nice woman, not a hot yoga instructor, but still. Besides, it wasn't fair that Chuck should have two women while Dean didn't even have one. His last girlfriend had moved to Chicago a year ago, and his new attempts at relationships seldom got past the second date. The mom duty didn't help matters any. If only he could see those flying angels at Halfway Falls. The sight would be a vision to bolster his spirit, an inner touchstone he could turn to when shadowed by tedium and disappointment. But Dean was not as fit as Chuck or Higby, and he found himself panting and lagging behind.

Chuck halted before a rock formation that he said looked like a face. Although Dean was thankful for a chance to catch his breath, he said the rock was nothing special, just some random fractured granite. Then Higby found something that might have been a face, but Dean opined that it looked like a squirrel, not Bob Hope. Dean looked off in the distance and saw a smooth rounded rock that looked like the comedian's profile, but he shuddered to think that unapproachable stone was the marker they sought, so he said nothing about his observation.

If only that couple had given them some idea of distances. It was now just before ten, and Higby proposed that they break for their meal. They found a flat rock and laid out their spreads. Chuck, now gloveless, produced a liter of green Gatorade, a big bag of organic soy chips, and a giant meatloaf sandwich with ketchup. He chomped into the sandwich with his very white teeth. They contrasted with his perpetual tan. Dean started on his ham sandwich first. It was a little salty, so he alternated bites with swigs of water from his blue canteen. Higby, they agreed, had the best lunch of all, although it was a rather delicate affair. His chef wife had packed him pâté de campagne on French bread with a container of cornichons. Then there was an assortment of cheeses, a strawberry tart, and lots of little cookies. Higby drank his Starbucks canned coffees and complained about his wife's business hours. She had no time for him at all, working sixty hours a week, and even when she was off duty on Mondays, she was on call for menu planning, food ordering, and various staff crises.

Dean stuck up for Higby's wife. It wasn't her fault, he said. It was the job's fault.

"Maybe you should try a side dish," suggested Chuck with a leer. He set his half-eaten sandwich down to chug some Gatorade. Just then a raven, which might have been the raven they met earlier, landed. It glared at Chuck. Then with its huge iron beak, it snapped up what was left of the meatloaf sandwich.

"Fuck you, raven! Fuck you!" yelled Chuck as he shook his meaty fist at the big black bird. It flapped away in triumph.

Dean and Higby laughed, but they also made sure they held onto their food. Dean offered Chuck half his PB&J.

Higby said, "Sometimes my wife will call me at four or five and say, 'Hey, I'm getting out of work early. Want to see a movie?' And I know I should feel grateful and wanted, but then I get pissed that I'm at her beck and call."

"Think of that food she packed for you," said Chuck. "My wife can't cook for shit."

"You guys don't know how good you have it," said Dean. "I have to cook for my mom and help her in the bathroom."

"Sorry, man," said Chuck.

"That's a tough break," said Higby.

"I love my mom. But I'm trapped. Or loyal. I don't know." Dean looked up at the clear blue sky.

They carefully collected their trash and placed it in their knapsacks. Dean tucked his food wrappers into the sandwich pocket of his vest. Odd that no one else was on the trail. They were like explorers in the New World. The air was fresh, sweet, and clear. The day was warming up.

Chuck once again remarked that there was something about the couple that didn't add up. Higby allowed that might be so, but here they were in the wilderness in the midst of the wonders of nature. As far as he was concerned, the journey was the thing. The Sierra Nevadas were spectacular. They hardly needed to get to the lookout or Halfway Falls, for that matter. Three hawks wheeled overhead. Dean viewed them through his binoculars and offered his friends a look.

Soon they came to a bean-shaped rock that was much larger than a human head. From the center, protruded a thin shard with a dip in it.

"This must be the Bob Hope rock," said Dean. "See the big forehead, the ski-jump nose, the prominent chin?"

"Nah, that just looks like a sideways pumpkin. Nothing funny about that rock at all," said Higby.

Pointing out the features, Dean again made his case that this was the Bob Hope rock.

"More like Chris Rock," quipped Chuck. They all laughed. "No way is that Bob Hope. Let's keep going.

Dean, you're just seeing things because want to get to that bogus falls."

"It is not a bogus falls. Just hard to find. I'm sure that this is the landmark," Dean said, wishing he were as certain as he tried to sound. At that moment, a raven, certainly the one that had been following them, landed on the rock in question.

"Bad omen," said Higby.

"Fuck you, raven! Fuck you!" shouted Chuck, who tossed a pebble at the big bird. "You stole my meatloaf."

"Cut that out," said Dean. "Maybe it's a sign to us." The raven nodded toward Dean. "Ravens are smart." The raven nodded again.

"Well, if it's smart, maybe it's telling you to give up on the falls," said Higby.

Dean didn't appreciate Higby's and Chuck's negativism. He offered a few more reasons why this had to be the turning point. His voice grew vehement. The two other men looked startled by Dean's passion, then gave in with a conciliatory shrug.

"Well, if it means that much to you," said Higby.

As the strangers had directed, the three turned left at this rock and marched into the trackless forest. So that they wouldn't get lost on the way back, Dean marked their path with triangles of stones and sticks. After half an hour of hearing no water and seeing no mountain lion rock, he began to doubt the truth of Halfway Falls. He thought of Ponce de León searching for the Fountain of Youth and Coronado vainly seeking the Seven Cities of Cíbola. It was almost eleven, and they all knew that if the strangers had spoken with a speck of truth, they'd be at Halfway Falls by now.

The sound of a cracking branch interrupted their march. The friends froze, listening for the next sound. Again they heard the crack of wood. Then many cracks, heavier and nearer. The low grunt of a bear came from somewhere in the brush. The grunt squeezed their hearts with terror. Had the bear picked up the scent of their food? Had they entered the creature's space?

They knew to stand their ground and gathered together to form a bigger presence. Through the trees about twenty-five yards away, they saw a sow emerging with her cub. Her huffing was clearer now, and she swatted the ground with her paws. Dean could not see her claws, but he recalled pictures of people mauled by bears. The men began yelling to scare the bear away. They yelled as loud as they could. The sow turned to them in what they hoped was a bluff charge. Dean frantically tore through one pocket after another in search of the bear horn: bandana, pocket knife, flashlight, hard candies, hand sanitizer. Stupid vest! God damn vest! Cell phone charger. Maps. At last, fingers trembling, Dean found the horn. He shot the sound in the direction of the huge brown sow. Dean shot the sound again and again. The sow sniffed the air, hesitated, and then retreated with her cub.

The men embraced each other. Relief washed over them like a waterfall.

"Atta boy, Mr. Pockets," said Higby running his hand through his blue-green hair. Chuck shook his head in amazement and went in again to give Dean another hug.

Just for good measure, Dean shot off the bear horn again. He felt enormous.

The emotion wrung out of them, their thoughts, most likely, on things both near and far away, the friends silently headed back the way they came, carefully following the trail markers that Dean had laid down.

It was now past two o'clock, and Dean knew that he'd never make it back to Fresno by four-thirty. He wondered how often his sister checked in on their mom. He could see their mom in her chair, staring at the TV, her walker nearby. She could get around a little with the walker, but she needed help to rise from the chair to use the device. He hoped she hadn't fallen or peed herself. His sister might abandon their mom at four-thirty sharp if Dean failed to return by then. His sister was harsh that way. All about herself.

"Guys, we have to make tracks," Dean broke in. He thought of the ridiculous flying angels and the ridiculous evaporating waterfall. And how stupid he was to chase after the rapturous lie. "My mom, you know. My sister's not all that reliable."

"Heard," said Higby.

Dean thought it was very nice that none of the guys blamed him for blowing his own deadline. Or for coaxing them into the perilous wild. The three men picked up their pace. It was downhill, and the descent was not as taxing for Dean. As they strode, the raven came back to accompany them, part strutting, part hopping, sometimes flying low alongside them.

"We had a good adventure," said Chuck, who was no longer inclined to cuss out the raven. "I don't regret it at all. And you saved us from the bear. And blazed our trail."

"Yeah," said Higby. "This was way more fun than going to the lookout."

That enormous feeling filled Dean again. What power did his sister have over him, he who had driven off the bear, who had laid the trail markers, who had prepared and provided with his many pockets?

"You guys. I love you guys."

"Back at you," said Chuck.

"Ditto," said Higby.

When they were a quarter mile from the parking area, Chuck, Higby, and Dean met up with another party of hikers. One man in the group wore a red hunting cap.

"Have you heard of a place called Halfway Falls?" asked the man in the red cap.

"Yeah," said Dean. "We tried to find it. Never did. It's just a tall tale."

"Just because you didn't find it doesn't mean it doesn't exist. Where's the logic in that?" challenged the man. "We heard all about it. We heard it was a magical sight."

"Maybe you'll find it," said Dean, and he gave the man in the red hat the same directions he'd received from the awestruck couple.

"Who's Bob Hope?" queried the man with a squint. One of the women in his party said she knew what the old comedian looked like. Stoked with this measure of confidence, the group turned toward the trail.

"You've got a raven with you," said the man in the red hat looking back at them.

Chuck, Higby, Dean, and the big black bird continued to the car park. When they reached Dean's van,

Dean opened one of his pockets and offered the raven a morsel of leftover sandwich. The creature snapped it up and fixed Dean with a dark and respectful gaze. Then it took off flapping its mighty cape. Dean watched the raven until he could not see it anymore. He felt as though he could rise above almost anything.

# The Husband and the Gypsy

As it falls to many adult children these days, it was my duty—and particularly mine being an only child—to move my parents out of the home they'd lived in for the past forty years and into a retirement community. I'd taken three days off from my social work job in Binghamton to help them, and while I was feeling wistful about the big move, my parents anticipated their new adventure as if it were a 'round-the-world cruise.

"We can hardly wait, Warren," my mother bubbled over the phone. "They have a hundred discussion clubs and reading groups, and for Daddy a music room and residents' orchestra." The latter was crucial. It meant that my father, a concert violinist, would remain in the embrace of the musical life, able to play—as much as his arthritis would permit—and maybe give lessons, too.

It was early September. Dusk had settled in as I drove down the Northeast Extension of the Pennsylvania Turnpike toward Philadelphia. Scanning the radio stations, I chanced upon a broadcast of Bach's *Partita No. 2 in D Minor*. The violinist was in the final movement, the Chaconne, a piece that still makes me quiver with an old and disturbing memory. At that very moment, three deer—they were the same color as the dusk—stepped out of the woods along the highway. They caught my eye, then darted back into the trees. My mother, my father, and me, I mused. Odd that our familiars should appear as if called to Bach's Chaconne, for when I was a teenager I believed that the piece had preserved our family.

***

Our family's drama began on a warm spring afternoon in May of 1979 when I was fourteen. I came home from school a little earlier than usual, completely bummed out. I was supposed to be feeling like a big shot: my father would soon be guest performing at my junior high, but I'd been a disaster at orchestra practice that day. I'd lost my place during "String of Pearls." As usual, I squeaked, and I couldn't blame it on the clarinet either.

I pushed open our front door, startled to hear a violinist in the house whirling through one of Brahms's Hungarian dances. The music pouring from the kitchen pulled my mood up on magical strings. It made me think of barefoot girls in low-cut blouses, swishing their skirts of paprika red. My father seldom performed such fiery pieces, preferring the formal transcendence of the Baroque. Besides, Dad was on tour. He was almost always on tour.

Clarinet case in hand, backpack on my back, I stood just behind the opening between the dining room and the kitchen. Mom, still in her pink bow blouse from work, sat at the table. Across from her stood the violinist, a compact man slightly younger than Dad. A gypsy, I thought. I had a hunch that he was one of Mom's Russian immigrant clients; he wore a black pullover, a red vest, and striped bell-bottomed jeans. Something foreign accented his musical style. He swept the bow across the strings with more weight and physical contact than Dad or any other string player I'd heard. I watched the stranger sway and dip. The black ringlets of his hair flew as if in a storm. He kept trying to hook Mom in his gaze. The magical strings that had lifted me up went slack.

The gypsy didn't notice me at first, but Mom did, and a blush of self-consciousness colored her face. She held her mouth in a stiff half-smile. Every so often she looked up to meet the guy's stare, I guessed to make him feel appreciated, but most of the time she seemed to study her fingernails or wedding ring or the pearly gray Formica of the kitchen table. On the table sat two quilted jelly jars of tea and a little plate of sugar cubes. Two *glezelekh tey* as Grandma Sarah would have said, but the *glezelekh* were also strange. Our family drank tea from cups, not glasses, and we used little packets of Sweet 'n Low.

I knew the guy's Svengali stare because some of the goofs in my class tried it out on girls who responded with scrunched noses and crossed eyes. As fourteen-year-old boys went, I was pretty naïve and inclined to give people the benefit of the doubt, but I felt this guy was bad news and wanted him out of the house. Besides, I couldn't figure out why he was there alone with Mom. Was she auditioning him for something? I imagined launching him from the house kung-fu style. But I dared not disturb his play. I respected musical performance more than anything.

At last, the gypsy finished the piece with a big flourish. He bowed deeply to Mom in a European way. Just as he was about to kiss her hand, I coughed. Loudly. The gypsy straightened up. I will not forget his eyes; they were greenish gray, the color of the sea on a cloudy day. Not quite as Svengali as I had assumed.

"Warren, I'd like you to meet Boris Nalibotsky, one of our refuseniks," Mom announced in a formal tone. "Boris used to have a chair in a very distinguished chamber orchestra in Leningrad."

I said hello and shook hands with the gypsy. I noticed

that his hands seemed small. Boris fixed me with his oceanic eyes. I complimented him on his performance and the great position he'd held. Of course, I was impressed. A chamber orchestra in Russia was a big deal, but I still couldn't figure out why he was in our kitchen serenading Mom and drinking glasses of tea. Besides, after my crappy band practice, I wasn't in the mood to entertain a stranger, let alone a musician. I was in the mood for chicken and home fries and some good TV, like *Happy Days* or *M*A*S*H*.

Not that Russians in the house weren't a regular occurrence. Mom was a social worker at Hatikvah House, a refugee resettlement agency for Soviet Jews in Northeast Philadelphia. Since Brezhnev had liberalized Jewish emigration, business was booming at Hatikvah House, and Mom, being generous and also lonely with Dad on tour all the time, often invited her clients to our home. As much as I yearned for freedom for the Soviet Jews, I loathed my mother's acts of hospitality. I always ended up getting sucked into awkward phrasebook conversations with the refugees. Why couldn't home be just us? I was looking forward to Sunday when Dad would return and we could be just us, a family—at least until his next tour.

"Warren Rappaport," said Boris in a deep baritone. "I

khear so mahch about you." Peering at him through my aviator-style glasses, I wondered how it was that I'd been a topic of their conversation. We chatted briefly about me and the clarinet, which was the last thing I wanted to talk about. Aside from his heavy accent, Boris spoke excellent English.

"I'm just a recreational player," I said, secretly fearing I might not even amount to that. "Nothing like my father. He's a virtuoso violinist. In the Rydal String Quartet." Mom aimed a crossbow stare at me.

Boris nodded in solemn acknowledgment and seemed to shrink for a split second. Then he brought himself back with a bright look. "Such a good boy this is, Leeendah." He tousled my longish hair. I recoiled at his touch. "One day we play duet, no?" That's right, I thought, no. But I mumbled some sort of feeble consent.

As Boris nestled his violin carefully in its old-fashioned figure-shaped case, I noticed with sorrow its scuffs and scratches. A poor immigrant, he had to make do with a beat-up, second-hand violin. The instrument seemed forlorn, not at all like Alma, Dad's gleaming Sergio Peresson. I wondered if the gypsy would find work as a musician in America or if he'd need to train for a new job like so many of the refugees did. I didn't like him invading our nest, but I didn't want his talent and training to go to waste either.

"It's not like he's an engineer," said Mom after Boris had left. She sipped her hot tea old-new style from a jelly jar. I noticed she was wearing red lipstick. "Boris is an artist. He has a deep soul." She sounded dreamy when she said that. I didn't get it. She was already married to an artist. A better one, in fact. And a better looking one whose group made recordings that got played on the radio. "Well, not that engineers don't have souls," Mom backtracked, "but you know what I mean. It's different for artists."

"Boris is a weird gypsy," I said. "He reminds me of those strolling minstrels in a restaurant that pour on the schmaltz, then eye you until you give them a tip. It's bad enough that you bring the couples home, but him?" I couldn't wait for Dad to come home. "Don't you think you're overdoing it with the cause?"

Now, I was no slouch when it came to activism. I'd written letters to refuseniks (like they ever got them), collected signatures on petitions, babysat for immigrant parents while they went to English classes, and, of course, I did a twinned bar mitzvah with a Soviet Jewish kid. Dad played his part, too. Once he brought tears to people's eyes when he performed Bloch's "Nigun" at a Free Soviet Jewry rally. Our family's fellow feeling for the Soviet Jews ran deep: we would have been Soviet Jews—well, we would have been lucky to have been Soviet Jews—if my great great grandparents hadn't escaped from Tsarist Russia. But neither Dad nor I consecrated our lives to the cause. Mom, on the other hand, pledged her nights and days to it. Looking back, I think that in her soul she was a refusenik.

Mom gave me a hot-eyed look and ladled out Boris's story like boiling chicken soup. Naturally the chamber orchestra fired him the second he'd requested his exit visa. It was official procedure. And then the same government that had him fired accused him of being a social parasite because he didn't have work! Typical twisted Soviet logic. And they'd confiscated his violin. That was standard procedure, too. Why allow a rebel musician to keep his cherished violin? The poor man scraped together a living giving music lessons. Practically a fiddler on the roof. "You don't know what I went through to find him that violin," she said yanking the key of the can opener.

I was feeling pretty rotten about Boris's plight and my lack of compassion and regretting laying it on thick to him about the great Mark Rappaport. Then when I thought things couldn't get any worse for the poor guy, they did.

"And on top of all this," said Mom, "Boris Nalibotsky's wife Yelena died of cancer before he came over. Can you imagine the heartbreak? All those dreams..." Mom's voice turned wistful and trailed off. She brushed her bangs off her forehead. I thought I saw a wisp of gray in her hair.

"I hope he finds a nice single lady," I said. "Maybe you could fix him up with someone." Mom shrugged.

"You don't need to mention this to Dad," said Mom offhandedly as she opened another can. "He thinks I get too involved with my clients, and he's got enough on his plate as it is." I looked down at my Manwich on bun and Green Giant green beans.

"Speaking of plates, Mom," I began but stopped it there. She brought out some potato chips to make it a balanced meal.

They were a pair my folks, each carrying on a separate romance: Mom with her mission to save the Jews, Dad with the elegant structures of his music and Alma, the Sergio Peresson violin he preferred even over the Guarneri a patron had offered to lend him.

Mom had done such a good job of guilting me about Boris that the next day, a Saturday blanketed with rain clouds, I roused myself from bed at the ridiculous hour of 8 a.m. to help her pick up donations for the immigrants. My mother collected clothing, dishes, linens, appliances, and toys from folks who were only too happy to declutter for a good cause. Our car loaded with boxes and bags, we made it to Hatikvah House by noon. And not a moment too soon: a bolt of lightning and a thunderclap announced us.

"I have a surprise for you," said Mom. A talent show, Mom called it a salon, was in progress in the social room. In spiraling tones, a man was declaiming a poem. People sipped tea, from Styrofoam cups not *glezelekh*, and noshed on sweets. Mom's clients waved me their greetings, and she bustled off somewhere. Relieved not to see Boris Nalibotsky, I wandered over to the spread of Russian goodies: a box of assorted chocolates and a vanilla torte. The snacks helped, but a grumpy mood was on me like smog. I had to practice my clarinet, a math quiz was breathing down my neck, and Odysseus demanded that I read about his exploits for Monday's mythology test. Held hostage at Hatikvah House, I silently steamed at Mom for costing me a Saturday.

I settled back in one of the folding chairs. After the poetry recitation, another man entered the performance circle and strummed some songs on a guitar. Then the gypsy—I guess he'd been tuning his violin in a back-room—emerged with my mother. A few of the Russians flicked a quick glance their way. I felt embarrassed and tricked. Mom hadn't mentioned that Boris would be at the party. Something about the way they entered the room made them seem like a couple. A sick vision of the gypsy as my stepfather and me living with Dad, alone most of the time while he toured, shrouded my future.

Boris, in his red vest, strode to the center of the circle and sliced into a folk tune, again with his heavy style of bowing. And again, as in our kitchen, he turned half musician, half magician. The humor and joy of his music blew away my clouded mood. Launched by the folk melody, two men jumped into a vigorous kazatsky, circling each other as they kicked. Rhythmic clapping broke out. Mom joined in, clapping like a regular Russian. In the moment, I found it hard to hate Boris. Then he began another folk dance, one less wild than the first, a type of circle dance that brought a group of men and women to the floor. A moment of sadness, a far-away look, passed over a few faces.

After Boris's set, a woman entered the performance circle and began to sing. I watched Mom and the gypsy disappear together down a hall. Once more, embarrassment warmed my cheeks. I felt unmanned somehow, part of my parentage stripped away. When Mom reappeared about ten minutes later, sans Boris, her hair a little mussed, her face dimmed with self-consciousness and maybe shame, I couldn't meet her eyes. Mom no longer seemed like Mom. Was she going to run off with him? When I thought of my mother in the arms of that gypsy, my chest tightened with a kind of anxiety I hadn't known before. I guess it was the way kids felt when they heard their parents were going to divorce. By a sheer act of will, I forced myself to stop thinking about Mom and Boris. We rode home together in silence, each of us staring straight out the windshield. I didn't know what I should do or say, or if I had the power to do anything at all.

When Dad came home Sunday evening from the Rydal's West Coast tour, I was curled on the couch reading about the return of Odysseus to Ithaca and Penelope's greedy suitors. I thought of patient pining Penelope. Well, it wasn't like my mom had to wait twenty years for her man to come home. I jumped up to help Dad with his suitcase while Mom stayed in her chair, afloat in a daydream, a Boris-inspired glass of tea in her hand.

"Hey, Mom, Dad's back!" I tried to nudge her from her trance with a peppy tone.

"Don't trouble yourself," said Dad. He ran his hand through his hair as if to massage away his annoyance. "I've only been away for the last six days playing my heart out and trying to earn a living." A tension line ran up my forehead. Dad had a steady temperament, but I couldn't blame him for feeling miffed, rejected even, by Mom's non-greeting. Because of Dad's many absences, I sympathized with Mom in a dozen ways, but now she was acting plenty weird, almost as if it didn't matter whether Dad stood there or not. I knew that Dad's travels wore her down. She didn't like playing second fiddle to Dad's fiddle or being abandoned in Northeast Philly while the Rydal String Quartet pursued perfection coast to coast. Some folks joked that Mom lived like an army wife and poked me on the shoulder saying, Warren, you're the man around the house. You look out for your Mom.

In retrospect, I think my father found it easier and more gratifying to live for Alma than for a real woman. How ennobling it must have been to interpret the very greatest music for the most cultured audiences, to perceive their delight, to cast a spell over their hearts. Art was a high calling, but to make art so much life had to be pushed aside.

"Hi, welcome home," Mom said, breaking through her torpor. She lifted her face to Dad. He walked a few paces to her and plunked a kiss, a disappointing kiss, I thought, on her forehead.

"What is that? Canadian Club?" he observed with an odd look at the jelly jar.

"It's tea," said Mom. "Russian style."

"Isn't that a dumb way to drink a hot liquid?" asked Dad. "Doesn't it burn your fingers?" Mom put down the tea and went to the laundry room to wash the clothes Dad had unpacked.

"What's gotten into your mother?" Dad asked me once we were alone in the living room. Dad glanced at a photo that hung above the piano. It was a black and white picture snapped after a recital. Dad, holding Alma in one hand, wore a tuxedo. Mom, glowing and beautiful in a long formal dress, stood at his other side.

"Heck if I know," I answered hoping not to sound false, wishing I could come up with a way to bring Mom to her senses.

"Anyhow, Warren," said Dad, "that music assembly of yours is the week after next, and I'm thinking of playing Bach's Chaconne." He saw my eyebrows levitate. "I'll be performing the *Partita Number 2 in D Minor* for a solo concert at Penn, and since I'm rehearsing it, well…" A little smile sparked the corner of Dad's mouth. He drew out the *well* to relish the excited look on my face. "You know the Chaconne, don't you? The piece Bach composed in memory of his first wife?"

Of course, I knew the Chaconne! It was the Everest of the solo violin repertoire, a competition piece. Its chord progression and elaborate variations called on every aspect of violin playing. Through its gorgeous depths, Bach explored the most profound territories of love and grief. My father would play this masterwork for the kids at Neil A. Armstrong Junior High. I felt like the son of the hero. And Mr. Casey, the music teacher, would flip.

"Mom will be at the assembly, won't she?" Dad asked.

"She'll be there. Unless she's not too busy being a cosmonaut." We shared a sardonic chuckle.

That night I couldn't sleep. Anticipation and pride about the music assembly kept clashing with dread about the state of my parents' marriage. To make the most of my insomnia, I decided to study for the next day's test on the Odyssey and soon came upon the portion in which Penelope, alone on the island of Ithaca and thinking her husband would never return home from Troy, devises an archery contest to defeat her many suitors. I read of Telemachus setting up the twelve axes through whose handle sockets only Odysseus could drive an arrow.

Then I saw it. A contest of strings and bow. Violin

strings and horsehair bow.

My father was Odysseus. Boris one of the suitors. My mother, though susceptible to temptation, was Penelope. I, as Telemachus, would set up the contest: I would make the music assembly a competition of strings and bow between my father and Boris, a match that my father would surely win. Mom would swoon over the Chaconne. Dad would defeat the gypsy. And Boris would be run out of our lives. I hoped it would not be too difficult to convince Mr. Casey to add Boris to the assembly program.

I felt like a genius and thanked old Homer. For a few seconds, I kept my hand on my paperback copy of the Odyssey, drawing power from it.

Monday couldn't dawn soon enough for me. Eager to launch my plot, I shook off my insomnia hangover. I aced the mythology test and could hardly wait for after-school orchestra practice.

I knew that Mr. Casey was a fervent anti-Communist, and I aimed to make that work in my favor. I arrived at the music room several minutes before the kids started drifting in. Even today, I can see the flocks of black music stands and gray folding chairs, the posters of musical terms and acoustic tiles on the walls, Mr. Casey's piano, and the busts of Bach, Mozart, Beethoven (who always seemed to be scowling). The scents of rosin and valve oil come back to me, the metallic tang of the brass instruments, the mossy feathery smell of the instrument cases. And the tuning up, that cacophonous collage of student sounds. But at the moment, only Mr. Casey and I stood in the room.

"Could I talk to you about something?" I began to perspire. The teacher looked at me as if I were about to spill something personal. I told him of Boris Nalibotsky, the extraordinary refugee violinist, the former concertmaster of the distinguished Leningrad Chamber Orchestra. Boris, I declared, was a protégé of my father's, and I asked, I begged Mr. Casey to add Boris to the music assembly. He would play something exciting, a piece of five minutes or less, and it was all perfectly okay with my dad. "When you think of all that talent locked behind the Iron Curtain, Mr. Casey," I said gazing at his American flag lapel pin, "and how so many Soviet artists must defect to be free..." Seeing that Casey was mulling things over, I stopped chattering for a moment. I'd made up the stuff about the protégé (well, the gypsy was Mom's protégé), Dad's approval, the concertmaster thing, and maybe even the official name of the orchestra. But Odysseus had lied a lot, too, so I figured it was okay to do for a good cause. The teacher shuffled some sheet music on his conductor's stand. I told him how the Soviet government had fired Boris from the chamber orchestra for being a dissident, took his violin away, charged him with social parasitism. "He's really been a victim of the Communist state, Mr. Casey," I said.

"How does your family know this violinist?" Mr. Casey sought my gaze. He had reddish brown eyebrows that reminded me of paintbrushes. I explained about Mom's social work with new immigrants.

The kids in the orchestra were taking their seats and opening up their instrument cases. "Okay, we can add Mr. Nal... Mr. Nab... Boris to the program," consented Mr. Casey. "As long as you can set it up, Warren. It's a go from this end." Electrified with joy, I thanked Mr. Casey at least five times. If only I could have honored him by playing better at practice. At last, my lack of sleep caught up with me and turned my mouth to rubber. I squeaked so much that the French horn player joked about a mouse in the house. And one girl climbed on her chair pretending to be afraid of the mouse. I had to admit that the cut-up stuff was pretty funny, and, anyhow, inside I felt like a dynamo. Then the challenge of inviting Boris to the contest of strings and bow clunked me on the head. If Mom found out before the assembly, she would surely try to talk

Boris out of performing or she'd boycott the assembly altogether. All this, on top of the tricky business of getting in touch with Boris.

When I arrived home, I found a note on the kitchen table and the scent of Mom's perfume in the air.

*Out to dinner with Daddy. Back around eight. Order yourself a pizza from Salvatore's.*

The note turned me into a grinning doofus. My parents were in love with each other. I had nothing to worry about after all. I ordered a mushroom pizza with extra cheese and considered telling Mr. Casey that Boris had backed out. Then even through my fatigue-addled brain, I realized that such a cancellation would be an insult to Mr. Casey. It would make the Rappaports look like schmucks and Boris like an ingrate. Boris may have been a lot of things, but he'd never back out of an opportunity to play. I would have to hunt down the guy's phone number and invite him.

I could not find any Nalibotskys in the White Pages and 411 had no listing for any either. Then I noticed, behind an easy chair near the piano, my mother's canvas attaché, the bag she took to work. Perhaps the gypsy's phone number was in there. Rummaging through the side pocket, I came up with pens, a lipstick, a comb, a collapsible umbrella, a receipt for shampoo from Thrift Drug, an accordion of assorted business cards, the Rydal String Quartet's concert schedule, keys, Kleenexes, an old raffle ticket, and some hard candies. In an outside zippered compartment, I found a yellow legal pad. Mom's field notes. Maybe Boris's number was there.

The notes fascinated me. Ioffe the dentist from Odessa was applying for work as a dental hygienist, and Sarah Dolinsky, the math teacher, found a job stocking shelves in a grocery store. M. L. Feldman, an engineer, was painting houses. I lost track of the time as I read their stories. Still, I found nothing of Boris. On the wall by the easy chair hung a photo of the four Rydal guys. They watched my every move.

The doorbell rang. In panic, I went klutzy. The yellow legal pad flew out of my hands like a canary. Trembling, I shoved it back into the bag, bending a few of the pages. I melted with relief to find the pizza guy at the door.

I scarfed a slice of pizza, washed the grease off my hands, and returned to my investigations. I pulled out Mom's calendar book and paged through the entries. On one of the pages for early March, I found the first mention of Boris Nalibotsky and his phone number. Bingo. I wrote the number on my hand with one of Mom's pens. Then I noticed a pink marble composition book and opened it. Pages and pages were covered in my mother's script. It was her diary. I hadn't known she'd kept one.

The diary began in January of 1979. Mom mused about Jimmy Carter and cheered the Rydal String Quartet's newest recording. She wrote, nearly obsessively, of Avital Shcharansky, the wife of the famous refusenik Anatoly Shcharansky, and of how the dark-eyed young bride traveled the globe pleading for her husband's release.

Then Mom jotted a funny story about a woman who was trying to coax her into hosting a Tupperware party and recounted a quarrel she and Dad had about his time away. Following that, more about Avital. Always Avital. It was as if Mom envied her suffering, the romance of her separation from Anatoly. Not that Mom wasn't in awe of Mark Rappaport. She carefully listed the Rydal's engagements in cities large and small, jotted Dad's comments about audience reception, noted the critics' reviews. She wrote of her own lonely nights and worried about how she'd cope if I went away to college instead of going to Drexel or Temple. I had some qualms about the snooping, but my curiosity about Mom's inner life compelled me to read on.

I took a break, ate another slice of pizza, again carefully washed my hands, and returned to the pink composition book. In early March as in the calendar book, the gypsy's name began to ink the pages of the diary.

*Boris Nalibotsky came to us this week, a widower and a violinist with no violin.*

From then on it was as if my mother could write of almost nothing else. Even Avital made fewer appearances in her journal. She recounted whole conversations with Boris. They spoke about Shostakovich, Stravinsky, and Ysaÿe, of Soviet propaganda, the dissidents Bonner and Sakharov and Slepak. How odd, she noted, that she was more political than Boris. Then Three Mile Island happened, and Mom wrote of her terror of a nuclear meltdown. But soon it was back to Boris: his late Yelena, the Nalibotskys who fought in the war and those who perished in the Holocaust. Avital, though less of a presence, never entirely disappeared from Mom's thoughts. Boris couldn't understand Mom's romantic fascination with Avital. "She's like some kind of fairy tale princess for you," he said. "But I'm here. You have your own Anatoly. That's me."

A sour entry followed: Mom found Boris's comment presumptuous, a mockery of the cause. I agreed.

Mom noted several calendar days in April and May, but nothing about their significance. Gaps appeared in the diary. And scratch-outs.

"I want to say yes, but I want to say no a hundred times more," she wrote. "And I super hate it when he speaks of Mark!"

I glanced at the clock. It was almost seven-thirty. Suspicion gathered like a lump in my throat. I didn't want to keep reading, but to stop would have been cowardly, like turning off the TV when bad news came on.

In America, the land of his dreams, Boris fretted about his future in music. So much competition, so many talented violinists. He worried that he'd chosen freedom over art and sometimes doubted his choice. Mom tried to buck him up. This was America, the *goldene medina*, the new promised land, the place of opportunity.

Then she recounted a coworker reminding her not to get involved with clients.

"That would be a hoot," Mom wrote. "Losing my job while trying to get one for him."

I don't know why losing her husband hadn't occurred to her in the same moment.

Today, I know of several marriages murdered by the written revelations of extra-marital passion: diary entries, text messages, emails, love letters. And to this day, I do not know why my mother, my smart, pretty, serious mother, risked so much by committing her relationship with Boris to that stupid pink marble composition book. Yet in another way, I understand her desire to preserve on the page, as if in amber, those moments of vividness and intensity.

I could tell that Mom wanted to back out of the relationship. It was more than she bargained for. And she was beginning to suspect, maybe rightly, maybe not, that Boris, though certainly a talented musician, might also be an opportunist who saw in this idealistic daughter of the free world a lucky stepping-stone. On top of all that, he might have loved her. How terribly lonely he must have been.

I shut the notebook. I can still hear its soft cardboard clap. I went to the kitchen to call Boris. From there, I'd be able to hear my parents come in the front door and hang up in a flash. I'd leave no trace. There was no caller ID or *69 back then. I looked at my hand. With a growl, I saw that I'd washed off Boris's number. Burning precious moments, I ran back to Mom's attaché and flipped through the calendar book, rewrote the number on my hand then, with a racing heart, dialed up the gypsy.

Boris's phone rang. After six rings, an answer machine came on with Boris's outgoing message in Russian. I hung up and tried every few minutes. At 7:50, knowing my folks could walk in at any second, I called for the twelfth time. Boris picked up. We exchanged halting hellos.

"I thought you deedn't lahk me," said Boris.

"I'm just a moody teenager," I replied, hoping my voice didn't sound shaky. "Listen, Boris, our junior high is having a music assembly next week, and Mr. Casey, the teacher, asked me to invite you. It's great that you play for the people at Hatikvah House, but you really deserve more exposure."

"Warren, this eez big honor," said Boris. "Tank you. This eez dyn-o-mite."

"Dyn-o-mite," I echoed and gave him Mr. Casey's phone number and the rest of the particulars.

"There's just one thing. You can't say a word about this to Mom. I want it to be a big surprise for her." Boris seemed confused but consented. At least he didn't ask me how I found his phone number.

Having Dad back in the house for those ten days was like a pleasure trip to the land of ordinary life. My father spent his time rehearsing and giving lessons. He even did a little yard work. His solo concert at Penn, the one at which he performed Bach's *Partita Number 2 in D Minor*, received a rave review in *The Philadelphia Inquirer*, and I knew he'd wallop Boris with the Chaconne at next Wednesday's music assembly. Although Mom continued her habit of sipping hot tea from jelly jars, she at least kept normal hours. It amused me to think that she, Dad, and Boris went about their business, unaware of my machinations. It never occurred to me that anyone would be angry at me afterward.

The day of the contest of strings and bow, we three Rappaports arrived at Neil A. Armstrong Junior High slightly late, delayed by unexpected traffic. Dad dressed in his typical concert attire, a black open-collar shirt with a charcoal-gray jacket. Mom wore a flowered skirt that Dad always liked.

Boris, clad in his red vest and some kind of big-collared shirt, was already seated when we entered the auditorium. He looked more like a gypsy than ever. When Mom saw him, her face went as holey as a Greek mask. Perplexed by her reaction, Boris attempted a hesitant smile, but Mom's face stayed masklike, and a wounded look drifted over Boris's sea-gray eyes. Dad, who was busy greeting Mr. Casey and tuning up Alma, saw nothing of the exchange. The room was loud with student chatter. The whole junior high was gathered in the auditorium. I could tell that the kids were very impressed to see me seated with my mom and famous dad.

Mr. Casey called for quiet and introduced the two violinists. When Mr. Casey announced that Mark Rappaport had taken the accomplished refugee under his wing, Dad tipped his head as if he hadn't heard right. Then Casey mentioned my helpful role, and Dad and Mom swiveled their regards upon me like two tanks aiming their guns.

Boris, being the warm-up act, took the stage first. He announced that he would play Fritz Kreisler's "La Gitana," the Gypsy Woman, and that Mr. Casey would accompany him on the piano.

Boris threw himself into his performance, whetting his bow across the strings in his dense Eastern Bloc style of playing. "La Gitana" was a short piece of three minutes or so, and it flowed from sweetness and tenderness to moments of gaiety and prancing. As Boris played, I could see a gypsy woman dancing by a campfire. Then the music grew into passionate, rose-in-the-teeth stuff, and Boris played it hot and heavy, fully present, knives flashing, flinging his curly hair this way and that. Once or twice, he winked at me as he played. I smiled and nodded, urging him on. He tried to catch my mother's eye, and though he failed at that, he had the audience firmly in his grip. He ended the piece with a flourish, thrusting his bow in the air like a victor would his sword. The kids applauded wildly. The teachers even louder. A few even shouted *bravo!*

When my father stood to play the Chaconne, I felt some trepidation. After all, the Bach was a longer piece, and it did not aim to wow like the Kreisler. But as my father dipped his bow into the golden well of Bach's chord progression and explored its complex variations, as he let the music plunge into the deepest pools of grief, I saw my mother's face transformed. My father drew from Alma a light and illuminated sound, very different from the gypsy's. Through the music, I could hear Bach cry out: *Oh beloved wife, why have you been taken from me?* The music sped up. It slowed down. It waterfalled over double stops and triple stops. It glided through realms of the ineffable. Although my father stood there and played, it was as though he were not there. Nor was my mother. Each seemed changed, their individual selves burned off by the music as if by refiner's fire. When my father drew the Chaconne down to its gossamer close, the students and teachers paused in silence. Only when my father took his second bow, did applause, reverent applause, break out.

My mother's face streamed with tears. Awestruck and vanquished, Boris appeared a shrunken soul. As Odysseus, my father had triumphed. He had regained his Penelope. Mom, however, would not look me, her cunning Telemachus. My parents left together, and I stayed behind to finish the day at school. It took several days before my mother would meet my eyes.

As the students exited the auditorium, I saw Mr. Casey enfold Boris with a fraternal arm. In July, I learned that Boris Nalibotsky no longer lived in Philadelphia. Mr. Casey had arranged an audition for him with the Lancaster Symphony Orchestra. The orchestra had hired him, and Boris Nalibotsky moved to Amish country. I believe that this was my first act as a social worker.

Upon my return from school, I had intended to tear out the incriminating pages in my mother's diary, but, search as I might, I could not find the guilty notebook. The next day, taking out the trash, I saw its pink marble cover through the white kitchen garbage bag. Rarely since have I known such peace.

Over time, I concluded that my mother never slept with Boris Nalibotsky. To be sure, there was necking and maybe a little more, but I always had the notion that the hundred no's she'd talked about meant a specific kind of no.

***

My parents were standing out in their front yard as I pulled up to the house. Mom, now very gray but still trim and attractive—you would call her a handsome woman—wore a pink T-shirt and a pair of pink-and-green flowered shorts. Dad, who looked merry but somewhat crouched, also wore a pink T-shirt. They looked like they were on the same team in their twin get-ups, though thankfully Dad wasn't wearing pink-and-green flowered shorts.

My mother and father have come to fit better into each other's lives. Sometimes they even seem like sweet-hearts, gifting each other with little compliments, deftly avoiding quarrels, relishing the little pleasures of togetherness. Hand in hand, they face the deaths of friends, the encroaching shadows, but also the *vita nuova* of the retirement community with all the cock-tail hours, clubs, the residents' orchestra, and the music room. Someone said that marriage is better after the first thirty years, and maybe that is so. If I ever marry, I might one day find that out for myself.

The kitchen was packed up, and I wondered if Mom

and Dad had donated their excess goods to Hatikvah House, which now served immigrants of many nations. I wondered where Boris Nalibotsky was, and if I should Google him to find out.

Oh, my fourteenth year. The year of Boris and Mom. The strangest year of my life, the one that stands a statue's head taller than all the rest. It was the first year I made a difference, the year I saved the family—or, at least, I thought I did.

On my way to Pho Palace to pick up Vietnamese takeout, I passed many billboards and shop signs for Russian restaurants, appliance stores, and dress shops. Perhaps I generalize, but these days the Russians I see in the neighborhood look fashionable and buff. In the *goldene medina*, the post-Soviets have taken to upward mobility in a big way.

Over a dinner of spring rolls, pho tai nam soup, and grilled chicken with rice, my parents spoke excitedly about their new apartment. "A two-bedroom model, Warren, with a guest room for you." That night I slept in my childhood room, in my old twin bed for the last time. It was like sleeping in the arms of a younger brother, or maybe the arms of my old self. Not that I hadn't stayed over countless times before, but this last night was different, a little sweet, a little sad. I dreamed about the three deer I'd seen on the turnpike when the Chaconne came on the radio. In my dream, the deer materialized in our living room. They caught my eye and sniffed the air, and I worried that they might run around the house and hurt themselves. But no harm came. They dissolved into a foggy part of my dream. And then I woke up.

# Tell Us about Your Experience

Jim Gulliford, wearing a white shirt and a slightly frayed blue tie, signed onto his computer at Union Analytics. As usual, surveys swarmed his inbox, all due ASAP: a Qualtrics about yesterday's meeting, a Doodle poll about the next meeting, a performance review for the new intern, an obligatory eval of an outside vendor with two dozen questions—this one even demanded that everyone rate the layout of the report, the background colors, and the size and font of the type. Every time Gulliford hit save, the vendor survey crashed, forcing him to start all over again.

Thirty-six and single, Jim had the face of a man seen from a distance, the face of a man in a crowd. Bartenders overlooked him. When raising his hand at meetings, he was ignored. On the plus side, because he blended in, panhandlers left him alone, and he could tailgate after others at keycard access doors. One of several data entry techs at Union, Gulliford spent his days in his cubicle, hands to keyboard, nose to screen, pumping numbers to analysts, who sat at nicer desks on better chairs and earned enough to buy themselves condos.

With all the busy work and make-work of surveys, when did the company expect him to do his job, which this week was logging in data about the sales of men's socks? No-show socks, athletic socks, mid-calf socks, and over-the-calf socks, with notably few sales for the over-the-calf kind. Then on to sock materials, then the styles: solids, bold solids, stripes, argyles, novelty patterns, and such. Really, quite a lot to men's socks. He glanced down at his own socks, which were gathering around his ankles on their way to bunching under his heels.

These days, you couldn't buy a bottle of booze or ask to have your modem reset without some wheedling robot pecking at you for praise: "Tell us about your experience," "Take a few minutes to help us serve you better," "Rate your satisfaction," "Write a review, "How are we doing?" And forget anonymous. Once Gulliford gave his banker an unsatisfactory review, and the next day the guy phoned to guilt him for costing him a bonus. This very morning, his cell phone lit up with a text message, but it wasn't from the woman he'd met at the singles volleyball meet-up. It was Frank's Service Center wanting to know how he felt about the repair they'd done on his vacuum cleaner. He respected (or maybe feared) the imperative and the interrogative, and he had an odd sense that the survey powers, like street cameras, were watching him. Therefore, he followed orders. Also, he liked to be helpful. There was that. Still, as he did his duty and filled out the surveys, he sometimes hated himself for wasting his time, his intellect, his freedom.

The hushed music of the office—soft clicks of typing and the fragments of muffled conversation— kept up its steady cadence. Barging into this came growls from Jim's stomach. No time to fix his breakfast today. Answering the vacuum cleaner repair survey sucked up all his time. He had to dash into a quick mart next to the office to pick up breakfast. As he toiled at the morning's surveys (sometimes ten meant worst, sometimes ten meant best), his Danish sweated in its cellophane, and his coffee, which was end-of-the-pot sludge to begin with, cooled to tar. Starving, his concentration interrupted by his gurgling gut, Gulliford plugged away at the latest time-sensitive survey, hoping eventually to get around to the Danish and the hosiery project. He glanced lovingly at the framed photo of Amber, his cat. She shed quite a bit, so the vacuum repair meant a lot to him.

As he selected the radio buttons, typed in his comments, and advanced through the screens, Jim's brain wandered to the more pleasant subject of socks. He wondered if the client, the American Consortium of Hosiery Informatics, had annual conventions where everyone showed off their socks. Did the companies have parties, and did they call them sock hops? Did they have holiday celebrations with contests for the best-decorated Christmas stockings? And did they have a podiatrist on retainer?

An email alert chimed: the deadline for the socks data was 3:30 p.m., which he very well knew, and he suspected that he might have to skip lunch in order to finish his project. He hadn't even had time to try the unappetizing Danish. Was it to be a day of fasting? A person could waste away.

After finishing the first several surveys, some imp inside Gulliford made him close the outside vendor survey (it was his third go) and delete the email that sent it. What a jolt he got hitting the delete key. He felt himself launched into a foreign space, exciting, scary, and free. Would management notice his rebellion? Would they even care? He thought about the watchful survey powers, then glanced at Amber, who gave him a supportive look.

Jim felt self-conscious about his sagging socks. He bent down to hike them up, frayed tie dangling.

Wham! His dipping motion upset the mechanism of his chair. The seat plunged. Something under the chair snatched the end of his tie and snagged him in a stranglehold.

Struggling for air, unable to speak, Jim gagged out *arggh* and then a tracheal *uhhh uhhh*. He smacked his desk and choked out a few muffled cries. With his waning strength, he again smacked the top of his desk.

"All good?" chirped Lora, the admin, from the other side of the partition. "What's all the racket?"

No, he wasn't all good. He was all bad. All dying. *Uhhh uhhh*, he tried the tracheal sound again. Life force ebbing, he clutched his tie and tipped himself all the way over so as to crash to the floor and make more noise. He lay on his side struggling for air, trying to skootch toward the chair to give his noose some slack.

"Good God," shrieked Lora, who came running with scissors and saved his life by cutting his tie in half. Jim rolled over gasping, the amputated neckwear lolling like a blue tongue in the chair works. His coworkers gathered around as he tried to catch his breath. Jeff from IT unbuttoned Gulliford's shirt collar, unknotted his tie, and chucked the garrote in the trash.

Jim didn't want to cry, but he felt like crying. Still gasping and hoarse from the trauma, he coughed his heartfelt thanks to Lora and Jeff. Now, there were two people who deserved great evals. He was amazed that Lora, whom he took for a dimwit, came running with scissors, which in this case was a totally genius thing to do. How life did surprise. Imagine dying in the office strangled by your tie. So different from wasting away in a cheap nursing home as he expected to do. Gulliford managed to stagger away from the chair, which he thought might snap at him again. Then he looked down at his troublemaking socks. What was that old saying, for the want of a horseshoe nail? He realized, as never before, the importance of quality men's hosiery. Jeff helped him to a spare chair, a traditional one, without mechanics. Someone brought over a cup of water.

Presently, Bronwen from HR came by. She had dark red nail polish with a white flourish on one of her nails. Jim hated her. She gazed at him with a prosecutor's eye, not a shred of sympathy or human kindness in her. She posed most of her questions in the negative. He wasn't injured was he? He didn't need to go to the hospital did he? He could tell that she wanted to dodge a worker's comp claim or trouble with OSHA. He doubted that she would ask operations to buy a new chair or talk to legal about suing the chair company or do whatever companies did when a guy nearly got killed by a piece of office furniture. She called someone to help Gulliford find a new cubicle. The chair lay on the floor like a somnolent bull. Gulliford rubbed his sore neck.

It was now noon. His near brush with death had swept away his appetite. He wished to return to the Zen of inputting sock data.

Then came a new round of surveys, a dragnet of them, chasing him down: "Rate your experience with HR," "Share your opinion of the Hands-Free Swivel Chair," "Tell us about your incident," "Teamwork and you: just a few questions." Delete. Delete. Delete. Delete. Trashing the surveys didn't give him the buzz he got before. Now when he hit the key, it was like a counterpunch. Three-thirty rolled around, his project nowhere near complete. An email came in, reminding him of the deadline. A hunger headache and a woozy feeling, low blood sugar he supposed, made it harder to concentrate, but he forged ahead with the socks project and left the office at 6:50 p.m. with still more work to do on the socks. Dragging himself from the bus to his apartment, he greeted Amber, freshened up her food, and, trembling from hunger, opened a can of tuna for himself.

The next day at work, the same incident questionnaires cluttered his inbox, this time with "high importance" tacked onto their subject lines. Again, he deleted each one. Whether this was passive resistance or passive aggression or the stubbornness of the imp, he didn't know, but he didn't love his rebellion as much as he did before. He didn't want to lose his job. He only wanted to do his job. He worked through lunch, inputting the socks data, his stomach gurgling. Once more, his job was starving him.

Bronwen materialized before him, gesturing with her flourished fingernail to his computer screen. "Jim, there seems to be some miscommunication. Yesterday, I sent you a number of questionnaires regarding your mishap. And today I resent them with high importance. You must complete them."

"I decline," said Jim, his stomach growling. Bronwen looked at him as if he came from outer space.

She began again, "You understand, Jim, that this is normal business practice. When you receive emails from management, you must respond to them."

"I decline to answer the surveys," Jim replied with blank look. He reached down to hitch up his socks, another recalcitrant pair. "I have work to do."

"What I am trying to tell you," she said in a severe voice, "is that you are obliged, that means you are required, to respond to the surveys."

"I decline," he said. Bronwen's eyes grew so wide that he could see the whites all around.

"As I said, this is not an offer you can decline. You don't have options. This company cannot operate with everyone doing willy-nilly what they please."

"I only wish to enter data," said Gulliford. "I decline to answer the surveys."

"Suit yourself then," she replied. Five minutes later, she zipped him an email that shouted, "TOP PRIORITY." He was now on probation. Also, he had finished the socks project and was now nostalgic for it. The present project dealt with furnace filters.

Three days later, he was summoned to a noontime meeting. Bronwen was there and so were the head of HR, the Chief Operations Officer, and Scott, the manager of the data entry technicians. Sitting in the corner, was a security man, dressed all in gray. Jim eyed the men's socks. Nothing really spectacular, but nothing saggy either. Black and navy mid-calfs judging from the good shin coverage. White athletic socks on the security guy.

"Funny, I hadn't noticed you before," said the COO, who went on to note that Gulliford's work was reported to be accurate, but that he'd missed a recent deadline, and procedures were procedures and noncompliance was noncompliance, and he had to respond to the surveys.

"Why don't you just fill in the surveys, Jim?" asked Scott.

"I decline to do that," replied Jim. He was in a pattern now, a kind of loop that he could not break.

"We don't want to lose you," said Scott.

Gulliford did not answer, but his stomach growled. Again, Union was forcing him to skip lunch. The steam had gone out of his rebellion, and yet he found it impossible to yield.

"Then will you resign? Or will you decline that too?" said Bronwen. Her boss squinted at her.

"You leave us no other option than to terminate you," said the head of HR with a look of pity and regret.

The security guard escorted Jim to his cubicle to collect his personal effects. His only personal effect was the photo of Amber. He told Jim to hand over his company ID and keycard. As they walked through the office, some coworkers turned their heads away, but Lora and Jeff looked on with sad faces. As the security man ushered Jim to the door, he said, "Don't you want to keep your job? How are you going to eat? What's up with you, man?"

The next morning, Jim Gulliford rode the bus to work as always. He tailgated behind someone with a keycard. He stopped to use the men's room and made his way to his cubicle amid a wave of confused stares. In his chair, he found a stranger, a guy in his twenties who said, "Hi, I'm Dewey. This is where they told me I sit, isn't that right?"

The security man approached Jim, his face tight as a

knot. Trailing after him was a policeman. The cop tied Jim's wrists in plastic cuffs and perp-walked him down the row of cubicles, all silent now, no typing sounds, no conversations. The cop drove him to the police station, but no one charged him with anything. They cut off his plastic cuffs and let him loose into the city.

Jim Gulliford had no plans except for the immediate, which was lunch. Spying a deli, he sat down at the counter and ordered himself a Reuben with extra cole slaw on the side and a 7Up. The Reuben was delicious. He savored every bit. The waitress left a survey with his check. He had plenty of time to do the survey, but he left it untouched on the table. Then he strolled into a department store and bought himself three pairs of novelty socks: one with blue and red diamonds, one with sandwiches, and another with cats. Naturally, the sales receipt asked him to rate his purchase.

Gulliford took off his shoes, pulled off his old socks, and changed into the pair with the cats. Then he walked out into the city, his belly full and his feet at peace. He must have been smiling as a few passersby caught his eye and with approving looks nodded his way.

# The Ask Sandwich

The TSA lady at Newark Airport had a nice touch, and Josie enjoyed the pat down. The blue gloves slid under her arms, along her sides, down one leg, then the other. They searched, discerned. They pleased with just the right amount of pressure. Josie thanked the TSA lady, who nodded back with very professional brown eyes.

In bed last night in Robert's apartment, it was their sixth time together, Josie had attempted the "ask sandwich," something she'd read about in a woman's magazine. First she told him how nice his cologne smelled and trailed her fingers playfully down his arm. That was the first slice of bread. Then she said she'd really love it if he rubbed her back. That was the sandwich filling. She would have praised him and reciprocated generously, which would have been the other slice of bread.

Instead he said, "You're really bossy, aren't you?"

Sheesh. She'd only done what the magazine had instructed. Josie curled away from Robert, then on his hard mattress, she recovered a little backbone. "I don't consider that so bossy."

"Well, I do." The atmosphere in the room wadded up like paper.

Pulling her carry-on bag, striding in beige pumps, Josie made her way to her gate. She tried to wall off the

Robert fiasco and focus on the nursing conference in Atlanta. She was looking forward to presenting her paper on pressure sores but hoped her seatmate would not inquire about her work. She'd about had it with folks who squinted and scrunched their faces when she told them about her field. Oh, you mean bedsores, they'd say using the old term. Didn't know they were that important. Well, they can be fatal, she'd retort. She would educate them a little about patients who were stuck in bed, about reduced blood supply, friction, cell death, complications. And that pretty much ended the conversation.

At first, she'd seen a future with Robert. They agreed on politics and comedians, hated remakes of classic films, and pork pie hats.

Maybe she should try being old school, passive. It wasn't like she was a thirty-three-year-old sensualist who only thought of touch. But she wasn't exactly a winner in the dating game—one six-month relationship and a lot of first dates with few follow-ups. Was it her or Match.com?

On the way to her gate, Josie passed a Hudson News. An array of cover girls beckoned her, fringed by come-on headlines: *Drive him wild tonight. Ten types of sex to try at least once. Better orgasms now*. Did everything have to be about the sack? Well, she would like to have some great sex before she died. Addicted to the promises on the cover, she bought a copy of *Cosmopolitan*.

Josie's seatmate was a fortyish man in a blue short-sleeved shirt and Phillies baseball cap. He said his name was Solly.

Josie said her name was Mimi.

Solly smelled freshly showered and had a dimple in his chin. They chatted about the weather and airplane coffee. When he asked her what she did for a living, she told him she booked models for fashion ads. With a light heart, she fibbed her way through a conversation about beauty, dieting, and divas. She'd met the famous Kate Upton. Yes, Karlie Kloss really was that skinny.

Solly said he didn't know who those women were, but he complimented Josie on her big career.

"Sometimes those girls are so beautiful and sexy they're unreal," said Josie.

"I like the real type," said Solly with a playful grin. "Real gals, like you." As he sipped his airplane coffee, Josie spied no wedding ring. The two laughed a lot. Each time she said something he found fetching, he touched her shoulder. He had a big paw, but his touch was gentle. It would have been nice to get to know him better. When it turned out they were both from central

Jersey, Solly asked if he could have her phone number. Could he call her sometime?

This Josie now desperately wanted, but her wardrobe of lies made it impossible. She gulped and rubbed her nose. She almost knocked her coffee off the little depression in her tray table.

"I guess with your schedule that would be hard to arrange," he said.

"I do travel a lot."

Solly opened his laptop and began to study some documents. Josie paged through her *Cosmo*. Her head felt hot. She was very cross with herself, whoever she was.

# Frieda and Her Golem

Not long ago, a poor and solitary rabbinical student named Frieda Goldstein decided that she would create for herself a being to serve as her helpmeet and companion, an affectionate partner, a support in times of stress and self-doubt. The two of them would live as one, eating together, relaxing at home, and should physical intimacy feel right, then that too. From the start of her first-year studies at the rabbinical college, Frieda's classmates, both the single ones and the married ones, aware that she was alone, invited her to coffee, Shabbat dinners, and movies. But Frieda, coveting her solitude and jealous of her time, always claimed other plans. Eventually, the invitations, which had first blown down like blossoms, withered away.

The rabbinical class had recently studied Jewish folklore and had thoroughly traced the legend of the Golem of Prague. It was said that a sixteenth-century mystic rabbi named Judah Loew, seeking to save the Jews of Prague from an antisemitic attack, fashioned a man-like creature from river clay. He animated it with an abracadabra of words and letters and sent it forth as a mighty protector. Once its mission was accomplished, however, the large and powerful golem developed free will and began to cause trouble. Rabbi Loew was forced to return the golem to an inert state. He did this by a clever move that again involved the mystical power of words and letters. When forming the magical savior, the rabbi had written *emet*, the Hebrew word for truth, on the golem's forehead. To deactivate the being, the rabbi removed the *e* from *emet*, which changed the spelling to *met*, the Hebrew word for dead. Thus, ended the golem.

Considering Jewish history, said everyone in the class, no sane person could ever believe in the fantasy of an animated statue coming to the rescue of the Jews. Still, the potential of a creature brought to life or almost life whispered in the ear of the imagination. The class discussion branched out into Mary Shelley's *Frankenstein*, the question of robots with minds of their own, computers that could write music, and the wonders of machine learning: algorithms capable of remembering your tastes and habits, codes that told you what you should buy and do. With fear and awe, the class agreed that artificial intelligence was taking over, seducing and controlling us in its hyper-logical way.

The class's conversation turned to ethics: To what extent should we let our inventions serve and direct us? How much should we toy with life? Nowadays, the disabled had robots to help them. What a superb and liberating force technology could be.

"Might it not," Frieda spoke up, "at least in the world

of make-believe, be morally acceptable to create a being—you could call it a golem if you like—to be your partner in life?"

Everyone in the class turned to her with startled looks.

"It would be a good golem, one that didn't cause mischief or commit violence," she continued to the dumbstruck faces. "Not a mindless automaton, but a golem that could be happy, have a purpose, and know that its existence meant something."

"Are you serious?" came a voice from across the room. No one else took up the argument, and the professor, adjusting his kippa, turned the discussion to the tale "The King's Three Daughters."

Disregarding her classmates' reaction, and refusing all reason and the wisdom of legend, Frieda Goldstein resolved to make herself a personal golem.

She would make it out of meatloaf, not river clay, and she would make it the coming Sunday. On the appointed day, a cold bright day in early January, Frieda Goldstein sauntered home to her apartment, swinging two canvas shopping bags filled with ingredients for the meatloaf. Her curly brown hair bobbed in the chilly breeze. Advancing with her right foot, she felt herself striding toward a golden destiny. But with each footfall of the left, she sensed herself pitching headlong to a deep and dark unknown. As she came to the dog park across from her apartment building, she paused to watch the breeds and the mixes chase tennis balls and sniff each other. She saw their owners bag the poo, break up dogfights, and dole out treats. Millions of people found love and companionship with dogs and cats. But it was so much trouble to take care of them. Better to fashion herself a neat and tidy one-and-only. With her helpmeet by her side, Frieda would have peaceful company, someone to handle the household chores, and loads of time to study. She would become a scholar rabbi, specializing in mystic texts.

Frieda preheated the oven to 350 degrees and mixed together ground beef, dried onion soup mix, oatmeal, egg, and water. A kosher recipe, to be sure. In the baking pan, she formed the feet, then the sturdy legs and hips. She gave the creature a yoni and breasts. She shaped the meat into arms that could both work and embrace. Then she lovingly molded the face, adding two pearl onions for eyes. Being white and luminescent, the pearl onion eyes, as yet sightless, seemed to stare at Frieda.

As Rabbi Loew had inscribed *emet* upon his golem's brow, so Frieda, using tiny strips of red bell pepper, pressed the word *friend* in English on her creature's forehead. She inserted a piece of paper with the name "Gittel" into the mouth and baked the figure for an hour. When she removed it from the oven, she circled it seven times in the way that a bride would circle her groom. Then she waved her hands over the human-like shape— it smelled so meaty and good— and said, "Blessed are you, O Lord our God, King of the Universe, who has made me a friend." With this, the creature blinked. Frieda, startled, jumped back. Gittel's eyes, while still white and translucent as the pearl onions, began to focus. Her skin changed from cooked meatloaf to an opaque sandy tone, as if she were wearing a beige bodysuit. She sat up, began to stretch and grow, slid out of the baking pan, off the table, and stood in Frieda's kitchen, beautiful, nude, no hair on her head or anywhere else. Trembling, unsure of how to act in this sacred moment, Frieda covered her face with her hands.

Gittel grew until she stood six feet tall. The red bell pepper strips that spelled "friend" clung weirdly to where her hairline would have started, if she had had hair. Frieda found her lovely and shapely, her features more refined than her own. She glowed in admiration of her work. This friend, or simulacrum of a friend, was now all hers. Gittel swallowed the piece of paper with her name.

With much fear and trembling, Frieda reached out and held the creature's hands and said the *shehecheyanu*, a prayer thanking God for bringing her to this occasion. Gittel repeated the blessing back in perfect Hebrew.

"You are Gittel. I have made you," said Frieda, barely able to believe her good fortune and magical power. "Gittel," said Frieda pressing a finger gently to her new friend's lips. "Frieda," she said pointing to her own mouth. Gittel mirrored her maker's gestures and uttered the names in clear English. And so, the journey toward language and understanding quickly began.

Yet their life together remained secret. Gittel's appearance was strange, and Frieda decided that she must not let others see the naked wonder who lived with her. She would get around to buying her tall women's clothes, but for now Gittel must be kept away from the world, and the world must be kept away from Gittel. Frieda drew the shades in her apartment and kept them down.

Gittel absorbed new vocabulary and grammar with ease, forgetting nothing. Evenings when Frieda could steal a little time from her studies, she would sit with Gittel on her brown corduroy couch, first reading her pre-school books with lots of pictures, then teaching her how to read. Together they moved on to children's classics, then Nathaniel Hawthorne, George Eliot, and Mark Twain. Frieda guided her friend's understanding of the needs and predicaments of the people in the books. For the first time in her life, or at least the first time that she would admit, Frieda knew closeness and saw with growing awfulness, regret, and sadness what she had been missing all along. She wanted nothing more than Gittel in her life. Well, that and becoming a famous mystical scholar.

The pair celebrated Shabbat each Friday night, Gittel blessing the candles, wine, and challah. When the winter holidays came up, the two of them relished dates, figs, and olives for the New Year of the Trees and ate hamentaschen for Purim. In the bedroom, they discovered each other's pleasures. Frieda stroked her friend's smooth body. There was so much of her to caress. And Gittel, instructed by Frieda, ministered to her mistress's desires. After lovemaking, each clung to the other.

Over the weeks, Gittel's awareness sprouted into many questions: Where did all the people in the books come from when there are only two of us? Why do those people in the books have so many problems?

Frieda began to wish that she had not educated Gittel through literary works. Better to have instructed her in basic arithmetic, abstract art, or geometric design, supplying paper, pencil, and crayons instead of schooling her in the ravelings of human lives.

Those were made-up people, explained Frieda, while the two of them were real. They were not lonely, and they did not have problems like the people in the books. Gittel looked at her maker through the knowing translucence of her pearl onion eyes. "Yes, we have each other," she said, and then observed her maker spending long hours at her desk and computer, engrossed in her studies, her mind in some faraway place.

Each book begot interest in other books. Gittel, being home all day and a hungry reader, tore through volume after volume. She drew up reading lists based on writers Frieda had mentioned: Walt Whitman, Albert Camus, Bernard Malamud, Toni Morrison, Margaret Atwood. Frieda gladly carried home stacks of library books for her friend. And thank goodness for libraries, as Frieda, who was barely scraping by on her stipend, could afford to buy nothing but her textbooks and only the most basic foods and supplies.

Frieda taught Gittel how to tidy up the apartment. How fine it felt, after a long day of studying rabbinic skills and commentaries on ancient law, to return to an apartment that was all swept, dusted, and shiny clean. Lovely to walk in the door, to kiss and be kissed. Frieda always smiled to see the red bell pepper strips that spelled *friend* upon Gittel's brow. But the knowing focus of those pearl onion eyes made her uneasy, and she would look at the being's brow or cheek or chin rather than meet the pale gaze.

At first, Frieda, who was at best a very basic cook, had to learn what Gittel would eat and what she would not. Beef, she would not touch—no surprise, considering her raw material. For the same reason, she refused eggs, onions, and oatmeal. Eager to honor her companion's tastes, Frieda became a vegetarian, and soon began to teach Gittel how to measure, mix, and use a knife. A quick learner with plenty of time on her hands, Gittel mastered easy, then elaborate recipes which Frieda pulled off the Internet. She prepared pakoras with potato and cauliflower filling, vegetable biryanis, chopped salads, humus and tahini, roasted carrots, and pizzas galore. Gittel wanted to learn more recipes, so Frieda taught her how to use the computer.

One evening in March, Frieda came home to find a tower of boxes by her door shipped from booksellers and purveyors of fine foods. Perplexed and suspecting fraud, she signed on to her credit card account and gasped as she read through hundreds of dollars of charges. Gittel cocked her head in confusion as Frieda broke down in tears. The red bell pepper letters spelling *friend* on the golem's forehead began to look taunting, even sarcastic.

"How could you do this?" she cried to Gittel. She clutched her chest. "You can't buy things. Only I can buy things. How am I going to pay for this? I can't pay for this." She pointed at the boxes. Was her companion going to take over her life?

"The computer said that based on the books I've read, I would like these books. And the recipes online said that because I made those recipes I would like other dishes like them, and the computer showed me how to get the things I wanted."

"You don't understand money," retorted Frieda. "You did something you had no right to do."

A new awareness lit Gittel's face. "This is what happens in books." She turned her terrible eyes to her maker. "This is people having a problem."

Frieda reported the spurious credit card charges to the bank, blaming them on a house guest who went way too far with computer privileges. She cancelled that credit card, requested a new one, followed the instructions for returning the merchandise, and changed her passwords. All deliberately in front of Gittel. That night, each rolled away from the other in bed. In the darkness, Frieda considered the story of the Golem of Prague, how it broke free from the rabbi's control and began to frighten the town. But her Gittel was a good learner, and now that she knew that buying things by herself was something she must not do—and because Frieda had put precautions in place—the conjurer was confident that Gittel would desist from future shopping sprees.

The next morning, they said little to each other.

Upon returning home, Frieda was horrified to find that Gittel had opened all the window shades and was sitting by the living room window, chin in hand, fixated upon the dog park across the street. *Oy gevalt*! Had others seen the smooth and naked figure staring out the window? Now that Gittel was aware of the world outside their apartment, what was to become of their couplehood? What of the fiction, the lie really, that Frieda had fed her: that only the two of them were real?

"We never open the shades," Frieda admonished her companion.

Gittel stared out the window, mesmerized by the sight of other humans and the four-legged furry things scurrying around them. "You said that there were only two of us. But there are so many others. So many others outside our home."

"I meant," said Frieda, "that for me there was only you, and for you there was only me. We are a couple.

But I kept much from you, and I am sorry." A veil of shame drifted over her face. She was unsure of how Gittel would see her now, unsure if their bond would hold. Gittel's awareness was growing on its own. Gittel, the marvelous invention, was transmogrifying into something as unpredictable as life itself. What was to become of Frieda's perfectly constructed life of study, domesticity, and companionship?

"And what are those brown and black creatures on four legs?"

"Those are dogs. You pet them and feed them, and they live with you and love you in return."

"Do they ever have problems?" asked Gittel.

"Sometimes. It's a lot of work to take care of them."

"I would like to visit the dogs and the people. Frieda, all day you go to school. All evening you stay at your desk. I feel alone when you are away, and alone when you are at your desk at home. I cook. I clean. I read. And now I see the outside, and I want the outside. I want to talk to those other people and pet their dogs."

On her way home the next day, Frieda stopped at a Goodwill store and bought a tall woman's outfit for Gittel. Shoes and socks, pants and a blouse, a winter jacket, and sunglasses. She also purchased gloves and a big headscarf printed with pink magnolias. She would need to keep her creature as covered up as possible.

The next Saturday, after she returned home from synagogue, Frieda dressed Gittel in the Goodwill outfit, explaining that this is what one had to wear when going outdoors. She stood on a chair and tied the headscarf as snugly and as fashionably as she could around Gittel's head so that the red bell pepper strips that spelled *friend* were covered by the scarf. Now she could pass for an Orthodox Jewish woman or maybe a cancer patient hiding hair loss. Frieda slid the sunglasses onto Gittel's face. That was better. Now Frieda could look at her friend head on, no need to shy away from the troubling eyes. She tied a scarf around her own head and donned a pair of sunglasses.

Gittel watched as Frieda turned the key in the lock. The two descended the stairs, walked across the street to the dog park and sat on a bench. They watched the owners throw balls and rings, saw the dogs slurp water from bowls, and heard the owners compliment one another's pets as they traded tips about dog food and vets. A smile broke over Gittel's face as she watched the romping. A woman in a red coat, who had a Boxer, sat down beside them on the bench and made small talk about the crisp day. Other dog people nodded their way. A dog park was a place for fellowship. Frieda did not sense that her golem smelled beefy, but soon a number of dogs trotted over to sniff her. Gittel watched people petting the dogs, and she imitated them. Soon she appeared popular with the dogs. Someone let her throw a stick for fetch. The pet people came and went, but the lady in the red coat stayed beside them. She complimented Gittel on her magnolia-printed scarf and showed her how to say "paw" so that she could shake hands with Sandy, her Boxer.

Gittel had so much fun that Frieda took her back to the dog park the following day, making sure that her friend was covered up as before. "Every time you go out," she said, "you must cover yourself up like this."

The lady in the red coat, whose name was Nan, was back, and she seemed especially interested in Gittel. She again admired her magnolia-printed scarf and made oblique references to healing. Pets, she said, improved one's health. They lowered your blood pressure. You lived longer if you had a pet. "For a long time, I never wanted a dog," Nan confessed. "Now I know what I was missing."

"I would like to have a dog," announced Gittel, caressing Sandy's silky head and floppy ears.

"They are a lot of work," countered Frieda.

"I would take care of the dog," said Gittel.

Sandy rested his head on Gittel's knee and looked up at her with his sad and loving eyes. He was a jowly beast and left a swipe of slobber on her pant leg. Frieda thought about the mess dogs made, shedding all over the place, flinging spittle on the floor and walls. And the chore of walking a dog, the cost of kibble and visits to the vet, and then the grief of putting the creature down when it was old and lame. Oh, and the barking, the scampering. She needed silence and peace in which to contemplate the divine, search for oneness, pour over mystic texts. Ultimate questions called her: Where did the soul reside? What did the soul do before life and after death? Were new souls born, and was heaven crowded with them? Questions ad infinitum, queries as vast as space, fit only for the greatest minds.

These park visits were wolfing down her study time. To the extent that Frieda was an introvert, Gittel was turning out to be an extrovert. She was far more sociable than Frieda. The young scholar began to fear that she might not be enough to fill her companion's heart. If only she could return to the early days when they were as two Eves, with no one else in their world.

The following day, Monday, returning from school, her mind cluttered with her studies and worries about

Gittel, Frieda approached her apartment door, then stopped short. The door was ajar. A break-in? Had Gittel escaped? Stoking her courage with a deep breath, she pushed open the door to find her beloved with Nan at the kitchen table and Sandy beneath it. Gittel looked at Frieda through her sunglasses. Thank God she was in her outdoor costume, her headscarf covering, just barely, the red bell pepper strips that spelled *friend*. Frieda's heart raced. The golem and human were drinking tea and eating the raisin apple pie that Gittel had made the night before. Nan was sitting in Frieda's place.

"Nan, what a surprise!" said Frieda unsmilingly. "Hey." She dropped her books on her desk.

Sandy woofed. The hair on his back rose up in a ridge. She felt unsafe in her own home. She was furious at Gittel. Who was she to invite a stranger into their home? Worse, their secret lay in wait under the edge of the scarf, a quarter inch from being revealed.

Nan petted the dog to calm him down and told him to be a good boy. She hurried to explain that Gittel had visited the park on her own and sought out Sandy at once.

"So nice to see her getting out, feeling strong, doing something on her own. Health returns little by little," she said. "I know. I've been there. Have a piece of pie."

So now this invader was offering her some of her own pie. It was a tiny apartment with limited seating, only two chairs at the kitchen table, one at the desk, and the small brown corduroy couch. Frieda walked to her desk and opened a book. She was facing a deadline, she explained.

"Frieda has to study, and I have to start dinner," said Gittel in a shrunken voice.

Nan's face narrowed. "I should get along myself." She slid into her red coat and took up Sandy's leash. The dog shook himself as if to rid the air of tension. Brisk as a broom, Nan swept herself out the door.

The fine order that Frieda had imposed on their life together was giving way. Gittel was making friends on her own, and there was no telling where this would lead. Nan might come by to visit. There she would find Gittel in her naked state, her pearl onion eyes uncovered, red bell pepper strips blazing. The monster revealed.

Gittel cleared the table, clattering the dishes on purpose.

"You brought someone into the apartment without asking me," said Frieda. "That was not okay."

"I was lonely. I wanted more friends, and I wanted to play with the dogs."

Pity touched Frieda's heart, but Gittel's new freedom

also seized her with alarm. Frieda tried to reason with her. The world was a dangerous place. She should never go outside alone.

No, returned Gittel. Outside there were new friends, people who asked what she thought and what she did, and they had pets. "If I want to go out, I will go out. But I will still cook and clean for you. You don't need to worry about that."

The pledge hit Frieda like a slap. She backed away from Gittel. Then she gasped as her companion put an acorn squash on the cutting board, took a butcher knife, and hacked it in two with one blow. Her golem, like all golems, was very strong. And now her golem was angry and did not love her anymore. She cursed the day she'd stirred this thing into existence. What a fool she had been to teach her creature language and instruct her in the ways of human need. Now she had agency and desires of her own. Maybe a soul had evolved within her. With foolish magic Frieda had made this monster, and it was only a matter of time before the monster broke free.

Frieda thought of the Golem of Prague and knew what she had to do. That night as Gittel slept, Frieda, hands shaking, peeled the letters *f,r,i* from Gittel's forehead, leaving the word "end."

Gittel stirred, then rose from the bed and tried to speak, but only glugging sounds came from her throat. Before Frieda's eyes, the beautiful figure began to wrinkle and contract. Gittel looked at her maker with a final flash of consciousness, then collapsed on the bedroom floor in a formless mass.

Frieda fell to her knees before the ruined creature. She clutched her chest. Her heart curdled with guilt. What was it worth, her desire to ponder the great mysteries, or her longing for the starry realms? Was not Gittel her greatest work and her gravest loss? There were people who built relationships and lost them, but she had animated a being and instilled a soul into it. And then she'd destroyed what she had made. Was she a murderer? Had she killed a person? No, Gittel was not a person. Frieda tried to tell herself that. But that was not how she felt.

She cried all night. When morning seeped in through the edges of the shades, she gathered up the meat that had been Gittel, put it in a bag, stood and recited the Mourner's Kaddish, the prayer for the dead. Even though awash in sorrow, she was aware of her foolishness. How could she say Kaddish over this bag of meat, when one said Kaddish over a parent, sister, brother, spouse, or, God forbid, a child?

That morning she took the bag of what used to be Gittel to a creek and fed it to the fish. It was like *tashlich*, the way one sprinkled bread crumbs into a stream at Rosh Hashanah, a symbolic casting off of sin. She performed her ritual with the same mixture of grief and foolishness she felt when she had recited Kaddish. She did not sit shiva—who would come to call?—but mourned for seven days, covering the one mirror in her apartment, the bathroom mirror, and rending the sleeve of her shirt. Looking pale, her attention fixed on faraway things, she made it to all her classes, and when her fellow students asked what was wrong, she told them that a dear friend had passed away. They offered condolences, which she accepted with gratitude and even a faint smile, warmed by the normalness of their caring. She donated Gittel's clothes back to the Goodwill store.

How awful that the dog park was across the street from her apartment. Frieda had to look at the sky, her phone, or the sidewalk as she passed the congregation of dog people. Had she really instilled a soul in Gittel? Certainly, one had evolved. And if the soul had a beginning, did it also have an end, or did it go on existing in some kind of afterlife? Here were those questions again, but they did not lift her mind as they had before. She wondered if the idea of an eternal soul was a universal fantasy in response to the universal fact of death. She wanted to curl up like a snail with a primitive brain and live in a shell.

Shortly before her week of mourning was over, she heard unfamiliar footsteps on her landing and the scratch of nails. Then came a knock at the door. It was Nan with Sandy.

Frieda let them in. "Sorry to bother you, but I haven't seen Gittel around. Maybe she'd like to take a walk with Sandy and me." Nan looked around the room, perceiving the vacancy.

"We broke up," announced Frieda. "She moved away. Things weren't working out."

Nan's expression widened in surprise. Then she swallowed a little as if to contain her feelings.

"I'm so sorry. This must be rough. So rough," said Nan. Her words tumbled quickly. "Rough for me, too. I mean not as rough as for you. She was a new friend." Sandy sniffed the air. He stood by Nan and did not lie down or sit. "She didn't even stop by the park to say good-bye."

"It was all very sudden," said Frieda.

"I hope she's okay. It looked like she'd been through a lot, what with the hair loss, the skin situation, the vision issue."

"She wanted her freedom."

"But to vanish like that."

The two spoke a few more minutes about friends and break-ups, and how people got over them. Frieda looked at Nan. She was the forward type, but how else do you make new friends? And friends are so hard to find. It seemed that all the connections were already knitted.

Nan, as if anticipating that Frieda would soon hint that she should leave, announced that she would be getting on her way. The dog needed his walk.

"Gittel would be happy to know that you came by."

"But to vanish like that," repeated Nan.

Was she wondering if Frieda had murdered her friend? Locked her up in a basement somewhere?

"She did what she had to do," replied Frieda. "She wanted her freedom."

And except for the fact that Gittel lay trapped in her maker's heart, the great creation, unlike her maker, was now free from pain, and loneliness, and thought.

# The Dirty Martini

The day of his wife's forty-fifth birthday party, Norbie Bernbaum let Jerry Rosen talk him into an afternoon at the Dirty Martini, a strip club on the edge of downtown where Hot Pantz, Double Dee, and The Bride seduced the clientele to one degree or another. Rosen had been there a couple of times, mostly during weekdays, and he made the place sound so irresistible—the women were just like showgirls—that Norbie was panting to go.

"But what about Donna's party?" Norbie groaned as Schpilkes, the family dog, came by and leaned against him.

"Just tell her you're going out to buy her a gift," advised Rosen. "You'll be back in time for brisket with the in-laws. I promise."

Norbie hadn't bought Donna a birthday present, so this sounded like a plan. He hurriedly splashed on a bit of cologne, brushed his teeth, and scooped his keys off the top of the bureau, which was slightly dusty and decked with family photos. He nearly tripped on a toy police car that his son, Eddie, had left in the upstairs hall. Latin rap pulsed from his teenage daughter Annette's room. Through the slightly open door, Norbie saw her working her hips to some kind of chipotle-flavored belly dance and cringed. He had to pick up Rosen in twenty minutes.

An accountant in a medium-sized firm, Norbie was in good health and not bad looking: he had a full head of onyx hair and a slight cleft in his chin that could look playful and charming when he was feeling merry. But he had not felt merry in some time. Instead, a blue mold of boredom and resentment had crept over him. He began to wonder what accountancy meant in the big picture and what the big picture was anyway. The idea that he was squandering a third of his life on other people's numbers poked at him like a constant elbow. As for his marriage, he was bored and resentful of it, too. The easy passion he and Donna once felt for each other had subsided with the years and petty disgruntlements of matrimony. Norbie sometimes asked himself if this was a normal part of the passage or if he and Donna were just stringing each other along. The problem was that nothing much could gain traction in his soul. He felt like a man dangling and reaching out for something, but he didn't know what.

As Norbie sought relief from his funk, ideas of purpose would stir in his mind. He should coach Eddie's Little League team, learn Spanish, take up guitar, engage in a wild affair, maybe even try harder to appreciate what he had. But he only dreamed of these things. He didn't act on them—neither the good things nor the bad. The idea of the affair he dismissed as too real, too intense, too risky. Sooner or later, each notion dissolved like the morning fog, and hard daylight only made him see the slag heap of his life more clearly.

Eventually, he figured that he should simply try to have more fun. And convinced that his opportunities for fun were speeding away from him like a Porsche down the highway, Norbie jumped whenever Jerry Rosen called with a new adventure. So grateful was Norbie for these invitations that he tried not to mind that Rosen was always a few dollars short for beer or greens fees, that he usually had Norbie chauffeur, or that Rosen kept him waiting as he finished his shower, went through his mail, or yakked on the phone with his girlfriends, some of whom were married. Compared to Norbie's life, Rosen's seemed so various and full.

Donna Bernbaum, Norbie's wife of sixteen years, worked as a paralegal in a small suburban law practice. A devoted mother and a loyal spouse, Donna also numbered (how could she not?) Norbie's small abuses—no-showing for dinner without bothering to call, playfully putting her down in front of the neighbors, opting for outings with Rosen over dates with her. Now on her birthday, Norbie avoided eye contact with Donna as he strode toward his red Toyota Camry. He aimed his electronic key at the car like a ray gun.

It was a fruitful May, the air heavily peppered with pollen, and Donna had a bad case of hay fever. Before she could utter a word, a sneeze tornadoed through her body. Recovering, she arraigned her husband, "You're off with that Rosen, Norbie. I know it." She fixed him with a narrow look. Behind her accusing tone, Norbie sensed the fluttering flags of insecurity and fear.

Ever since Rosen had entered their lives, Donna had felt herself weirdly in competition with him for Norbie's love and attention. This Saturday, his flight on her birthday made her feel even more sidelined and insulted. Not that a man wasn't entitled to his free time. And her birthday party was hours away. When, however, her tormented nostrils caught the scent of cologne, a new anxiety pricked her. She hadn't known Norbie to cheat, but under Rosen's tutelage anything was possible.

"And what's that smell? Where are you going on a Saturday afternoon that you have to wear cologne?"

Schpilkes trotted up to Norbie for a good sniff. The dog's tail accelerated to a quick tick-tock. He looked expectantly at his master.

Norbie made no reply but lobbed a you-must-beparanoid look at Donna and made the loco sign so she could see it. He knew that being a little mean would make Donna shut up. He slid into his car and started the engine. Today, it was easier for him not to feel so annoyed or judged by her. After all, he would soon be in the bosom of topless dancers.

"We have to be at my sister's by six. It *is* my birthday," she said, fighting suspicion and another oncoming sneeze.

"Terrific. Thanks for the reminder," snapped Norbie. "If I have to spend time with your family, the least you can do is let me have a little fun first."

A wounded expression whitewashed Donna's face. Talk about a low blow, insulting her family like that.

"Maybe I'm just going out to get you a present. Unless you'd rather I didn't," he said glancing at his watch. What would Rosen think if he had to call and cancel just because he caved to his wife's nagging?

"You play in the dirt, you get dirty," warned Donna in just the sort of schoolmarmish tone that made Norbie jump into the fraternal arms of Rosen. As he backed down the driveway, he saw her brandishing a Kleenex. He definitely did not like the way she said "dirty." It was as if she knew where he was headed.

The thought of Donna's birthday party circled him

like a turkey vulture. He could barely tolerate Donna's family, a bunch of self-righteous socialists always hammering away with their politics and justice causes. If it wasn't the whales, it was the disabled or the undocumented immigrants. He needed an antidote to all that suffocating goodness, and he was now gladder than ever that Rosen had talked him into a visit to the strip joint.

Donna ducked into the house and told the kids she was off to the health club for a quick lift. For the last several months, whenever she felt Norbie was saying no to her and yes to Rosen, she went to the health club to weight train. She could now curl fifteen-pound dumbbells and bench press forty pounds, yet she lacked the power to cut Norbie's ties to Rosen. The fellows' friendship burgeoned. The lists of hurts grew longer.

It would be a busy Saturday. After the gym, she had to run Annette to dance class and Eddie to his ball game. And there was Norbie out and about who-knows-where, no help at all with errands—and on her birthday no less. Of course, he was going with that Rosen. It was scrawled all over his face like a signature on a bad check.

Donna Bernbaum detested Jerry Rosen. He was a know-it-all, a *schnorrer*, and he dripped enticements into Norbie's brain the way a bad factory leaked dioxin into a creek. A half-hearted salesman of uncertain skill, Rosen had, at various times, peddled ad space in magazines, vacation time shares, radon detection systems, and mortgages. Now he was selling hot tubs. He mostly lived off his wives when he had them and his girlfriends when he was single. Donna couldn't stand the way Rosen used women and the way he collected male followers like Norbie, guys who mistook the cheesy glow of Rosen's sporting company for a kind of glamour. She hated Rosen's stupid satanic-looking Vandyke. She hated the way his cigars stunk up their good car, his cocky self-confidence, and, if she had only known him better, she surely would have hated him more. Just hearing Norbie on the cell with that Rosen made her skin crawl like a roach in a diner. What skeeved her especially was that peculiarly light and eager tone her husband used only with Rosen. It was a voice he never used with her.

While Donna militantly believed in protest, she worried that today she had antagonized Norbie too much. It was something about the sight of him backing down the driveway and speeding off down the street. She stood for a moment in front of their house as she watched Norbie disappear. A pang of anxiety went through her.

***

Jerry Rosen kept Norbie Bernbaum waiting as he finished watching a golf tournament on TV. Norbie understood that Rosen was a tacky playboy, and he therefore secretly considered himself morally superior to his friend. Rosen for his part, liked Norbie well enough, but saw him as a watch to unwind, a pal to fill his loneliness, and, should he sell him a hot tub, a customer from whom he could profit.

Rosen seemed to be endowed with great bravado and self-esteem, yet inwardly he was not a happy man. On some level he knew he was self-centered, of little help to those around him, and below par on the job. He sought to blot out this sense of lack with pleasures and entertainments—women, golf, cards, dining out, shopping, movie going—and endless hours of chitchat: gossip, trivia, and dubious advice he foisted on his listeners. Yet after all of this, there was still the lack.

The golf match crept by slowly, and Norbie grew increasingly antsy. It was already after two in the afternoon. He instinctively felt a little bad at having treated Donna poorly, but he tried to delete those feelings. Then there was the matter of the birthday present. Norbie usually just bought Donna a card and maybe flowers, but now he was committed to buying her an actual gift. But what? A nightgown? A handbag? He hadn't a clue what she'd like.

"Hold your horses, bubbeleh," Rosen soothed as he pared his fingernails. "Those gorgeous gals aren't going anywhere."

The Dirty Martini was a low, flat building that might have once been a factory or a grocery store. An easel-style marquee in front announced, "Philadelphia's Bachelor Party Headquarters. Congratulations, Brad." Another sign in the parking lot read, "Police and Dirty Martini Parking." Although it was early afternoon, all the parking spaces were filled. Cops or no cops, it was a dodgy neighborhood, so Norbie didn't want to park the red Camry on the street. "Here's a space," said Rosen pointing to a spot designated for disabled parking.

"Are you crazy?" replied Norbie. "It says a minimum fifty-dollar fine, plus towing at the owner's expense."

Rosen minced his lips and rolled his eyes heavenward. "Listen, do you really think some gimp in a van is coming to the Dirty Martini? They have to put a handicapped space there. It's a federal law or something. Just park for crying out loud. You don't have all day." Then he looked at Norbie meaningfully and added, "Well, if it will make you feel better, limp in and, if anyone asks, say you twisted your ankle."

So Norbie did as Rosen instructed, parked in the handicapped space, and made his way into the club half jumping, half limping. Like Hopalong Cassidy on his way to the bordello. He felt very foolish.

Two plaster statues of female nudes pillared the entrance to the club. In the parking lot, a number of men lingered talking on their cell phones. Inside, a huge bouncer, who looked like a body builder, had Norbie and Rosen pass through a metal detector. Rosen sauntered through. Norbie kept up his limping act. By the metal detector were signs that warned against cameras and touching the girls. Norbie was surprised at all the security. It made him kind of nervous. He heard raucous laughter coming from a curtained-off room. Peeking in, he saw several girls in fishnets and black leather bustiers wheeling in a big box that was iced like a cake. He felt sure that a girl would pop out of that cake.

"Craaazy, craaazy," yearned a female voice over the sound system in the cavernous main room, which smelled faintly of a moist mustiness. One wall of the club was mirrored. The other was hung with a number of flat-screen TVs tuned, audio off, to a baseball game. The patrons were mostly middle-aged white men. Some were seated on shell-shaped cushioned chairs; others perched on barstools along the polished runway, a black stretch bordered in red lights that rolled out through the center of the room like a long tongue. There was a brass pole in the middle of the walk. Overhead pulsing spotlights splashed the strippers in red, green, blue, and yellow.

The Dirty Martini was like something Norbie had seen in a movie or a TV show, only it was better and real. The door to a deeper, darker, nastier side of sex opened to him, and he felt big, elevated, male. There to be served by juicy little teases who sometimes acted submissive and sometimes acted like they were begging for it.

The two friends settled into bar stools along the catwalk and ordered beers. The DJ played mostly sultry R&B and announced girl after girl. There seemed to be an endless stream of dancers of all races, skin tones, breast sizes, and hair colors. Each came in with her gauzy wrap and five-inch Lucite heels. The Lucite high heels were definitely a very big item. Then inch by inch, each girl unpeeled her wrap until she wore nothing but a thong or a G-string, see-through pasties, and those skyscraper Lucite heels. Then the slow grind. And the embrace of the pole.

Hot Pantz, a very fit Black girl in a leopard thong, thrust herself up against the brass pole. Norbie wished he were that pole. Then Hot Pantz climbed the pole and suspended herself upside down. Her legs were like boa constrictors. She had amazing abs. She did all sorts of acrobatic moves. Just like Cirque du Soleil, mused Norbie. Then she slid down the pole and began to stalk catlike on all fours. One man put a bill in her thong. She purred.

From the corner of his eye, he saw a patron leave the club with one of the girls.

A tall blonde with huge breasts came on and slowly gyrated to "Nasty Girl." "That's Double Dee," Rosen whispered. Double Dee did a backbend, lowered herself to the catwalk floor, then knees bent she pumped her beautiful and shapely legs open and closed like a giant butterfly. Shaved, fit, and incredibly tight was all Norbie could think. The kind of girl you can't get at home. His heart was pounding, and a big erection took root in his pants. He watched as she went down on all fours and crawled up to a patron who lovingly tucked bills in her little pink thong. She smiled at Norbie. He wanted to be a bill in her thong. He took a dollar from his wallet, and she held her side string open for him. His fingers grazed her hip, which was warm and round and smooth. He was mesmerized, lost in a hormonal haze.

"Hey, give me a bill," Rosen broke in, rubbing his fingers together. Norbie hesitated but, reluctant to seem a poor sport, he handed Rosen a single. "Gimme a five, at least. They like bigger bills," wheedled Rosen who proceeded to insert Norbie's five-spot into Double Dee's thong. Double Dee swung her silky golden tresses and worked the two cupcakes of her ass.

"And now, gentlemen," announced the velvety voiced DJ as organ tones of the "Wedding March" began, "Here comes the Bride."

The Bride, petite and virginal, began to step demurely down the runway. She wore a white G-string, a white garter, and a snowy shawl over her small breasts. Dangling from her arm was a white beaded drawstring pouch, the kind brides carry to collect wedding checks. A hush drifted over the crowd, but this was soon disturbed by some rustling at the back of the room.

A grizzled male voice ripped through the sultry atmosphere. "Lawbreaking prick!" The man's tone spiraled louder with mounting indignation. "Lawbreaking prick!"

The "Wedding March" kept playing, but the DJ fell silent and The Bride froze. The yelling was coming from a guy in a wheelchair. "Whose red Camry is that?" he raged. "You're in a disabled zone. You're gonna pay for this, asshole! Management, too."

Working the hand controls on his wheelchair, the disabled man, a guy in his mid thirties with stringy hair, motored deeper into the club. Fear dug its red polished nails into Norbie's chest. The huge bouncer lumbered into the room.

A contingent of strippers, now in halter tops and miniskirts (how plain they seemed off the stage!), filtered through the crowd to comfort the disabled guy. Their kindness caused him to lose his tough edge. His voice began to break. "I just wanted to see you girls dance. And some bastard with a working prick..."

Two cops came up to the man in the wheelchair. One took out a notepad and began to write a report.

"Bubbeleh, looks like you're up shit's creek," said Rosen as he took a pull at his beer.

"You're the one who told me park there," retorted Norbie lamely.

Having run a license plate check, one cop began to bellow, "Norbert Bernbaum! Is there a Norbert Bernbaum here! Red Toyota Camry!" Norbie was frantic with shame; fine beads of sweat broke out on his forehead. He hopelessly prayed for deliverance. Trembling, he looked at his watch. It was after five o'clock. The party. The present. And he was about to get a citation in a strip club.

The limping excuse did not work with the cops. Then the strippers gathered around Norbie and started to yell at him. "Don't you have any respect for those less fortunate than yourself?" scolded Hot Pantz. "Shame on you."

"And I thought you were a nice guy!" hissed Double Dee curling her collagen-plumped lips.

The Bride glared at him and smacked him with her white drawstring purse. "Go back to your wife, you dick!" she shrieked.

The cops assessed him a seventy-five-dollar fine, twenty-five more than the minimum. When the bouncer escorted Norbie and Rosen to the door, Norbie saw that his red Camry was being hauled away on a tow truck. It would cost a hundred-and-fifty dollars to get it out of impoundment, and he'd have to pay for a taxi to the lot, too. He fumbled with his cell phone and was finally able to call a cab. There were six missed calls from Donna and one bitter voice message. "If you don't think enough of me to get home in time for my birthday party, then I think that is pretty disgusting. But I understand your priorities. And don't bother coming to my sister's."

The ride to the impoundment lot was a long tour of the city's rundown riverfront streets. The lot, no surprise, was attended by some unsavory types and a couple of pit bulls. Nothing like the sweet-tempered Schpilkes. Forced to pay with his credit card, Norbie knew he'd need to intercept the statement before Donna could see it and interrogate him. Not that he'd have to account to her. She wasn't his mother. And if Donna did see the statement with the impoundment charge, he prayed she would not use her paralegal skills to get to the root of the story. The fine for illegal parking, he'd pay with cash.

The drive back to Rosen's place was bleak. Norbie imagined Donna's family at dinner, drinking wine, talking politics, tsk-tsking when his name came up, or maybe not speaking of him at all. "Shit happens," offered Rosen seeking to break the silence and minimize the situation. "All you wanted to do was be happy and have a little fun. Is that such a crime? You'll buy the wife a nice gift, that's all. And you'll say you screwed up. You'll say you went to a sports bar and lost track of the time."

Norbie made no reply. Shame was on him like sloshed beer, and a sick stomachache churned in his gut. Over and over, he saw those censorious whores and the paraplegic man with stringy hair and a life that was so much harder than everyone else's. If only he had refused Rosen's idea and looked harder for a parking spot. That fucking Rosen! And fuck me, fumed Norbie. Fuck me!

"I really think you should help me out with the cost of the fine and the towing," Norbie said to Rosen.

"I don't make bank like you, my friend. From each according to his ability, you know what they say," declared Rosen. He blew a smoke ring with his cigar, a big fat zero in the air. "But I'll see what I can do. Here," he said and handed Norbie a ten-dollar bill. Minus the five bucks for the thong money, Norbie calculated that his companion had really chipped in a measly five.

***

Down and depressed, partly angry, partly worried, feeling not at all like a birthday girl, Donna fed Schpilkes his dinner and drove with Eddie and Annette to her sister's. In the car, the children were very quiet.

When they arrived at her sister's house, Donna preemptively announced that Norbie would not be coming, and after that no one spoke his name. At least being with her side of the family was a comfort. Over eggplant salad, they talked about movies, and as dinner progressed they moved on to Iraq and Afghanistan and the miracles orthopedists were working on injured soldiers. As her mom and dad and her sister sang "Happy Birthday," Donna felt weirdly girlish and unmarried. When she blew out the candles on the pink-and-white cake, she could barely muster her traditional wish: that lightning would strike Jerry Rosen.

No longer in a hurry to get home, Norbie drove to a McDonald's and ordered a vanilla milkshake hoping it would settle his stomach. Amidst the loud primary colors of the McDonald's, he imagined being yelled at by Donna. He drove to a Walgreens and browsed through the gift items—big candles, jars of potpourri, Whitman's Samplers—and ended up buying a bubble bath and dusting powder set, a humorous birthday card, and a festive gift bag for the presentation. He planned on using that excuse about the sports bar.

Schpilkes wagged his tail energetically when Norbie came home and nosed his master's pant legs curious about the unfamiliar odors. When the family arrived home, Eddie bounded up to his dad, hugged him, and asked him where he'd been. Annette was sullen. Donna, her face drawn and colorless, barely looked at her husband.

"Happy birthday," Norbie said attempting cheer and

tried to kiss Donna, who backed away from him. He apologized, offered the sports bar alibi, then handed her the gift bag. He half expected her to clobber him with it à la The Bride, but she merely mumbled thanks and placed the gift bag on the dining room table without peeking inside. There was no yelling. Donna's eerie politeness troubled Norbie; a rant or at least a quick curse would have helped him justify his escapade.

"It must have been a very exciting game," remarked Donna dryly. She wondered how much of Norbie's story she should believe. She had always seen sharply through falseness and remarked on it quickly, but now that falseness seemed so close upon her, she found herself looking for ways to justify Norbie's version of events.

That night, they lay restlessly in their double bed, a shadowy wall between them. Some day this turned out to be, thought Donna, inhaling the new atmosphere of mistrust. Yet as angry as she was with Norbie, she was glad that he had returned, comforted that he had not abandoned her, relieved that he had not been in a car accident. Then she detected the fading whisper of Norbie's cologne. She opened her eyes in the darkness. Cologne? A sports bar? She twitched her nose for the scent of another woman. Finding none, she drifted for a while on a current of bitter thoughts, then fell asleep.

On his side of the bed, Norbie tossed and turned. What is wrong with me, he thought, that I cannot be happy with what I have? Why do I want more? And what do I want more of? Visions of Hot Pantz, Double Dee, and The Bride swam up to him like evil spirits. What a dumb shit he'd been. What rotten luck to be caught by the disabled guy, a man frozen from the waist down, who nevertheless had the power to cause him such anguish.

Norbie reached out to Donna's slumbering form, hoping that she would not wake and shake him off. She was warm, and she was there, and down the hall the children slept, and Schpilkes snoozed, his simple canine mind at peace.

If Donna had known about Norbie's afternoon at the Dirty Martini, she would have been more appalled…and then less. She would have approved grimly of Norbie's comeuppance by the feisty man in the wheelchair. She would have reasoned that at least Norbie didn't buy a lap dance or, horrors, contract with a girl for sex. As for the business about the bill in the thong, well that was practically expected of him as a red-blooded patron, no worse than a woman slipping a dollar into a Chippendale's mankini. But Donna knew none of this, thought none of this. What turned the bad key over and over in her mind was the simple fact that on her birthday her husband had preferred Rosen over her.

A week passed of work and chores and not much talk between them. Donna could not bring herself to use the bubble bath and dusting powder, but she wasn't the type to throw good items in the trash. Unsure of what to do, Donna left the birthday present on the dining room table. At first it glared at her from its brightly colored gift bag, then it seemed to turn into something funky like an overlooked bag of groceries. After a week it practically ossified into a cast. Eventually, she decided to donate it to a women's shelter.

A gauzy mist overcast the sky as Donna, who had taken a half-day off, drove to the shelter office (the actual location of the safe house was kept confidential). In the haze, the sun looked moonlike and opalescent. The route took her down some unfamiliar roads, and, after a while, Donna came upon a white wooden lawn sign planted in some landscaping. The sign read: "7-Day Spa—Massage and Reflexology."

A treatment would feel good, she thought. A way to do something nice for herself. So, she pulled into the parking lot and entered the spa, which looked a lot like a suburban insurance or real estate office. The place was very plain and seemed deserted. Not a receptionist or client in sight. How did they stay in business? Then with a frown, Donna wondered if this could be a happy-endings parlor.

After a moment, a woman emerged from a back room and showed Donna a menu of services. She settled on a half-hour deep tissue massage. The therapist, Rose, was plain-looking and her long mane was grasped in a pink hair claw. She had Donna strip down to her panties and lie face down on the table, which was covered with a white sheet. Rose smoothed massage oil over Donna's back. Her hands were warm, meaty, assertive. Flute and harp music trickled from a portable CD player. This was meant to make the clients zone out, but the plinking and the blowing just irritated Donna. An aromatherapy machine cloyed the air with a heavy vanilla scent. She sneezed a few times.

At first Rose's hands fluttered over Donna's back. Not bad, thought Donna. She could get into this. But it had been a while since she'd had touch, so the niceness also made her feel a little sad. Then Rose began to dig. "You work out?" she asked observing Donna's body tone. "But lots of tension," she said. "Lots of knots." Instead of easing away the tension, the treatment hurt. Was it supposed to feel this way? Perhaps she should ask Rose to stop or go a little lighter. But then she figured that this was what a deep-tissue massage was, so she toughed it out, paid the bill, and, minding her manners, gave Rose a tip. Her back was so sore she had to take a couple of Advil, which luckily she had in her purse. Still, she ached all the way to the women's shelter office. How she regretted that massage. What a stupid thing it turned out to be.

"Of course, our clients would be delighted to have these things. The children will love the bubble bath," said the receptionist at the shelter office, a friendly but cautious woman who took the toiletries, gift bag and all, and didn't ask any questions about the provenance. Donna immediately began to feel better. The receptionist offered a tax receipt, which Donna declined. No sense in letting Norbie know that she had visited a women's shelter, much less donated the birthday present to it.

As Donna drove home, a sense of lightness came over her. The haze had evaporated, and the sun was as yellow as the middle of a daisy. The Advil must have been working because her back didn't hurt as much, and she felt satisfied by her secret deed. In fact, she found its secretness especially pleasing.

When Norbie returned home that evening, he was glad to see the bubble bath and dusting powder gone from the dining room table. He assumed that his wife had come to her senses and had made good use of the gift.

# THE LADY
# WITH A HUNDRED POCKETS

Doris and Mickey drove to the recreational complex in separate cars. They arranged to meet at the playground and cut through to the picnic area where the day-of-fun benefit for Cameron Ferderbar was taking place. Cameron, Doris's neighbor, had fallen off a ladder when cleaning out his roof gutters, and now he was laid up in a rehab facility, which, let's face it, was actually a nursing home that smelled like diapers. Bankruptcy was pawing at the family's door, and the GoFundMe had come up short, so Cameron's men's club was putting on the benefit hoping to cover some of the healthcare bills.

Doris arrived at the playground wearing a Quality Sugar sun visor, a red-and-white striped shirt, and white slacks. Quality processed sugar, and Doris worked in inventory control. As she waited for Mickey, Doris noticed children crowding around a woman dressed in an enormous multicolored patchwork skirt covered in rows of pockets. Next to her was a sign on a chair that read, "The Lady with a Hundred Pockets. Fifty cents per chance."

The woman smelled like a tropical fruit salad. She reminded Doris of a fertility goddess. She wore her hair in a massive braid, thick as a bicycle tire, that she fixed in a circle on top of her head like an Italian Easter bread, except there was no pink or blue dyed egg in it.

Children were begging their adults for change and darting over to the pocket lady. After she zipped their coins into her belt bag, she let them plunge their hands into her pockets. They came up with mini pinwheels, plastic knights, frogs, lions, junk jewelry, and tiny squirt guns. A few kids liked their loot, at least for a moment, but some did not. They wanted to put the junk back and try again. But the pocket lady tilted her head, shook her finger, and said, "For another chance, you must pay again." Most of the adults shelled out for two chances, but when the kids wanted more money, their adults escorted them to the play equipment, and, if they kept making a fuss, back to the car.

Mickey showed up twenty minutes late, but at least he showed up. It was a hot August afternoon, and he was mopping his brow. Doris offered him an air hug. Like Doris, Mickey was in his early sixties. They had met two months ago on a dating site for mature people. Age was just a number, that's what everyone said. Like it was only about age.

Doris had been through one divorce, Mickey three. A solidly built man, he wore his thinning iron-gray hair in comb-over. Not a ridiculous comb-over, one of those trimmer comb-overs. He was a delivery driver for UPS.

"Who's the gypsy?" he asked.

"That's the Lady with a Hundred Pockets. For fifty cents, you get to pick one of her pockets. I'm going to try my luck."

She meant this to sound playful, but Mickey mumbled something about her acting ridiculous and like a little kid and there being better ways to spend money. He stood with his hands in the side pockets of his plaid knee-length shorts while Doris gave the woman two quarters. The lady told her to go for it. Doris stuck her hand into a paisley pocket and pulled out a gold plastic ring with a big faceted plastic ruby in it.

She showed it to Mickey. "My lucky ring. Maybe it will grant me three wishes."

Mickey gave her a whatever look. "Now I know something new about you. You believe in wishes and luck." He mopped his brow again.

"I do happen to believe in wishes and luck," she said, and Mickey gave her another whatever look. It would have been nice if he played along in the spirit of fun, but he evidently did not budge on his principles. She began to think of her wishes, but she kept them to herself. She wished for a caring guy with a sense of humor, speedy healing for Cameron, and a winning state lottery ticket for the Ferderbars. Maybe a winning lottery ticket for herself, too. What did she spend, maybe ten or twenty dollars a week on the state lottery?

"Why don't you put that silly thing back and let a kid get it?"

This made Doris feel ashamed. She put the ring back in its paisley pocket. Maybe some little girl would pull it out and be delighted.

"You don't have to put it back," said the lady. Doris shrugged like it wasn't a big deal. Then she saw the lady aim an evil eye at Mickey. It was like a laser locking onto a target. Maybe she had real gypsy powers. Doris hoped that things would improve during the day of fun.

She had paid for the beef-and-beer tickets, which was only right since this was her cause and the decision to go had been her idea. She wondered what it would be like, Mickey meeting so many of her friends all at once. Maybe he was skittish about that. So far, their dates had been one on one, your basic dinner-and-a-movie thing, and they always went halfsies. It would be nice if he treated her now and then.

The men's club had produced a shindig. A sound system played country music. There was a dunk tank, horseshoes, drawings for gift baskets, bingo for prizes, and a bean bag game called cornhole. It cost extra for the games. There was a prayer station, too. No charge for that, of course. Connie Ferderbar sat in a lawn chair with a giant get-well card that everyone signed. The aroma of barbeque wafted through the air.

Doris and Mickey headed to the food table, Doris waving to acquaintances along the way. There must have been two hundred people there—neighbors, friends, people from the community.

"Didn't Cameron have health insurance?" asked Mickey.

"Connie said he dropped their coverage as soon as the government lifted the no-insurance tax penalty. Not too swift, I know."

"Talk about false economy. And they didn't find him for three hours? He lay there for three hours? Working alone on a ladder, no spotter?"

"He took risks. But you can fall off a ladder even if you have a spotter," remarked Doris.

"The guy's an idiot," said Mickey. "You take precautions. You carry coverage." A yellow jacket flew up to Mickey, and he swatted it away.

"There's good luck and bad luck." Doris thought of all the times Cameron and Connie had been there for her both during her divorce and after. Cameron had helped her with a leaky faucet, a busted screen door. He'd helped her change lightbulbs she couldn't reach.

"Well, he's my friend, and that's the reason we're here. Do you really have to call him an idiot?"

Mickey loaded his plate with a heap of barbequed beef, big mounds of macaroni salad and cole slaw, and stuck tortilla chips into the salads. He took a can of Pabst and headed to the picnic tables, which were under a pavilion. Worried that Mickey had taken more than his share, Doris took less than she wanted, then sat down next to Mickey.

The Chens, the Rothmans, and the DiPietros joined them. After the introductions, Frances Chen updated everyone on Cameron's situation. He'd broken a leg and three ribs, screwed up a shoulder, suffered a concussion, and, worst of all, had a spinal cord injury. The spinal cord injury made it hard to predict if he would walk again. Plus, an infection had cropped up in the diaper-smelling rehab. Don't even ask about the bills. Before the accident, Cameron had managed a restaurant.

"How do you guys know each other?" asked Rose Rothman inclining with interest toward Doris and Mickey.

Marrieds always asked. Singles also asked each other how they met. But that was different, everyone on the same playing field.

"Online dating. That's the way people find each other these days," replied Doris. She spoke in the kind of voice that said she wanted to move on from that topic.

Bea DiPietro said she'd heard quite a few stories about online dating, women meeting creeps and such. Sometimes nice guys too, countered Doris. Bea wanted to know what site she used, and Doris replied in a general way that it was one of the over-fifty sites. In truth, she couldn't recall if it she'd met Mickey on SilverSingles, or OurTime, or one of the others. No law against having two or three accounts at once. It increased your possibility of finding Mr. Right or, at least, Mr. Available. Sometimes Doris saw the same guys overlapping on the sites. Maybe they noticed her overlapping, too.

"That's how it's done now," said Mickey, rescuing Doris. He took a swig of beer. "You meet people online."

"Mickey's a pitcher in a softball league," Doris piped up, and the husbands, clearly impressed, picked up on the sports theme.

After lunch, Doris and Mickey ambled over to the activities area. Doris bought some chances on gift certificates for local hair salons and restaurants. Mickey said she was wasting her money, why not just patronize the places directly? Doris stared at him.

"You do it to help them raise money," she explained like he was some kind of dolt who didn't get it. "The guy had an accident, and now everybody's helping out."

"Well, the guy didn't play his cards right. So now everyone has to bail him out?"

"You think you always deal your own cards, Mickey?" Doris was surprised at her sharp tone. "What about a flood or a hurricane? What about cancer?"

"You buy insurance for those things. You don't buy a house in a flood plain. You manage your risks."

Now he was acting ridiculous. And hard-hearted.

"You can't always control what happens to you. What if you go to a festival and a shooter opens fire?"

"Do you know something I don't?" he said, trying to be funny.

They walked past the horseshoes and the dunk tank to the bean bag toss with the weird name. Mickey wanted to show his pitching chops. The game was popular, and they took their place in line. Doris wondered if he would pay, since cornhole was his idea, or if, at least, they'd go halfsies. The fellow in charge explained the rules of the game, which were fairly involved with all sorts of scoring levels. You aimed to toss the bean bag into the hole, and the holes were on two slanted boards. One board had a sun, the other a moon.

"Hey, Sugar," said a voice behind Doris. There stood Louella from work, also sporting a Quality sun visor. She was with a fellow named John, whom Doris had dated in the past. They had met on OurTime. Or was it SilverSingles? Louella and John were holding hands.

The women made the introductions.

"How do you do?" said Doris, trying to act as if she were meeting John for the first time.

"Pleased to meet you, Doris," returned John. They discovered that they were each there to support Cameron, who was a mutual friend. "A good time for a good cause, but a good cause for a sad reason."

They decided to play teams. First girls against boys, then couples. John took out his wallet. Mickey left his wallet in his pants.

Doris's bean bags kept landing on the grass. Louella had slightly better aim, but the boys won, Mickey landing all this throws right in the hole. Doris noticed that Louella wore a slender gold ring with a tiny red gemstone, a garnet or ruby, on her right ring finger. "A promise ring," said Louella with a glint in her eye.

Doris took the singles prerogative and asked how they met.

"Online dating," said Louella.

"What a coincidence. That's how we met." What had she missed in John? She had thought him boring and stodgy and let things trail off after two dates. What a gentleman he was and clearly in love with Louella.

They changed to couples teams. Louella and John tried impromptu rituals each time they prepared to throw their bean bags, touching an ankle for good luck, doing a few Charleston steps, each breathing on the promise ring. They racked up points, but again Mickey landed all four of his bags in the hole. He tried to help Doris improve her aim, advising her to shoot to the left since her tendency was to pitch to the right, but that did not help. She finally turned around and threw backwards. Shockingly, her last bean bag made the hole.

Mickey shook his head in amazement. "Gotta say, dumb luck won that time."

Doris did a little happy dance.

After the game, Louella and John moseyed off in the direction of the food table, and Doris and Mickey headed to the dunk tank. There was a big crowd there too, and one of the neighbors sat on the platform of the dunk tank cage egging people on, "We want a pitcher, not a glass of water! We want a pitcher, not a belly itcher!" Everyone was missing the target. "You pays your money and you takes your chances," yelled the guy collecting the money. It cost ten bucks for three tries.

"Sugar, I'd like a shot at that dunk tank. Bet I could sink the guy," said Mickey.

"I bet you could," said Doris. "Show 'em what you got."

Mickey stood there with an expectant look. Then he rubbed his fingers together in a where's-the-money gesture.

Doris blinked. "Pretty much, Mickey," said Doris, "it's your turn to pay for some of the entertainment. To be fair, I mean, looking at the whole afternoon."

"The laid-up guy is your friend. It's a conflict of interest for me. I don't believe in paying the bills for people who got themselves into their messes. Ethically, you should pay."

"Ethically? Ethically, there's something called sharing and generosity." She looked at him for a response. He looked at her. It was a standoff. "Come on, Mickey. Come *on*," said Doris. "Don't be cheap and childish. You're acting like a little kid asking his mom for money. Like those kids with the pocket lady."

Mickey blazed a look at Doris. She had called him on his behavior, maybe overdid it, and he more than didn't like it. He looked ferocious, and it scared her.

He tore a ten-dollar bill from his wallet and thrust it at the carnival barker guy. People noticed his rapid movements. He was making a scene.

Maybe she should have paid the ten bucks and afterward called it quits between them. A one-time appeasement. But something in her made her say what she said and in the tone that she said it.

Everyone stepped back as Mickey wound up for the pitch. Doris knew his skill, but the others did not. They only saw his aggression, the hard set of his mouth, and Doris standing by with a crooked smile. She knew that in the privacy of a home, which they would never ever share, he would always be right, even if he were not right. She knew that type. The type that called disagreement starting a fight.

Mickey launched his meanest fastball and hit the bullseye hard. It was assault by proxy. She could feel it. He smiled a triumphant smile. Normally people would clap and laugh as the guy in the dunk tank dropped into the drink. Instead, silence settled over the crowd. "You really know how to spoil an afternoon," he snapped loud enough for others to hear. "Don't bother to call." With that, Mickey stalked off in the direction of the playground.

Her face reddened with embarrassment, but it would have been worse if Louella and John had witnessed the drama. How lucky that she and Mickey had come in separate cars.

Abandoned, or was it liberated? Doris wandered around the grounds. "Old Town Road" played on the sound system. She looked at her cell phone and watched other people play bingo and lawn games. She joined Connie Ferderbar and chatted with her about the great turnout, the tasty barbeque, and the loving and supportive friends.

Frances Chen, Rose Rothman, and Bea DiPietro joined them. Had they observed the scene at the dunk tank?

"Where's your friend?" asked Bea.

"He had to go somewhere," replied Doris, trying to look stoic. The women nodded.

"I don't know how anyone finds anyone in this world," said Frances.

"It takes a miracle, but you have to believe in miracles," said Rose.

Doris did not stick around for the prize drawings. She said her farewells and made her way toward the playground and the parking lot. She'd taken a chance on Mickey, and it wasn't a winning chance. Or maybe she had chosen Mickey, and it turned out to be a bad choice. Her thoughts turned to poor Cameron, and she considered how much more serious other peoples' problems could be.

The lady with a hundred pockets was packing up. She recognized Doris and waved to her. She didn't smell like a tropical fruit salad anymore and her elaborate Easter bread hairdo was falling apart. She still wore the face of a seer, but now she looked more world weary.

"Where's your man friend?"

"He couldn't stay," replied Doris. "He had to leave."

"That dude was a jerk. You can do better. Here, have another try at a pocket. It's on me."

Doris found the same paisley pocket in which she'd found the ring. Lo and behold, the golden piece of junk, the trinket that Mickey had shamed her into giving back, was still there. She smiled and slid the clunky thing onto her finger. As Doris drove back home, she felt safe. She had never felt safer. And she thought of her wishes, which were pretty things and well worth wishing for, even though they might never come true.

# Little Secrets

Maurice Warminster, the winner of practically every major poetry prize in the country, the man to whom Kerrie Shapiro had dedicated *Little Secrets*, her first collection of poems; the man who was Kerrie's cherished thesis advisor, who told her to give herself over to poetry, that sideways was the best way into a poem, to make the strange familiar and the familiar strange; the man who, in defiance of the MFA program's very strict policy, had bedded her many times including once, memorably, at a conference in San Miguel de Allende; Maurice Warminster, who declined to recommend Kerrie's manuscript to his friend Jack at Stonington Press or Melvin at Megillah Press, claiming that he had made a new year's resolution not to pull strings for students (even as Kerrie knew that he was a consummate puller of strings); Maurice Warminster, who also had begged off blurbing her book, though Kerrie made the case that their closeness should mean something to him; Kerrie's own Maurice, whom she loved still and anyway, was to give the John Keats Society reading at Gailor College where Kerrie was now an adjunct in English comp. The news that Maurice was coming shot through her breast like a golden arrow.

Gailor spared no expense sprucing up the campus for the honored guest. The buildings and grounds crew repainted, in a handsome shade of ochre, the auditorium in which Maurice Warminster would speak. Workers varnished the old and slightly wobbly wooden lectern from which he would deliver his complex meditations on love and independence, his political poems, and the narratives of his working-class youth.

Kerrie found a publisher for *Little Secrets*. The book, released four months before by a small literary press in Evanston, had a lovely lime green cover. On the back were laudatory blurbs by three well-known poets. Kerrie could have mailed the book to Maurice, but hearing of his visit to Gailor, she set her heart on placing an inscribed copy in his hands. The scene floated before her eyes: they would sit together on a secluded garden bench, renewing if only for half an hour, their intellectual, if not physical, passion. She had so much to tell him, longed for his advice, missed his gray eyes, his hippyish chin-length hair, the practiced feel of his embrace. They had not seen each other for a year.

Aware that Maurice never replied to emails or letters, Kerrie phoned him two weeks before the reading and left a message suggesting lunch at her apartment or perhaps a visit to Gailor's English garden. He did not call back. Undeterred, she called him several more times and finally reached him days before his arrival. After her flurry of I-miss-you's and I-love-you's followed by Maurice's cunning elided retorts— "And I you"—Kerrie scaled back her get-together ideas to simply coffee or a stroll through campus. Gailor was lovely in early fall, the green of the trees and lawns against the red and orange brick of the buildings called to mind the work of Kazimir Malevich, a Russian painter he admired. She could not wait to give him her book.

"There won't be time, dear. I only have half a day." He spoke in a voice of false regret. She recognized the voice. She'd heard him use it when dismissing other people. A darkness, like the shadow of a bird, passed over her.

"But surely you'll have a little time for me, Maurice." For they had been naked together, meandered for hours deep in discussions of poetry, politics, life, and love. He had shared secrets: who had affairs with whom, who showed great promise then disappeared from the scene, who was bipolar, who divorced. Such gossip from Helicon, outrageous, hilarious, sorrowful.

Kerrie yearned to tell Maurice of her poet's life, not so much secrets but things that would make him proud—her work in progress, writers she met, where she was publishing. And the good reviews her book had received—written mostly by friends, but still. And she had a small following on campus, was mentoring an especially talented student. Sure, her Amazon sales sucked, but didn't every poet's Amazon sales suck?

"The department head has scheduled every moment for us, Kerrie dear."

Again, the bird shadow. "Who is 'us'?" she asked carefully.

"By 'us,' I mean Olivia and me. Olivia is the woman I am seeing. Didn't you hear about Olivia? She's marvelous. A poet, the best in the program. She speaks three languages. And paints. And plays competitive golf." He chuckled mentioning the golf. Kerrie was teed off.

"Did you have to bring her here? This is my place, Maurice."

"She's my partner. We travel together. That's how it works. That's what we used to do, remember?"

Kerrie parried the idea that the partner travel was planned out of meanness, though she suspected that it was. Maurice could cut with a sly knife. Weren't his refusals of a publishing connection and a blurb just those sorts of jabs? Time, separation, sparser and sparser phone conversations had diminished their intimacy, flattened their heart-to-hearts to cordialities. Twice before she had protested his shrinking interest in her and tried to revive their bond: once by publishing a pithy essay about his work, once by abject pleading. She could not turn his mind. Now their tie was as split and withered as a dead squash vine, and he would come to trample on its remains.

Even so, the memory of their affair strode through her thoughts. The lyrics of *Little Secrets* stood as a record of their passion. She thought of the inscription she had penned in his copy, "To Maurice, mentor and true friend, forever in my heart, this book is for you, for us. All my love, Kerrie." How those words gurgled over the top. She wondered if she should give him an uninscribed copy. Or no book at all. She dismissed the latter. Why gift him with relief, especially when he was about to parade his new favorite before her? "To M. W." was printed, at this point it glared like a typo, on the dedication page. The bolder statement, the truer statement, would be to present him with the book. Anything else would be denial, an act of yielding, of scampering away in defeat.

"Won't I see you at the dinner before the event?" asked Maurice.

"The dinner," she repeated as evenly as possible. Of course, there would be a dinner. There was always a dinner, but Kerrie had received no such invitation.

"The dinner at the home of the departmental chair. I thought you'd be on the list. Or maybe only tenured people. The chair—what's her name?—Donna Something, knows you studied with me. But you understand how these things work, hierarchies, protocols, whose ass needs kissing, et cetera, et cetera."

Again, the Maurice of the sly knife. A discreet suggestion to the chair, Donna Grabowski, with that chuckle of his, about skirting an awkward situation. Or perhaps he preempted the issue with a generous little speech about his desire to meet her full-time and tenured people. Kerrie, humiliated, the tip of her ear burning, managed to sign off without sobbing. That came in the privacy of her apartment.

Alone in her bed, shifting from side to side, Kerrie wept on and off for an hour, strewing damp white Kleenexes about her floor. Maurice could very well have asked Donna Grabowski to include her at the dinner—or to exclude her. And Donna would have complied out of courtesy and deference. How Kerrie would have liked to have seen herself at the gathering, hob-nobbing with senior faculty, talking about poets and writers, chatting amiably with Maurice, being nice enough to Olivia while boiling inside. She might have impressed her bosses, earned consideration for a lit class or a creative writing workshop. She didn't want to be relegated to comp for the rest of her life. Not that there was anything wrong with comp.

Her tears dried. Kerrie's thoughts then swerved back to the old affair, which no longer seemed as ardent as before. She gathered up the Kleenexes. They looked like a bouquet of wilted white carnations. She chucked them in the garbage.

The evening of Maurice Warminster's John Keats Society reading at Gailor College, Kerrie chose a flattering knit dress of hunter green, which she accessorized with small gold hoop earrings and a paisley scarf. She came early and took an aisle seat in the second row. He would have to look her in the eye, at least for a moment. She would give him the book.

Donna, Maurice, Olivia, who was a beautiful woman, tanned, fit, smooth and poised, entered the auditorium followed by the rest of the departmental dignitaries. Students, faculty, community people, poets from the local flourishing coffeehouse scene, all chatting excitedly, packed the room. Kerrie waved to some friends. Trina, the student Kerrie was mentoring, beamed at her and gave her a thumbs up. Did she find it odd, knowing of Professor Shapiro's ties to Maurice, that she was not part of the retinue?

As Warminster, wearing a black sport coat and dusky-blue turtleneck that betrayed a slight paunch, took his seat, Kerrie darted over to give him a hug. He smelled leathery. She whispered how good it was to see him. She pressed *Little Secrets* into his hand. He accepted her offering with a tentative smile, congratulated her, scanned the blurbs.

"And how good to see you, Kerrie." His tone was formal, clipped. "Too long, too long. Have you met Olivia?" Olivia extended her bronzed hand and grasped Kerrie's like the grip of a golf club. Then Warminster handed Olivia the copy of *Little Secrets*. Kerrie sizzled.

Donna Grabowski approached the old lectern, which had a short corner. The moment she touched it, it wobbled. The water in the speaker's glass jiggled as if from a mild earthquake. She welcomed the audience and introduced Warminster with wit, well-chosen quotations, a list of his major awards. Applause rose up when he approached the lectern. As soon as Warminster leaned his heft against the stand, it rocked and the water glass shook precipitously. "That lectern must be nervous," he quipped. A wavelet of amusement rolled over the audience.

Then Warminster gripped the old and beautifully varnished wooden stand more forcefully, which made it seesaw even more due to its short corner. He seized the water glass before it fell on his books and papers. "Olivia, darling, could you find something to put under that corner?" Immediately, athletically, Olivia jumped up and jammed Kerrie's book under the corner to stabilize the lectern. "Ah, at last a practical use for poetry," said Warminster. The crowd tittered.

Incensed that *Little Secrets* had been cast to the ground and used as a shim, Kerrie, though not as gracefully as Olivia, sprang from her seat. People stared. Kerrie froze. Self-consciousness held her back, but only for a split second. Heart speeding, she dashed up and snatched her book from under the lectern. "How dare you shove my book under that stand!" she fired at Olivia.

A hush fell over the crowd.

"*Excuse me.* This is a reading by Maurice Warminster," Olivia said severely.

"Now, Kerrie, come now," chimed Maurice in mock admonishment. "Are you not a supporter of the arts?" Kerrie glared at him. Clucks of laughter rose from a few in the audience.

"That's my book. The book I wrote about us!" blurted Kerrie. "I will not have my book treated like that."

Some shame noises, *whoa*'s and *tsk*'s, spun up from

a few in the audience. But the crowd was not all of the same mind. Other people stirred in their seats and spoke.

"Stand up for your book, miss," someone called out.

"Don't throw her book on the floor!" shouted Trina.

"Hey, you, sit down," barked a male voice. "Show some respect to Dr. Warminster."

"They should respect the book!" sounded a voice.

Astounded, Kerrie turned to face the audience. Though the *tsk*'ers still *tsk*'ed and hand-motioned her to sit down, a number of others clapped. Kerrie Shapiro felt jittery, vindicated, heated, and excited by the attention.

Then someone pointed to Warminster. Kerrie spun around. As if he were Sir Walter Raleigh with his cape, the poet bent down and with a flourish slid one of his own books under the troublesome corner of the stand. "Look!" he announced with stagey gallantry. "Now I am a supporter of the arts." A small swell of high-brow chuckling rose from the crowd.

Kerrie's mood slid downward. Now he was getting the best of it. Well, good for him. Red-faced, gripping the book, she made her way down the center aisle, everyone turning their heads to stare. One step landed with shaky pride, one step in a puddle of embarrassment. When she made it back to her apartment, she had to use one hand to unclench the other hand that held *Little Secrets.*

Unable to stand the sight of the book, she hid it under a pile of student essays. It seemed to smoke. She transferred it to a canvas book satchel. But there it seemed like a rabbit that might jump out of a hat. She finally zipped it into a suitcase, drank three glasses of wine, and passed out.

The next morning, her head a gray balloon, Kerrie found her social media packed with comments about the night before. Someone had swapped his own Warminster book for Maurice's under-the-lectern copy, and the show had gone on, though it lacked a certain verve. Once the high comedy of the Kerrie kerfuffle passed, the poet's patter fell flat. The post-reading buzz was all about Kerrie's standup moment. Trina posted that the instant the reading ending, cell phones lit up all over the room like fireflies. Kerrie scrolled through the postings on her Facebook wall.

*-Glad you rose up, Kerrie.*

*-Way to go.*

*-You were the best part of the night. Gawd, MW was so booorring.*

*-You caused quite a flap, ha!*

*-Everyone wants to buy your book.*

A blogger took up Kerrie's cause. By noon her Amazon rank shot way up. No such thing as bad PR. She was unsure of how much of all of this was scandal, how much triumph. But who cared? She smiled to herself, reveling in her newfound notice.

Still, the dedicated book, the troublemaker, the one in her suitcase, felt nuclear. But dump it in the recycling she would not. Forcing herself from bed, she took a hot shower, packed up for her afternoon comp class, put the copy of *Little Secrets* into a bag, and headed for the Gailor College library. The autumn air felt fresh and cool. The afternoon sun showered gold on the velvety campus lawns. She told the acquisitions librarian, a man she'd seen a few times at coffeehouse poetry events, that she wanted to donate the book to the college library.

"Is this *the* book from last night?" he asked with an inhale of surprise. The librarian, a pale man with interested eyes, looked at Kerrie. "Are you sure you want to donate it?"

"Absolutely." Relief washed over her as she pulled the fateful copy of *Little Secrets* from the bag. The librarian handled the book as if it were a precious artifact.

He explained to her that the book was part of literary history, at least as far as Gailor College was concerned. It would go into Special Collections. It would live in a locked glass case alongside other rare books, and, although it would not circulate, Kerrie could visit it whenever she liked. Kerrie thanked him, but she doubted that she should ever wish to touch that copy again. Still, the book's new status as a museum piece appealed to her. She saw it as a beautiful green bird, killed by an arrow, taxidermied, protected under glass. Never to be thrown on the floor or cast aside. Meanwhile, all the others of its kind were free to fly.

# Student Rebellion

9:15 a.m.

The revolt against the humanities faculty begins as student rebels halt professors in the middle of class and usher them to the quad. Some of the professors assume that they are being led to an assembly honoring them for their service.

Rebel leader Gillian Jones passes around a box and orders the professors to hand over their pens and paper.

"From now on, no writing on dead trees," orders Gillian.

"And no reading from them either," chimes in cellphone poet Billy "Bullz" Rohrer.

"How are we to jot down a thought?" Dr. Leon Babbage wonders aloud.

"Or write in our planners?" asks Dr. Nia Stone.

9:40 a.m.

The captive faculty mingle nervously as rebels march another group of professors into the quad.

"The more the merrier," says Dr. Kelly Donaldson.

"I love a good mass roundup," says Dr. Gloria Jiménez.

"Detain them in the library," commands Gillian.

"Not the library," counters co-leader Franklin Li. "They love the library."

"Yeah, no," replies Bullz. "Lock 'em in the computer center. They hate computers."

"No, yeah," says Karim Mohammed.

"Yeah, no," says Yael Cohen.

Gillian, Franklin, Bullz, Karim, and Yael herd the teachers into the computer center.

Stone says that she needs to use the ladies' room.

Gillian hastily tapes a "Gender Neutral Bathroom" sign on the nearest men's room. Glowering, Stone stomps into the facilities and strides past the urinals, some of them in use. Grateful to find a stall with a door, Stone tends to business. Why the term "gender"? What's wrong with the word "sex"? Does sex sound too sexy to them? When she was in college, she was all about sex. Had a lot of it, was a big fan. Yes, those were the days.

11:00 a.m.

The rebels torture the professors by forcing them to learn a new online teaching platform. Once the professors have mastered some of the basics, the young radicals send through an update that completely changes the system.

"We still have the power of grades," whispers Jiménez to Dr. Louis Greenbaum.

"Whom do you think you're kidding?" says Greenbaum. "They'll grind us down with their wheedling emails like they always do until we put through a grade change."

"I'm starving," moans Babbage.

"Hang in there, Leon. Maybe they'll bring in some non-allergenic, non-GMO, nut-free, gluten-free, organic, soy food," encourages Dr. Rita Chang. Images from the movie *Soylent Green* float into the consciousness of several of the faculty.

12:30 p.m.

Gillian arraigns the detainees. "We hereby charge you with criminal use of the sexist pronouns 'he, him, his' and 'she, her, hers' and your anti-progressive refusal to accept 'they, them, their' as universal gender-free singulars. We condemn your refusal to use the terms 'Latinx' and 'alumnx,' and we condemn, in advance, your refusal to use any x-suffix inclusive terms yet to be invented."

She takes a breath, "We call for an end to the time-wasting teaching of long works, such as novels and epic poems."

"From now on, it's flash fiction, haiku, and tweets," interjects Bullz.

"Furthermore, any so-called textbooks are to be provided free online."

"There go the royalties," sighs Babbage.

"You get royalties?" asks Donaldson, shooting Babbage a jealous glance.

"Our PDF Liberation Organization will upload all books to free open-access websites," says Franklin.

"That's theft of intellectual property!"

"Piracy!"

"Copyright violation!"

The professors shout out their protests, knowing that they are helpless before the tech-savvy rebels.

"And no more essay writing. Multiple choice tests and PowerPoint decks only," adds social media chief Elsie "L-Z" Lockhart, scrolling through their cell phone.

"How are you going to learn anything?" challenges Greenbaum.

"EduSnack Packs," Karim replies. "All prepackaged and free online. Gives students the highlights. Easy as popping Skittles."

"At least I won't get a backache from toting twelve pounds of books in my knapsack," says Chang. "My arthritis is killing me."

"And my bursitis. Don't get me started about my bursitis," adds Dr. Pete Milano.

"Does anyone know a good cataract surgeon?" inquires Stone. "Getting to be that time for me."

The young rebels shake their heads in pity. Karim fiddles with their nose ring. Yael adjusts their "Cancel Gender!" button.

"We furthermore accuse you," says Gillian, "of white privilege, Black privilege, Asian privilege, Latinx privilege, and Boomer privilege. We accuse you of homophobia, heterophobia, transphobia, and all the other phobias now known or yet to be developed. You stand accused of Islamophobia and antisemitism, the teaching of dead white male writers and live white male writers. We call for an end to syllabx and lecturx." The manifesto covers a dozen more biases and insensitivities.

"No lecturx?" says a perplexed Babbage. "How will I share my knowledge?"

"You give lecturx?" says Chang. "Leon, no wonder you're exhausted. You should just show videos in class like me."

2:00 p.m.

The rebels mercifully allow the professors to order their own lunches by old-fashioned phone calls. After lunch, the captives must face the horror of the gender-neutral necessary.

Yael, Karim, and Bullz break the professors into groups for intense self-criticism sessions. The professors apologize for their sexist and non-progressive use of outdated forms of grammar, obsolete pedagogy, flagrant use of paper, failure to offer trigger warnings before discussing disturbing material, unconscionable tolerance of opposing opinions, rejection of cancel culture, and every other social offense and insensitivity, real, imagined, or future.

"We trust that you will take this re-education session with the utmost seriousness," declares Gillian.

"Remember," warns social media chief L-Z, brandishing their cell phone, "we have command of Twitter, TikTok, Snapchat, Instagram, Facebook, and all the other platforms, plus we're on every professor-rating website."

A shudder runs through the captives. How often had they been pilloried on the professor-rating sites, always surprised by what mild remarks ignited fierce offense?

"We can hack anything," says L-Z.

Gillian makes a hand motion as if to tell the powerful social media chief to tamp it down.

"Remember when we used to say don't trust anyone over thirty?" Stone whispers to Babbage.

"Now, it's people under thirty," he laments. "It's either that or depend on them."

"Remember when we protested the war in Vietnam? Remember Black lib, gay lib, women's lib, and farmworkers rights?" says Jiménez.

"Now I feel so nostalgic," says Chang with a faraway smile. "My husband and I met at a sit-in."

"Maybe we brought this on ourselves," muses Milano.

"You think?" says Stone.

4:50 p.m.

The student rebels order the teachers to pose for a group mugshot. Milano extends his middle finger and covers it with the fist of his other hand. He nudges his colleagues to do the same. Soon all the professors, wearing sly smiles, display the secret gesture.

L-Z snaps photos and posts them on social media.

A torrent of responses pours in about the hand signal.

"Are you making some kind of elitist, Boomer privilege, retro hippie, white power, racist hand signal?" accuses Gillian.

"Not at all," 'splains Milano. "This is a sign of solidarity among the people of the remote Brazilian Amazon.

Quite well known in progressive academia. Trending, really."

"We should try that," says L-Z. "We need to be more woke."

All the rebels form the gesture and salute each other with it, their faces glowing with new conviction.

5:00 p.m.

"I have to get to my job," says Yael.

"I have a midterm tomorrow," says Karim.

"My parents are expecting me for dinner," Bullz pipes up.

"I could use a martini," says Babbage.

Gillian gathers the rebels. They all give each other the secret gesture. Gillian dismisses the professors.

"We'd like our pens and paper back," says Chang feeling bold.

"Fine," concedes Gillian. "Just don't use them to write anything."

"We hope this will not affect our grades," says Franklin.

"No, yeah," says Greenbaum, attempting the senseless affirmative-negative collation popular with the youth.

Franklin stares darkly at Greenbaum as if double-crossed.

"I mean, yeah, no," Greenbaum corrects himself.

"No, yeah," says Karim.

"Yeah, no," says Yael.

"No, yeah," Babbage jumps in, thinking that logically the interjections should negate each other. Then he wonders if the "no" is a serious "no" or if the "yeah" could be a "yeah" of goodwill followed by the "no" of gentle disagreement. Gentle disagreement. That would be nice, but was the world ready for it?

# Mothers and Daughters

When the midnight owl hooted and cast its sharp eyes on all my worries and cares, when insomnia quelled my normal inhibitions, and when, not to sound too self-pitying, I also felt rather lonesome, I went on the Internet and looked up people I used to know. Scrolling through their golden lives made me feel worse than ever. Jeanne Chatham, the theater major I knew in college, was now the vice president of an insurance company. Jeff Stone, the PR chief from my old job at the art supply store, made millions as a land developer in Arizona. Barry Cutler, plain and timid in high school, beamed in his tuxedo in his son's wedding photos. Once morose and chubby, Sookie Billingsley from my old diet club glammed like a movie star in her exercise videos. Every once in a while, I looked up my ex-husband Dave. Still selling cars at the dealership and living with his new wife in their high-rise apartment with panoramic views of the Delaware. Under my name, I found a White Pages listing and the usual people-finder ads but nothing else about the life of Faye Glassman.

I never contacted any of these people. But almost every day, I emailed my daughter Petra with news of cat food recalls, phishing scams, shootings, house fires, and other perils. I loved her so much.

Petra had unfriended me on Facebook, blocked my phone calls, and, I guessed, deleted my emails or flagged them as spam.

"Take a chill pill, Mom. I can't talk to you anymore. You're using up my qi," she announced four months ago, and that was the last time we spoke.

Anyhow, I kept up with her after a fashion. To gaze at her lovely face, I visited the website of the elementary school where she taught. I read her lesson plans, smiled at the daily enthusiasms that festooned her class calendar. Framed photos of Petra greeted me in every room of my house. Petra baking cookies. Petra in her soccer uniform. Petra as high school grad, a college grade, Petra and her boyfriend, Bob. Although we lived outside of Philadelphia, no more than three miles apart, I had not seen her since Thanksgiving when she and Bob presented me with a pumpkin pie then ran off to dinner at Dave's.

January of 2020 came with whispers of a new respiratory illness in China, a threat so remote we thought it hardly mattered. But now it was March, and the new coronavirus was rolling over the defenseless globe. My emails to Petra turned medical. Did she have a dry cough, a fever, chills, a feeling of exhaustion? Did she see the reports about Italy and Spain? Did she think the virus came from the horseshoe bat?

In order to halt the spread of the virus, Pennsylvania locked down in the middle of March: schools, libraries, offices and stores, gyms and hair salons, the museum where I worked part-time at the visitors' desk, and all the other museums, everything nonessential went from on to off. You hardly saw a plane in the sky or a car on the road. Every day dawned like early Sunday morning, quiet but for birdsong, and, happily, the air was alive with that. I sheltered in my home, fearful of breathing in the virus or touching a door handle that might be coated with the spiky little balls of the disease. When I had cabin fever, I screwed up my courage and ventured out for a walk.

"I used to think that a nuclear war or an asteroid smash would end life as we know it. Now look," I wrote to Petra. "Some enemy RNA is going to worm its way into our cells and finish us off. Can you imagine?" Petra sent me no response.

I had always lived in an ambient state of fear, but now so did everyone. For once, I was right in step with the status quo. I reminded Petra of the lifespan of the virus on paper, plastic, glass, and metal, of how far it could fly through the air. Could I run an errand for her?

Hand sanitizer was in short supply, but I could hunt some down for her or mix up a batch myself. She must be overwhelmed with all her online teaching. Had she seen the mass graves of unclaimed victims in New York?

She could have written me to say: Mom, I'm fine. Mom, you'll be fine. Take some cleansing breaths.

But she didn't.

If I had a close friend or two, I would not have leaned on Petra so, but my social life bounced around on short-hop conversations between coworkers and minor acquaintances. It wasn't easy to make new friends after the divorce: my few attempts made me feel as if I were nosing into other people's lives. Now, however, that the threat of contagion sent everyone into isolation, lots of people felt lonely. Again, I was right in step with the status quo. Living by myself, I hardly uttered a word aloud. Pleasing chats with Ted across the street and Bonnie next door and the clerks at the supermarket only went so far. Everyone ended conversations by saying, "Stay safe."

The newscasters and features writers began to encourage people to check in on each other, offer to run errands, phone to say hello. This call to action perked me up. Not only could I contact people I knew, I *should* contact them. It wouldn't seem weird. It was my civic duty.

I stopped trolling the Internet for updates on the denizens of my past and instead scrolled through the contacts in my cell phone. I embarked on my mission with relish, texting my coworkers at the museum, my neighbors, my neighbors who had moved away, women from my old garden club, distant relatives, ex-relatives.

"Hi Clarence/Jane/Maryanne/Paula/Linda/Terry/Robert/Rachel/Bess/Deborah/Mimi/or any of twenty other names! Faye Glassman here, checking in. How's it going? I hope this message finds you well. If you need anything, just call."

My spirits soared at the chime of their replies. Some sent emojis: a smiley face, a thumbs up. Others gifted me with words: "Working from home. So busy!" "Baking bread." "Bingeing on Netflix." "About to Facetime with my grandkids." "Thanks for checking in. Hope you're well." The texts made me smile like the tiny yellow celandines of early spring, and like celandines they bloomed but once.

I hoped to hear from everyone, but some people did not text back, and some replies brought horrid news. Jane Lincoln said, "We can only wave to my father from his nursing home window." Rachel Barsky wrote of her mother's death. "We're quarantining now. Terrible times." Why did I not think ahead to the possibility that my eager shout-outs might reap some grim replies?

I emailed Petra with the latest infection totals and death statistics. Did she know how unreliable the Covid-19 tests were? So many false negatives. But it still made sense to get a test at CVS, especially with Bob going in and out of her apartment. Did she consider that he could be a vector? Had her auto insurance company reduced her premium? Less driving, fewer accidents, now there was an upside to the lockdown. As usual, my daughter did not respond.

My texting mission, with its bright pops of cheer and black bursts of awfulness, could not last long for I soon ran through all my cell phone contacts and thought it prudent not to bug my respondents with another round of texts. Craving conversation, I decided to call people who still had landlines.

I retrieved my tattered green address book. As a precaution, I checked the names against online obituary listings before I placed my calls. I found no deceased but unhappily few landlines still in service. As for phones that did ring, how very exciting when some old acquaintances said hello. I hooked some conversations with nonplussed folks who must have blinked in astonishment to hear my voice. "Hi, it's Faye Glassman. Long time, I know. Now that we're all hunkered in our bunkers, I thought I'd catch you at home, ha ha, and see how you're doing in these strange times. Safe and well, I trust." Then I'd pause for their reply. While I annoyed a handful of people who dispatched me with a terse "What can I do for you?" or "Super busy, working from home," I netted some who caught me up on their doings.

"We're moving to North Carolina. At least, that's the plan. You okay?" replied Chip Elverson. He asked if I were conducting a psychological survey or working for the Census.

I was half glad to be bored by Nina Cohen, who droned on about her online grocery orders, her wiping and washing, her canceled trip, all the books she'd read, her son's promotion, her adorable grandchildren, her husband and his crossword puzzles. I had to find an excuse to get off the line.

"Nice to have a call from you out of the blue," said Sandy Sherman. "No, not too weird at all. These are weird times, and they call for weird measures."

When Sandy asked how I was holding up, I grew shy and brief: why darken this friendly conversation with my worries and fears? Instead, I pivoted to Petra, who was great. Teaching third-graders online. What a world, right?

Did you hear, I emailed Petra, that pets can get covid and that people could get covid from their pets? How do you teach remotely if there is a power failure or computer crash? And was this the end of brick-and-mortar schools? And what about office towers, libraries, college campuses, and museums, for pity's sake? Do you remember when I was so worried about my arthritis? Those were the days. Maybe she read the email, maybe not.

I dusted the house from top to bottom, swept and vacuumed, watched all of *Grace and Frankie* and *The Marvelous Mrs. Maisel*. I read the *Bucks County Courier Times*, my *AARP Bulletin,* and the free circulars that came in the mail. One article in a little shopper paper caught my eye. A county agency was inviting isolated elders to sign up to receive phone calls from volunteers. Surely, they needed friendly people to make the outreach calls. Now I could call someone who *wanted* to be called.

I dialed the number of the county agency, my heart rate picking up a bit as if I were telephoning someone for a date.

"We'd be happy to have one of our community volunteers call you, Mrs. Glassman," said the staffer.

"Oh, not for myself. I'm perfectly fine. I want to be a volunteer. You must need more volunteers."

Yes, he said, provided that the volunteers could commit to their elder for a minimum of a month. The clients looked forward to the calls. I assured him that I was the dedicated type. Reaching out was what I did best. He gave me the link to the application form.

A week later after a background check and a video interview, the man from the agency got back to me with the good news. I was accepted! They gave me the phone number of Mrs. Lucy Shawmont, a widow, age eighty-seven, who resided at Autumn Woods, a senior-living community. The sort of place I guessed I'd end up one day.

"Lucy is 'with it,'" the volunteers' coordinator explained, but one part of her background was strange. "She says she has a daughter who lives out West somewhere, but she has no contact information for her. We don't know what to make of it."

Our first chat was to be no more than twenty minutes, the staffer explained, and from there I should set up a regular phone schedule. A phone date you can both look forward to, he said, and emailed me a list of ice breakers and some discreet quality-of-life questions, as well some don't-go-there items, such as politics and religion. He also advised that I not ask Lucy about her daughter. You never know what kind of gopher hole you might step into, he said.

I composed a message to Petra but told her nothing about my new role as an elder-caller. Did she have enough masks? Did she watch the conferences with Dr. Fauci and Dr. Birx? The death rate of covid patients on ventilators was over twenty percent. Could she taste and smell things? That was the latest: covid could take away your senses of taste and smell. Out went my message into the electronic void.

At ten the next morning, I dialed up Mrs. Lucy Shawmont. She answered on the first ring. Excitement rushed through her voice, matching my own anticipation. After the first bright greetings, however, an awkward pause set in, so I followed the agency's introductory script that asked about health, mood, appetite, and general getting around.

Lucy soon took the lead. She felt okay, normal aches and pains considered. Sure, she had enough to eat. Too much in fact. Leftovers crammed her fridge. Out of fear of contagion, Autumn Woods had closed down the dining room. Attendants delivered heaping meal trays to the rooms, but no one was allowed out of their rooms.

"It's like we're bad children having to go to our rooms and stay there. House arrest, really. All but the ankle monitor. We can't even go out for fresh air or walk in the halls. You hope for a doctor's appointment, just to get an hour of freedom."

"They want to keep you safe." I tried to sound positive.

"They want to avoid a liability case, that's all. Besides, being a prisoner isn't my idea of safe. Takes all the living out of you."

Lucy asked me about myself. Was I married? Did I have children?

"Teaching, bless her," Lucy said of Petra. "She must have a sweet temperament and a lot of patience."

I agreed that Petra was sweet and patient.

And did she live nearby? Did we see each other often?

These days not so much with the stay-at-home guidelines.

Mrs. Shawmont said that talking to me was jolly good. I should call her Lucy, and we set up our next call. I looked forward to it. I knew that she did, too.

I felt restored and lively. I took a long walk. Amazing

what you could discover when you went on foot: jonquils around mailboxes, garden gnomes, kids on their trikes, but none on the tot lots. Signs warned you away from high-touch surfaces. People crossed the street or stepped wide if another walker approached. You did your best not to exhale near others.

The weeks of lockdown crept fretfully by. Now it was early May. We were in our third month of staying at home. I was in my second month as Lucy's phone companion. On the news, I watched the country's death toll mount toward 100,000, a number we thought—how wrong we were—would top the worst tally the statisticians could predict. On her online class page, Petra instructed her students to list five things that made them happy. A nice conversation starter for me and Lucy.

"Did you hear," I wrote to Petra, "Dr. Fauci said that this coronavirus was his worst nightmare? Did you see the case totals? How will we ever get out of this mess?" Not that I expected her to answer.

I began to see my calls to Lucy as special occasions. I put on lipstick, a nice blouse, the way I dressed to work at the visitors' desk at the museum. I thought of all the paintings staring at each other, wondering where the humans went.

I asked Lucy to name five things that made her happy.

"Talking to you makes me happy. Also, I am fond of cinnamon raisin coffeecake, the sing-a-longs and lectures we used to have in our community room, most of all, shooting the breeze with my neighbors, especially Sadie Miller." Lucy cleared her throat. I hoped it was only that and not a cough.

"Oh, look. Mr. Hirsch is making his getaway." Lucy described the little parade: Mr. Hirsch on his walker, his daughter and grandchildren behind him toting suitcases, a lamp, and a TV to the car. "Escapees almost every day. I see them from my window." Lucy coughed. There was no mistaking it for throat clearing. "If you test negative for the virus, they'll let you go. But you can't come back until the plague is over, and who knows when that will be."

"I'm going to bake you a cinnamon raisin coffeecake."

"And bake one for yourself," added Lucy. "Then we can have coffee and cake together over the phone. And if you don't mind, I'll share mine with Sadie Miller. Sometimes we sneak out of our apartments after the night patrol has passed and visit each other. We sit six feet apart and whisper."

"Why you, rebel, you. I'm impressed." I was happy for her and a little jealous that she had a best friend. I was also quite concerned about her cough.

Lucy gave me the address of Autumn Woods and her apartment number. She explained that I must clearly mark the package with her name and apartment number and place it on the designated drop-off table outside the front entrance. The mailman had to put the post there, too. No visitors were allowed inside the doors, only staff and emergency people. Upper management now worked from home.

"But don't the staff go in and out? Returning to their families when they go off duty?" They could be vectors, I thought.

"Don't get me started," said Lucy interrupting herself with a cough.

"Lucy, about that cough..."

"Oh, it's nothing," she said. She asked if it would be okay if she called me sometimes. "I won't be a burden. I imagine you have so much to do." I gave her my number with pleasure. "Call any time," I said. She coughed again.

I baked two cinnamon raisin coffeecakes and treated myself to the first warm delicious slice. I packaged Lucy's cake and jotted a note to tuck inside: "So glad that the County Department of Aging has brought us together." Then I worried that the staff might open the package, read the note, and conclude that Lucy was complaining about Autumn Woods. I tore up that note and wrote a new one that said cheerful things about friendship and cake, then I drew flowers on the page.

I drove to Autumn Woods, a trip that was not nearly as fraught as going to the grocery store. Wearing my blue mask, I deposited the cake on the table. A staff person, masked and gloved, recorded the drop-off. A family was moving an elderly woman out. Just as Lucy said, the place was emptying. I looked up and waved to some windows, not knowing which might be Lucy's or if she was at her watch post. What if Sadie's family moved her out? Lucy would lose her best friend. I wondered what it must be like to be one of a dwindling number of residents.

So consumed was I with Lucy that I had not written my daughter for several days. I composed an email: "Petra, how do the young mothers cope, working from home with all the daycare centers closed? And what if the parents were laid off? Even more terrible." What was the use in writing her? I saved the email to drafts.

The following day, Lucy called to say that the staff had brought her the cake, and she had shared it with Sadie that night. Sadie raved and said it smelled and tasted divine. "But I don't have much of an appetite," Lucy confessed. "Or it's my tastebuds. I don't get the same enjoyment out of food." Loss of taste and smell. And her little cough. Covid symptoms. It was beginning to add up. Lucy said that she was feeling weary and needed to lie down. I insisted that she call her doctor after her nap. I would phone her tomorrow morning as usual. I feared that this could go nowhere but worse. I rubbed my brow in worry.

It took many rings before Lucy answered the phone. She'd given the cake to Sadie. No sense wasting something wonderful. "Now it's Mrs. Altamiri moving out. Her daughter's putting her in the car. I always liked her daughter. Lovely girl."

Although, the volunteers' coordinator had warned me not to ask about Lucy's daughter, all this talk about elders being rescued by their children naturally led to the topic.

"What about you, Lucy? Do you have children?"

A black silence opened between us. That gopher hole. An instant pang of remorse gripped my chest.

At last Lucy replied. Her voice sounded slow and far away. "I do have a daughter…and I don't have a daughter. Her name is Dana. I have not seen her in twenty-eight years."

I sat at my kitchen table, almost paralyzed, nearly forgetting to breathe. Twenty-eight years. What could that mean? Had the girl been kidnapped, was she jailed in a foreign country, did she hate her mother? Lucy seemed smart and reasonable. Had there been something she had done or failed to do? Often parents were to blame for things like this. Abusers were. But Lucy?

"Don't feel bad about asking, Faye." There followed a series of coughs. "We're friends now, and it's all right for me to talk about Dana. Not many people know our story nowadays.

"She is in a cult. That's why I never see her. They call themselves the Gates to the High Place of Radiance. They elevated her—that's what they call it when they take you in—when she was thirty. She calls me on my birthday. They let her do that, but she talks with an odd accent like she's from an imaginary land, like she's not in herself anymore. When it's my birthday, I sit by the phone all day waiting for her call."

"A cult." I was dumbfounded. "You hardly hear of them these days."

"Oh, they're around," said Lucy. "Some last for decades, like the one Dana's in."

"Oh, Lucy. I can't even imagine..." What was my separation from Petra compared to this?

"They do something to your ego when you're in a cult. But I don't think she minds that."

Lucy coughed harder this time. She had to catch her breath before continuing. "My husband Don and I adored Dana, doted on her as much as any mother and father could. She was a good student, never any trouble, but there was a shadow in her heart. She hadn't many friends, at least not ones that stuck.

"Dana didn't finish college, but that was fine with Don and me. She found a job in sales, supported herself here in Philadelphia, had her own apartment. And then she met Lloyd." Lucy spoke the name as if it were poison. She paused Dana's story, coughed a few times. She observed that an ambulance was pulling up to Autumn Woods. It was either the EMTs or the relatives coming to get you, she said dryly. Then she coughed some more.

"Dana never had a real boyfriend until she met that terrible man. They moved in together, but things were always shaky. You never knew what would set Lloyd off. Sometimes an anvil wouldn't, sometimes a feather would. She'd tell us how much she loved him, how she'd apologized, cried, begged, pledged to be more respectful about whatever line she crossed. That was romance, she said. It was what the songs on the radio were all about. No, it wasn't, we told her. This was being tied up with a short-fused son-of-a-gun who didn't care about her feelings and punished her for speaking up. We pleaded with her to leave him and move in with us, but Lloyd was her first boyfriend, and she wasn't about to give up on him.

"Then he got her a ring. They set a date. We rented a hall for them. Got the invitations printed. It was bound to happen. One day she said something he didn't like, maybe a criticism, an opinion, a request. Then down came the hammer. He called off the wedding. Boom. Just like that. Thank goodness we hadn't mailed the invitations." Lucy broke into a coughing fit, but she was determined to get her story out.

"I suspect she went through her usual weeping, apologizing, begging, and he grudgingly consented to take her back. They set a new date. We rented a hall again. Same story. Only this time we'd mailed the invitations."

"Oh God, Lucy."

"It only got worse. Lloyd's company transferred him to California. Dana moved with him. They set a new date. She bought a wedding gown. Then Lloyd did it again and called the wedding off. Can you imagine? And Dana so far from home.

"She called me from a bus station gasping between

sobs. Then in the background, I heard someone offering to buy her a cup of coffee. An hour later, she called me back from the same pay phone, sounding like the rays of dawn had filled her heart.

"'I'm better now, Mom,' she said. 'I have a new friend.' The leaders of the Gates to the High Place of Radiance sent out members to recruit lost souls, and they knew just where to find them." Lucy began to cough again. The coughs came faster.

I offered to call the front desk, to phone her doctor for her, or an ambulance. Lucy said not to. The coughing was just coughing, and it would pass. It always did.

"You take a nap," I said. "I'll call you back later." I started to call the front desk, then halted. I knew that Lucy hated the way management controlled the lives of the residents.

My fingers trembling on the keys, I typed an email to Petra. Had she read about the doctors and nurses living in their garages or in hotels, fearful of bringing the virus home to their families? And what about those anti-maskers? You know what was next? I wrote. Wars over who would get the covid vaccine first. Oh, I could see that coming. I said nothing of Lucy. I did not think Petra would care. I felt proud of myself for not hitting "send."

I set about cleaning some bathroom drawers. The things I found: twenty-five-year-old Vicks VapoRub, long-expired children's cough syrup, old stick-on bandages with rainbows and stars on them. I watched a Marie Kondo video about tidying up. I loved the way she folded clothes. Still, even as I cleared and straightened, fears for Lucy piled up in my mind.

I called her back. She sounded more rested and filled in more of Dana's story. The Gates to the High Place of Radiance had compounds out West, owned property, but she and Don were never able to find out where.

"We wanted to hire a deprogrammer and a rescuer, but without an address our efforts were useless, and a lawyer said that even if we did find her, the cult would fight back, claiming freedom of religion, charging us with abduction. Besides, she was a consenting adult."

Just then there was a knock at Lucy's door, an attendant with her dinner tray. No sense in starving, she said, even if the food tasted like cornstarch and cardboard.

By the next morning, we were off the subject of Dana, and Lucy had turned the conversation to me.

"Faye, let's talk about how you are doing. I get the impression that you are a bit of an anxious Annie."

The kindness of her interest melted over me, though I wondered how I had exposed my signature trait. I was about to confess that I breathed much easier when we spoke, but before I could say a word, she broke out in a cry of pain.

A pressure headache had hit her. She yelped again. Hurt like the devil.

"Do you have Tylenol? Lucy, take some Tylenol."

The coughing started up again. She couldn't catch her breath. She couldn't speak.

"That does it, Lucy. I'm calling you an ambulance. And I'm driving over to Autumn Woods." I dialed 911 then jumped in my car. My hands shook so violently that it was hard to grip the steering wheel. I swerved into Lucy's complex just as the ambulance arrived, blue and red lights flashing.

"Lucy Shawmont!" I shouted her apartment number to the attendant. He grabbed a set of keys and ran, the EMTs barreling after him with the gurney.

Fifteen minutes later, they wheeled Lucy out, a little white bundle, hooked up to an IV, an oxygen cannula in her nose.

"Lucy! Lucy!" I cried, waving my arms wildly as they slid her in the ambulance. "It's me, Faye. Your friend Faye!"

Lucy turned her head to me, her gray eyes catching mine.

That was the first and last time I saw my friend.

I chased the ambulance to the hospital and ran, heart pounding out of my chest, across the parking lot to the special covid entrance.

A guard stopped me at once. I could barely speak for sobbing and shaking.

"Ma'am, I know you're upset, but no visitors allowed. They're taking good care of your loved one." He handed me a card with covid precautions and the number of the patient information desk. Was that all he could do?

On the walkway, I saw a group of people standing together. We nodded to each other in sorrowful acknowledgment. Storm clouds were gathering in the west. I had nothing to do but drive home, trying not to cry, as I struggled to stay in my lane.

"Yes, we have admitted Lucy Shawmont," said the woman at patient information. "Are you next of kin?" I told her that the patient was my outreach client from the county agency. I thought that might help me break through the bureaucracy and privacy regulations, but it did not. "You could have your agency fill out some paperwork about guardianship, if that applied. We'd pass that on to legal. Then maybe..."

"But I'm her friend!" I burst out.

The lady took pity and gave me the number of the

covid unit, and when I called to see how Lucy was doing, I was again asked if I were next of kin. Well, then, did I have power of attorney? Did the patient have a living will? Who *is* Mrs. Shawmont's next of kin? Can you tell us how to reach them? The same bureaucratic walls all over again. I ended the phone call in despair.

The cinnamon raisin coffee cake sat on the counter in its plastic keeper. I dialed Autumn Woods to ask for Sadie Miller's number. Who could understand but the two of us?

When I identified myself, the receptionist's voice turned icy.

"Are you the one that called the ambulance? You're supposed to have us do that. And I cannot give out a resident's phone number."

I clicked off the call. I imagined Lucy in covid intensive care, monitors beeping. No Dana to hold her hand, but no visitors allowed anyway. Was she awake and thinking? And what was she thinking about? Perhaps they had put her in a coma and intubated her. I called the county agency, but it was after hours. Leave us a voice mail. Visit our website. Thunder rolled in from the spring storm. I slept in fits and starts. I had a covid dream, something about an angry mob and broken glass.

The volunteers' coordinator at the county agency offered me sympathy. He was sure that Lucy was in good hands and asked if I wanted some counseling. Or maybe, I would like an outreach volunteer to call me?

I'd think about it, I said. Maybe it wouldn't sound too lame to say yes.

I knew that there was no use in asking the agency to intercede with the hospital. Day after day, I called the number of the covid unit. And day after day, Lucy was still there. I don't know why but several times a day, I called Lucy's number at Autumn Woods. It went to voice mail until one day a recording announced that the number was not in service. They were turning over Lucy's apartment.

I had not sent Petra an email in two weeks.

I paced out my days in silence and fear. At least, I did not disrupt my daughter's peace.

One day, the person who answered the phone at the covid unit at the hospital told me that they had no patient by the name of Lucy Shawmont.

"Yes, she's there," I insisted. "An elderly woman." The person double-checked then said that I would need to speak to the patient's family. That's all she could tell me.

Yes, the family, I thought. I broke down in tears.

I hoped that a nurse had held my friend's hand as she passed away.

I'd read about the protocols for the unclaimed deceased. Lucy would be in a morgue somewhere or maybe in a refrigerated truck for overflow storage. Then to the medical examiner. Then to a group burial. I thought of those group burials of yellow fever victims in Philadelphia hundreds of years ago. Maybe a pastor would say some prayers. Lucy. Good Lucy, my motherly old lady friend.

I put my head in my hands. Then I lay down on my bed. I fell into a black and dreamless sleep.

At last, I pulled myself awake, told myself to get on with it.

I wondered when Lucy's birthday was, when Dana would place her once-a-year call. What a jolt that would give her. Then she'd be sorry. Or maybe she wouldn't be sorry. Maybe she didn't even care. I resolved to make a memorial service for Lucy. Maybe the county agency helped with that sort of thing.

At night, I watched more cleaning videos. My days of looking up people I used to know had long since passed, but I kept up with my decluttering: shredding old checks and ancient receipts, giving away things I never used. The heavy work of casting out the souvenirs of my life was almost done. If I had to sell the house and move into senior housing, it would be easy now. But I sure as hell would not move into Autumn Woods. I kept myself from emailing Petra. Every day I held off was a day that I did not drive her further from me. The thing was not to lose your daughter. That was the thing.

It was not quite the end of May. Covid cases were falling, and the state allowed some businesses to open. A feeling of lightness suffused the air. We felt that we'd chased the virus back, starved it of hosts even as the experts warned us that, vaccine or no vaccine, the virus now lived among us and would rally its forces again to send us back in hiding to save our lives.

I made myself a cup of coffee and signed onto my email. I could draft another message to Petra, tell her of my friend who died, but I abstained. Just more talk of suffering. Petra wouldn't want to hear about it.

Maybe I'd call the county agency and volunteer again. Or even sign up to have a volunteer call me. About that memorial service, I'd ask for help with that: a group service conducted by us elder-callers. No doubt, some of our number would have names to add.

I scrolled through the newsletters and account notices in my inbox.

I drew back when I saw it. An email from Petra.

"Hi, Mom" said the subject line. "No dire digests from you…" appeared in the preview. There might have been more to the message or maybe not. Some invisible hand kept me from opening it.

Anticipation quickened my heart. I felt something I had not felt in a long while: maybe it was relief, maybe it was joy. Look how my daughter has returned to me after my long silence! I thought of how much closer we would grow the longer I held myself apart. Then I judged myself for that sad and pitiable thought. Better to see things some other way, but what was that other way? I would open Petra's email, but not today. The longer I left the email unread, the more precious it seemed, like a gift before it was opened, like a necklace in box. The sun shone through my window. The social heartbreak, the demonstrations, and destruction that were to shatter our city and many others were days away. The second wave of the virus, and who knew how many other waves, had yet to come. And what more, what more?

I turned away from the computer and opened the window. The May air felt cool and fresh. I looked at the blue sky. I took a deep breath.

# Baby and Gorilla

A new Spiffycuts has opened in town. They need someone to walk around the shopping center in a gorilla suit to spread the word, and I am the man for the job. Pay is off the books, less than minimum wage, a temp job, but I'm not choosy. My drug arrest makes it hard for me to pass a background check, and Spiffycuts hasn't asked too many questions.

On my first day, I shuffle to the back room where they store the towels and shampoo. The manager suits me up in my fur costume. One of the stylists fastens the yellow pinney that says "SPIFFYCUTS GRAND OPENING" in front and "CELEBRATION SPECIALS" on the back. I pull on the grinning gorilla mask.

"Hey, everyone, meet our newest associate," calls the manager. I practice my welcome wave as I big-foot it through the salon.

"Tell me I'm not going to leave here looking like him," jokes one lady.

"I think a vampire would attract a better class of customers. Don't you?" says another lady like she's a marketing expert or something.

I respond in character with some grunts and strike a fashion pose. Yeah, mock this big hairy beast all you want. He's going to do his monkey job and then wash dishes at the Greek diner afterward with the caballeros.

I am practically a caballero myself, not very documented and working for cash.

I have a lot going for me as an ape. I like the outdoors, and it's April, so not too hot in the costume. The suit has a big plastic chest that makes me look mighty. Inside the big black pecs, my heart's a flat tire. I have a court date and a lame public defender. I could get sent upstate. Possession and receiving stolen property. Not that bad, but enough to fuck up the rest of my life.

Pointing to the announcements on my yellow pinney, wearing my big ape grin, I stroll up and down the shopping center, which also happens to be a drug hotspot. I see some of my old user friends. They have no idea it's me in the gorilla suit.

"Hey, Harambe," jeers a junkie named Weezer. "Where's Cecil the lion?"

I continue on my rounds, past the pizzeria, the pretzel shop, the pay-day loans joint, the hardware store, the urgent-care clinic. I wave to shoppers. Some wave back. Some even check out Spiffycuts.

You learn a lot about people when you're an ape. And the kids. Don't get me started on the kids. Some scream in terror when they see me. One kid hugged me. One kid kicked me. I acted wounded and wiped my gorilla eyes. "Be nice to the gorilla," the mom said. "There's a person in there."

Not that I see her very often, but with my mom it's always, "Grant, are you going to meetings? Grant, are you going to jail? Grant, are you still on methadone? Are you going to be on methadone for the rest of your life?"

So, it's my last day as a gorilla. I'm waving my fond farewells to the shoppers when a teen mom appears. She's bug-eyed, jumpier than a grasshopper, high as the moon. She's swinging a pink-and-blue-flowered diaper bag on one arm, and in the other arm, football style, she's carrying a tiny baby. Then she swings the diaper bag too high and twenty, maybe thirty, tiny bags fly out of her satchel. Plus, a couple of diapers. She falls to her knees, puts the baby on the concrete, and scrambles to pick up her dope.

"What are you looking at?" she says, her voice hot with menace. Her gaze is like the muzzle of a gun.

I hold out my arms for the baby and give what I think might be a gorilla daddy coo. I huff. I coo again. The girl figures out that she can give me the baby, so she does. It's a baby boy. He's wearing blue. He's crying now. I rock him. I've never felt so sad in all my days, or so human.

# You Take Care Now, Mary Jones

I bounce from Aperitivo with $215 in tips and the credit card numbers and security codes of three patrons in my back pocket. The patrons still have their plastic. This is my favorite moment. The future reels with promise. I picture glossy fashion magazines and make a mental list of the goods I can buy: designer handbags, swank watches, gift cards from stores both modest and luxe. My boyfriend Lon and I collaborate. I don't buy swell gifts for myself. Well, hardly ever. I mostly buy items to resell for cash. Lon, on the other hand, craves the finer things. He pampers himself with presents, like every other day's his birthday.

My dad used to say, "Don't shit where you eat." Each time I score off the patrons, his warning whines in my ear. But I let bigger music drown the small voice out. Soon, I'll be quitting Aperitivo. Natalie, the ace waitress, the one who gets extra in sympathy tips because she's minus a pinkie finger, will be outta here like a home run from Camden Yards.

I'm building a nest egg for after college, hence the fencing. But the minute I graduate, I'll go legit. Because—well, at least half the time—I can't stand what I do. Often when I use stolen numbers, the chilly feeling comes that a detective from the Baltimore PD will tap me on the shoulder and duck my head into a cop car.

Yet when I pull off a heist, I sense my superpowers. I feel triumphant and untouchable, a girl of ghost particles, a woman who can walk through walls.

Playing with purloined credit, Lon and I have dined on prime aged steaks, flown to Florida, and cruised the Caribbean on a giant ship in an elegant cabin with a pricey ocean view. Lon has a degree in business administration from a good school in the Mid-South. He's a junior executive at a pharmaceutical benefits company downtown and makes enough to support a family, so his need to heist is something of a mystery.

Though I have my theories: such as he dislikes spending his own money and grooves on the thrill of getting away with a well-executed crime. As for the well-executed part, Lon knows how to genius-up the operation with multiple names and accounts. Only one purchase per stolen card, of course. Lon adores using aliases, revels in not being himself. We have a lot in common that way.

Anyhow, the sleek leather seating in Lon's apartment, his state-of-the-art media center, his hand-knotted Oriental rug—all billed to Messrs. X, Y, and Mme. Z. What have I bought for myself? A navy suit for job interviews, a leather portfolio case for same. Nothing too showy, nothing that would provoke frowns of disapproval. I'm at Moresmith University on scholarship, a full ride, and people would think poorly of me if they saw me squandering the little dough I have. The Tahitian Fantasy Dusting Powder was an exception. The Gauguin beauty on the little hatbox container charmed me; its sugary spicy scent drove me dizzy. I charged it to another student's credit card. She'd left her plastic by the bags of strawberry Twizzlers at the college snack bar. Talk about scatterbrained. Anyway, I palmed it, copied the numbers, wiped off my fingerprints, and put her card back on the Twizzlers. I ordered online, and in a few days the treasure was mine. I had the powder sent to one of our mail drops held under one of our made-up names. Tahitian Fantasy contains pulverized diamonds and pearls. I love to poof myself with that fairy dust. Right now, I can't wait to get back to the dorm to shower. I smell like the bread dip at Aperitivo, a nose full of olive oil and garlic.

The April breeze blows softly tonight, and the Bradford pears, clothed in their white blossoms and funky-sweet perfume, line the street like petticoats. I'm about to call Lon on my cell when I hear the determined dig of boot heels on the sidewalk. The footsteps aren't Mom's. But they could belong to a hooker who wants my cash. Or to an angry patron. The street is deserted, and all the stores are closed. Nowhere to duck into. I pick up my pace. Heel-and-toe picks up her pace. I pretend to be on my cell phone. As if I would really call 911.

"Natalie Vest? Hey, are you Natalie Vest?" she yells like she's the town crier. Her voice is young. I halt just so she'll quit megaphoning my name. "You lost your ID."

I turn to find a student from Moresmith, a woman I vaguely recognize. She wears hoop earrings, fashionable boots, and a Peacemonger button on her tight scoop-neck T-shirt.

I dig for my ID in my right jeans pocket. Nothing. I dig deeper. Nothing. Left pocket. The same nothing. The shock of not-there hits me the way it must hit Lon's victims as they frantically pat themselves down or dump out their handbags searching for their missing wallets. The woman hands me my student ID. I thank her at least six times. Between gasps of gratitude, I imagine dreadful scenes: not being able to get into my dorm room, needing to call security to let me in, strangers and miscreants using my card to gain access to campus buildings.

"It's not the end of the world," she reassures me. "But you wouldn't want anyone using that around campus."

The woman with the Peacemonger button practices Moresmith ethics: you intervene, you go out of your way to help. A few days ago, I gave a guy a couple of bucks when he was short on cash at the bookstore. But the ethics imperative really requires more than that. At Moresmith they expect you to have a cause, like keeping it green or tutoring disadvantaged people. Last year I taught poetry appreciation to some kids in a foster care group, but mostly my cause is me. Protecting myself from my mom is my cause. These days she shares an apartment with someone in Fells Point, a long bus ride away from Moresmith. I have a protective order against her, but it doesn't help. Last week, Mom accosted me in a secluded area of campus, demanding cash as per usual. I forked over forty bucks, which wasn't enough, so she kicked me in the shin fast and hard, threatened to get back at me if I had her arrested again. A few yards away, a campus security guard tooled by on his Segway. The purple and yellow blotches from that bruise still linger on my leg.

My savior and I walk back to campus, both of us relieved not to be alone. I reach into my back pocket with my good hand and find, to my great relief, the little scrap of paper with the copied credit card numbers.

At eight-thirty the next morning, I roll out of bed and stumble on my roommate's butterfly net. I land on my butt among the dust bunnies. I sneeze. I curse. I do a rewind. Roll back into bed and look up at the row of Polly Pocket dolls on my bureau. Fathoms down in her morning meditation, Gretchen does not move. She studies comparative religion and presides over Moresmith's PETA chapter. Wears her hair in ropy white-girl dreads that make her look like she has an octopus on her head. Despite her fierce appearance, she would never hurt a fly. Literally. With the butterfly net, she captures flies and moths that stray into our room. Then she swooshes them out the window. I've never stolen a thing from her, not even a paperclip.

Refreshed from her trance, Gretchen dives into breakfast, dark brown lumps that look like large roaches.

"Want some? High in vitamins and fiber." She peers through her dreads, holding out a cellophane bag.

Gretchen Larrabee and I have been roommates since sophomore year. We're like sisters. We commiserate about men, talk about diets, moan about homework, bitch about profs. I proofread all her papers for her. Some nights, we stay up late and talk in bed when the lights are out. She's taught me how to write a thank-you note and how to make polite introductions. Gretch knows about my mom and how I lost my pinkie. She knows about my disadvantaged past. She has no idea that in my locked desk drawer are a David Yurman necklace, a Rolex watch, a blonde wig, the legal documents for my new name, ATM cards for my pseudonymous bank accounts, and a page of yet-to-be-used credit card numbers.

Last month I took a bus to the county courthouse in Towson and had my name changed. I did it to be free of Mom and the family name. If I merely moved away, Mom would surely try to track me down, shrilling: *I must find my child!* Therefore, I decided to embark upon my post-college future untrackable, untraceable, to come up as zero results in the directory searches. Let no one think my mother is a stupid woman. She'd stalk the databases for Natalie Vest, even put my face on milk cartons and coupon mailers. Not because she loves me, but because she is my pursuer. But I also changed my name because I wanted a future with everything innocent, everything new. I just haven't figured out when to stop being Natalie and when to emerge as Mary Jones.

I knew the courthouse building well. I'd been there to start the protective order against Mom and to enforce it. With its rectangular windows and concrete frame, I always thought the courthouse looked like a stack of dentures. How did I feel about sending Mom to the big house? Powerful, justified, unfilial, somewhat rotten. On the other hand, as a guest of the state, she got free food, clothing and shelter, so that was a benefit for her. Each visit kept her away from me for several months until she came raging back like an attack dog.

As I walked to the judge's chambers to present my petition, my armpits poured sweat. My heart banged like a caged bird. A criminal? No, to them I was a stressed-out young woman trying for a fresh start.

The judge was sympathetic. I showed him the stub of my pinkie, told him about Mom and Dad and kinship care. The scholarship for promising students from disadvantaged backgrounds. The protective order. Mom's violations. "After college, Your Honor, I want to leave all that behind. I want a new start." I presented the paperwork, my birth certificate, my Moresmith ID. I signed my new name, which I had practiced many times. Mary Jones. Mary Jones. Try Googling that. Sixty-first most common name in the USA.

"No one's going to find you with a name like that," the judge said looking a little deflated. "But don't you want to choose a first name with some flair? Like Cecily or Jillian? Jillian Jones? That has a ring to it." The judge looked hopeful.

I returned a faint smile that meant I was holding my ground. I brushed some invisible lint off my cardigan. "Plain vanilla is good enough for me, Your Honor."

The judge's kindness was making me feel squirmy. All I wanted was a name I could vanish into. The application required me to certify that I was not changing my name for a fraudulent purpose. I so certified.

"Bet you'll marry in a few years, change your name again." I could see that behind those serious silver-rimmed bifocals the judge was a good-hearted man. But the marriage stuff only brought to mind girls who had fiancés or steady boyfriends, and that depressed me because my life was not like that.

With a tilt of his head and a smile of concession, the judge signed the papers. "Pleased to meet you, Ms. Jones," he said. I thanked him and extended my four-fingered right hand, which he accepted delicately, not knowing quite how to clasp it.

For a moment, I glowed with the aura of a new self. Then nostalgia for the old Natalie crept over me like a shadow. I felt sad about sloughing off the former me. Life had been a rock climb for old Natalie, but she'd scrambled on. I turned to leave the judge's chambers on strange new feet. The blind future scared me.

Just as I approached the threshold, the judge called out, "You take care now, Mary Jones." It took a second to sink in that he meant me.

The next day, as required by law, I took out an ad in the paper to publish my new name and hoped no one would notice the announcement. I applied for my state photo identification card. I have told no one of my new name. I keep my new-self documents in my locked desk drawer.

***

After Gretchen leaves for class, I zap a mug of water in our microwave, make a cup of Earl Gray tea, open my laptop, and sign on to the account I use with Lon. I find an email he sent me at 2 a.m. last night:

*N,*

*Gorgeous, miss you so much I can't sleep. Miss your arms, your lips, your Botticelli bod. Can't wait to see you for dinner Friday night, but only after you've finished your Works Cited. Call me at work.*

*Big sloppy kisses,*

*L*

"Work" is code for one of our pre-paid phones. I don't know why he says big sloppy kisses. Lon's kiss is so expert it could be in the movies.

I call Lon my boyfriend, but maybe what we have is closer to a business romance. Our relationship, he says, is what it is. Whatever that means. No way will he give up his job and apartment to run off to Far-Away-From-Natalie's-Mom, USA. We hail from very different sides of the tracks. I hail from the side of the tracks near the railroad museum in Pigtown, by the big black steam locomotives and the permanently parked silver Baltimore & Ohio trains. Lon's family, the van de Bogaerts, live in a five-bedroom Colonial in Northern Virginia with an in-ground pool, about a mile of driveway, and acres of lawn. I've never been invited to the family seat, but Lon's shown me pictures. His dad is the vice president of something. His mom does volunteer work. My dad was a baker and worked nights. He was sad and drank a lot, but Mom was Hannah Hatchet. She used to have steady work chopping meat and butchering rump roasts at the Safeway. She had an affinity for knives. Then the pinkie incident occurred, and Dad, Pete, and I went to live with Grandma Vest in her red brick house on Scott Street. Even though it has a funny name, Pigtown's very nice. The people paint their doors every color you can name. The streets look like boxes of crayons.

Here's how we operate. Lon and I have our goods sent to pack-and-ship stores. They give you real street addresses and let you list yourself under any name you choose, so we set up the addresses to look like apartments with our various fake names. Then we match our fake-name shipping store addresses with fake-name bank accounts and fake sets of personal data for the online sites.

Lon photographs the goods and posts them for sale online. The buyers remit to one of our camouflage accounts. Sometimes we ship the buyers their merchandise. Sometimes we don't. I deposit my share of the money into one of my bank accounts; only one of them is in my real name. Between us, we have six aliases.

Lon is honorable in his own way. He never helps himself to my share of the joint cash. If he wants a new suit, a new gadget, he simply five fingers another victim. If they ever make a pickpocket hall of fame, Lon van de Bogaert will be in it.

My stomach's growling. I munch on some leftover Cheetos and dream of a crab feast. A place with brown paper on the tables, where you pound spiced steamed crabs with a mallet. Sides of onion rings and corn on the cob, plenty of cold beer. Hope Lon's up for that. I set one of the rock star Pollies—I always buy my Pollies with legally earned cash—by my laptop. I begin to type. This works-cited stuff is a pain in the neck. The title of my thesis is "The Girls Look Back: Anne Sexton and Sharon Olds Write of Their Youth." My problem parent was my mom. I had a good dad. I'd give another pinkie finger to know where he is. Sometimes I think I see him on a passing bus. Most likely he died drunk in a woods or a field, nameless. One day, I suspect a hiker will come upon his bones.

***

When I was twelve, my mother chopped off my right pinkie because I shoplifted a Polly Pocket doll. Not that she hadn't battered me before. Once she cold-cocked me for not doing the dinner dishes, and when I came to it was the next day, a sack of no-longer frozen peas—our family's ice bag—by the side of my throbbing head. Still, Mom bested herself with the pinkie episode.

At twelve, I guess I was too old to love dolls, but they still promised me happiness and comfort. Maybe I was emotionally immature. Maybe I just liked cute things. I was partial to Polly Pockets. And at that particular time, I craved the Snow Mountain Polly. She wore silver-rimmed sunglasses, an orange ski jacket, sported a blond ponytail. Mom and I were in a toy store buying a present for someone, and I asked Mom to buy me that

Polly with my next-week's allowance. She refused, so I pocketed the Polly. When Mom discovered what I'd done, she got her game face on. She said she'd teach me a lesson I'd never forget. With silver duct tape, she bound my right hand to our butcher block table, bunching my thumb and three fingers to one side. I kept screaming, "Mom, I'll be good! Don't, Mom, I'll be good!" She told me to shut up and hold still, that moving would only make it worse. I can still remember the touch of her hand as she spread my pinkie from the other taped digits. Then she whacked with the meat cleaver. She had to whack two more times.

I did not pass out. A blessed numbness buzzed over the hand. I looked down with a kind of awe. Blood pumped from where my pinkie used to be, and the pinkie lay on the butcher block like a little white grub. I hyperventilated, then I wretched. One second you have a finger. The next second you don't. I didn't cry. Crying never helped.

"Next time it'll be your thumb," Mom panted as if she'd had a workout, then unpeeled the duct tape. I lowered my arm. Blood ran from my hand like red juice from a squirt gun. "Put some ice on it," she said absurdly. But I couldn't open the freezer because my other hand wasn't working right either. "Then hold your arm in the air," she said. I looked like the Statue of Liberty in a horror movie. Then Mom collapsed at my feet and wrapped her arms around my legs.

"My baby. I'm so sorry. Sorry. Sorry," she wailed.

Awakened by all the commotion, Dad staggered into the kitchen. After a few seconds, the reality of the situation gonged him. He kicked Mom off of me.

Mom got some sort of suspended sentence, parenting classes, and counseling. Go figure: you maim your kid, you get a nice understanding counselor to talk to. Only Mom backslid; the protective order followed, plus a couple of sojourns in the county jail. Dad, Pete, and I moved in with Grandma Vest. But Grandma couldn't let bad enough alone. She kept yelling at Dad for marrying Mom and not being man enough to divorce her. Then one day he went to work and never came back. As for Pete, Mom never raised a hand to him.

With the protective order, Mom was not allowed unsupervised visits with me, but she'd pop up like a jack-in-the-box from time to time, mostly when I was walking home from school. I'd freak out. I'd run into traffic. I'd cling to strangers, and she'd say, "My poor daughter. She's a little disturbed. Come to Mommy, baby."

A couple years ago when I told Gretchen the story of Snow Mountain Polly and my pinkie, she said that if she were me she'd never want to see a Polly Pocket as long as she lived. "How can those dolls be your talismans?" she asked, petting my weird hand with sorrow and wonder.

***

I sip my tea. The bergamot perfumes the air. How to describe the high of completing my senior thesis? I feel as one walking into a room of dazzling light.

I'm in my bra and panties searching for something to wear when Gretchen breezes into the room, her boyfriend Big News behind her. I clutch my arms around myself. "Yikes. Sorry, Nat," apologizes Gretchen, "I didn't think you'd still be in the room." Big News helps himself to a lingering peep before he steps out into the hall.

I pull on a peasant blouse and denim skirt. Big News comes back and settles into a desk chair. From her canvas eco-tote, the very spiritual Gretchen unpacks her texts–*A History of God*, *Why Religion Matters*, *The Sacred Canopy*.

Big News's name is really Zbigniew Malinowksi. He writes for the school newspaper, hence the nickname. He's also king size. When he hugs you, you feel bear hugged. Big News doesn't care for Lon. Says there's something too slick about him.

"Got any breaking news?" I ask itching to scram. I have to deliver my thesis by 2 p.m.

"Two students were just elected to Phi Beta Kappa, so yay them." Gretchen and I nod approvingly.

"I know. Why wasn't it us?" Big News sighs. "But here's something really juicy," he dangles a pause before us. "Three Moresmith students have reported to security that bogus charges have shown up on their credit card statements."

Gretchen's eyes pop a little in surprise. I imitate her reaction. I wonder if some other operator, a wily competitor, could be at work. I wonder if Lon has been hunting on campus. Or if some of those purchases were mine. The Rolex, the Yurman necklace, the harvested account numbers hide out like criminals in my locked desk drawer. I can almost hear them breathing.

"I'm investigating the scammer story. I'm on it like a hound." Big News rolls out a comic "ruff ruff," shows a little fang, makes a pretend pounce. Then a fly buzzes in through the open window, and Big News swats it with his reporter's notebook.

"Big!" Gretchen whines. "Living things. Living things," she reminds him pointing to her butterfly net.

He rolls his eyes. "You ladies, best be wary. This crook has fancy taste. Racks up charges for prestige-brand jewelry, a designer handbag. Some sixty-five-dollar bath powder called Tahitian Fantasy. All shipped to apartments in the suburbs."

"Nat, isn't that the same powder you use? Your new powder?" Gretchen exclaims. Big News's face perks up like a pot of coffee. "Nat swoons over her Tahitian Fantasy." Gretchen rolls her eyes in comic ecstasy. "It contains crushed diamonds and pearls," she enthuses. "Plus, it's cruelty-free."

I pull my mouth into a faint smile, but a fine mist of mortal fear moistens my forehead and upper lip. I should not have pampered myself with that luxury gift. "I went a little overboard," I confess with a shrug. "Bought myself a graduation present. Everyone wants Tahitian Fantasy now. It's the hot new thing."

"Where did you buy it?" asks Big News.

"Big, I don't remember. It was a spur of the moment thing. Lots of stores carry it."

"You don't remember where you bought it?" he retorts.

As I slide my thesis into my knapsack, Big News tilts his head and tries to catch my eye. I loathe leaving the room. I know he'll try to snoop. I hope Gretchen will try to stop him. I can see him driving out to the "apartments in the suburbs" only to discover that they are pack-and-ship stores.

"Well, here goes nothing," I say in my best throwaway tone. "I'm off to see Brenner."

"You take care now, Natalie Vest," says Big News. I shiver as I hear him echo the judge's final words to me. "Good luck with that thesis presentation," he says, rising to pat me on the shoulder. His touch weighs a ton.

In the brick-bordered campus gardens, pink and white tulips nod. A storm is brewing, and a sick stomachache has taken up residence in my gut. So much for my dreams of spiced steamed crabs, onion rings, and cold beer. I long to chuck the Tahitian Fantasy into the trash, but that would only invite suspicion. On the other hand, to keep using it would be like covering myself in fingerprint powder. Perfect time for Mom to burst in on my scene, I muse ruefully. I'd love to confide in Lon just so he'd comfort me, tell me that our scheme is solid and safe. But I have no idea how he'd react. A poem by Anne Sexton comes to mind, the one where she tells herself to flee, flee on her donkey.

Moresmith's English department occupies a musty old mansion, trimmed in dark woodwork. Its atmosphere is as gloomy as a gothic tale. The gloom had always suited my nature. Now with mounting anxiety, I climb the stairs to Dr. Brenner's office. I had been looking forward to this moment, proud to present my thesis, eager to have one more conversation with him about literature and life. Now all I want to do is graduate and leave. Leave campus, Baltimore, the whole state.

Augustus Brenner, who is in his early seventies, is fixing himself a brown cocktail, prune juice with a shot of Old Grand Dad. He offers me a drink, and I say, sure, as long as I can opt out of the prune juice. He pours a finger of booze into a quilted jelly jar and hands it to me. "To your future," he toasts. We raise our cups.

"You look a little pale, Natalie. Are you feeling well?" His old-man face looks saggy and soft, but a deep look of concern inhabits his gaze.

"Pre-graduation jitters, I guess. It's the old what-am-I-going-to-do-with-my-life angst."

"As if anyone with any sense knows what he's going to do with his life," he says and takes a sip of his concoction.

Brenner knows about my pinkie and Mom's stalking and why I feel so sisterly to Sexton and Olds. He once had a brief fling with Sexton back in his Boston days. Beautiful, insecure, tormented Anne.

"Any thoughts of grad school? What about job hunting? You can count on me for a magnificent recommendation," he says, which makes me feel even more rotten and bogus. Imagine, one of his last students, a disadvantaged kid he'd thought would make it, turning out to be a scammer.

"Maybe I'll travel," I say. "But I have no idea where I'll go. I think I'll flee, flee on my donkey."

"Natalie, surely it's not as bad as all that."

I smile. We chat about school and discuss my senior thesis. We give each other a little good-bye hug. "Go forth and wander, Natalie," he says. "Maybe a little wandering will do you good."

I trudge off to Aperitivo to give notice. Ever the loyal employee, I tell them I'll work two more shifts, but my boss says, no worries. Says she knows the graduating seniors are off to bigger and better things. This makes me feel extra cruddy about copying the patrons' card numbers. It occurs to me that a data detective could find that a certain set of victims dined at Aperitivo, at dates and times that could connect to me.

I pull a bandanna out of my bag and tie it on to hide my dark brown hair. Per Lon's instructions, I stop by an ATM and withdraw three hundred dollars from one of our alias accounts. I'm a blonde at this bank, but with Gretchen and Big News in the room my Bombshell

Blonde wig had to sit tight in my secure drawer. I still need to open a new checking account in another neighborhood in the name of Mary Jones.

From the corner of my eye, I see them approaching, hunched and hulking, backgrounded by storm clouds. Mom and a strange man. Lucky after all that I am not in the blonde wig. So, what no good are you up to? she would have said.

The guy wears a plaid shirt and navy-blue work pants. His skin is bad. He's missing a front tooth. Mom bounds up to me with a hug, and I imagine I am a tree so that I won't feel the press of her body. Her arms are like strangle vines. Forget that she's forbidden to have contact with me, much less body contact. After a moment, the vines unwrap. I feel itchy.

"Malcolm, this is my brilliant daughter, Natalie. She's the brains in the family." A smile slices Mom's face. I notice that Mom is going gray, a shock of white, like a nest of pipe cleaners, has sprouted by the part in her hair.

I wave at Malcolm in lieu of shaking hands. He registers that something is odd about my hand. He nods like he doesn't want to be roped into the how-do-you-do's and takes out a box cutter. He starts to clean his fingernails with the blade.

Mom needs money to pay her phone bill, one hundred dollars, which she'll pay back as soon as a friend who owes her money gets her paycheck and cashes it. In two weeks.

"Come on, sweetie. I can't afford to have my phone cut off," she simpers, and there I am with my deck of twenties fresh from the ATM. I wonder how they trailed me. Mom was always so good at trailing me.

I reach in my pocket trying not to take all the bills out. "Never let people see your money," Dad always advised. Naturally, the whole wad of twenties comes out, and their eyes enlarge with eagerness.

"Since you're flush," says Mom, "can you spot me two hundred?" Malcolm holds the box cutter out as if to examine the blade, then puffs on it. It dawns on me that this is armed robbery. A band of heat sears my forehead.

That money is mine, and now they want to take it from me. I want to rebel, to refuse. But I also would like not to be cut because it hurts to be cut, and it takes a long time to heal. So, I count out two hundred into Mom's outstretched, five-fingered, right hand, my head fizzing with hatred, outrage, and grief. Mom kisses me on the cheek. Her breath smells like gum disease. As soon as they head off, I hurry back to my dorm thinking flight. Flight and survival. I turn around and in the far distance, I see Mom handing Malcolm some of the twenties.

***

Lon and I met at a rock concert when I was a junior. What struck me was how symmetrically handsome he was: even teeth, a straight nose, sandy hair zipped into a neat part. When he asked me for my phone number, I nearly flipped with joy.

On our third date, he took me to a very fancy restaurant and paid for the dinner with a credit card. When the waiter said, "Thank you, Mr. Logron," I opened my mouth to tell the waiter he'd used the wrong card. But Lon put his finger to his lips and said, "You're worth it, Natalie. Not another word." On our way home, I stared out the car window feeling cheap and shabby, like I wasn't good enough for his own money. Lon claimed the guy had left his credit card in a gas station bathroom. Not to worry, said Lon. Mr. Logron, whoever he was, would dispute the charges and wouldn't have to shell out a cent. So, I thought, well okay. How often do I get to sip a red Meritage wine from Napa or savor prime rib and Grand Marnier soufflé? We slept together for the first time that night. Naked in his mirror the morning after, I saw someone who looked like me but wasn't quite me. And that woman had a handsome naughty boyfriend. Her life was dangerous fun. I was surprised at what a pushover my conscience could be.

Lon almost never paid for our dates with his own money. When I mentioned to him that I'd rather go on cheaper legit dates, he replied that everything is a tradeoff: that by accepting those illegally paid-for dates I had become an accomplice. His tone was neutral, matter of fact.

For a week or so I wouldn't answer his calls; I deleted his emails. Then I caved. I missed the oxygen-filled, high-definition feeling of being in a romance. I missed Lon van de Bogaert. He was the only longish-term boyfriend I'd ever had. So, we started up again as a couple, only this time he wanted me to help him scam. Moral arguments never worked with Lon, so I pointed to my pinkie-less right hand. "In case you're wondering why I demur..." I explained about Snow Mountain Polly, Mom, and the pinkie.

Lon's expression fell in shock. "That's child abuse. That's torture," he said, and he meant it. "I always assumed that was a birth defect, so I never asked." He cradled my bad hand as if it were a kitten.

***

Lon wears a brown suede jacket and khakis. He smells of aftershave. His face is smooth. Mint frosts his breath. He kisses me and hands me a gift-wrapped Polly Pocket. "Congrats on the senior thesis. Bought with my salary money. Okay? No worries." He's in the mood to celebrate, then sees I can barely winch up a smile. I tell him about Mom, Malcolm, and the box cutter. But nothing about the student reports of mysterious credit card charges.

"You finished your thesis and you got held up!" He reaches out to touch my shoulder in sympathy. "Natalie, your luck will change. I know it will."

"It better," I reply.

The restaurant is a special-occasion place with white tablecloths and little vases with white carnations. Lon's choice and just as well. He's the one with the appetite. He slurps down oysters and tries to talk to me about school things, movies, things that would make me feel good. Every so often lightning flashes, and when the thunder cracks I jump a little.

I wonder what Big News is up to. I wonder if he could plant suspicious thoughts in Gretch. Lon asks if

I want to sleep over. And I do. The last place I want to be is the dorm.

"You're not eating," observes Lon. "You should eat something."

I take a sip of wine. I stir my salad. I feel bad that in my distracted state I can't absorb Lon's attention. I start to obsess about opening an account in the name of Mary Jones. With a made-up social? With my own social? I need to print out my grade reports. Should I close out my alias accounts or keep them open? Everything's a question.

Lon taps my bread plate with his butter knife. "What is up with you?" he says with a pinch of annoyance.

I lean toward him and whisper, "I want you to take the Yurman necklace and the Rolex. You can sell them and keep all the money."

"But you don't have to clear out of your dorm for another couple weeks." He looks at me sideways. Then he draws back. "Are you breaking up with me? Now?"

"I wish you could come away with me," I say bringing up our old differences. "We could stay together and start over in a new city." I reach for his hand with my good hand. A gold Chopard watch armors his wrist. His skin feels cool.

Lon shakes his head. "Not gonna happen, babe. But

like I told you from the start, you are always free to go."

I allow my face to drop with resignation. It would be better to have Lon out of my life. Through the plate glass window of the restaurant, I see the rain sheeting down.

"We'll still have email and Skype, right?" I ask.

"Yeah, sure," he says. He hunches forward. "You're not in trouble, are you?"

"Oh, no. Nothing like that." To avoid his eyes, I open my phone. I find a text from Gretchen:

*Heading up to the room with Big News right now. Be clothed.*

That night in Lon's spectacular apartment, between his expensive sheets, I cling to his warm lean body. Lon wants sex. I just want to be held. My lack of lust makes him grumpy. He drifts off to sleep, but guilt, fear, and questions take turns keeping me awake. Should I tell the registrar of my name change? Should I graduate as Mary or Natalie? I stress about finals and two more essays I have to write. What if, in cap and gown, I step down from the stage into the embrace of the law? Or my mom. Of course, the college will cooperate with law enforcement. First they'll put my student status on hold. Then they'll kick me out. So much for Natalie Vest. So much for graduating from Moresmith University. Unless the investigations meet dead-ends. Unless Lon's fail-safes really work.

***

Lon and I get back to campus by nine the next morning. The ground is still soaked, but the clouds are wisping to cotton. We stride across campus in silence, faster than usual. In the accent gardens, the pink and white tulips bear the drops of last night's rain. A few joggers pass by. I feel hazy from lack of sleep, and my head aches. If only I had shown fortitude, not let myself be seduced by Lon and his heisty schemes.

Gretchen's away, but I find the room air odd. My desk is angled slightly out of place. My Polly Pockets are not in order. A light coating of Tahitian Fantasy dusts the floor. I begin to tremble. Perspiration wets my pits. I shrug repeatedly as if to cast off my panic. Lon watches me, his expression souring. I yank my locked desk drawer. Still locked. My tremble progresses to shakes. I step on Gretch's stupid butterfly net, and the handle zooms up and smacks me on the elbow. I curse and kick it, catching my shoe in the green gauze, ripping the fabric.

"Geez, Natalie, what is it? You're acting like a mental case. Take a chill pill."

I want to tell him someone's rifled through my possessions, but I don't. Instead, I wail about finals and papers. A vision of Big News like a Macy's parade balloon floats over my head. I see his fat fingers all over my things. I wonder if Gretchen helped him in the name of truth-seeking or tried to stop him out of loyalty to a friend. Maybe she told him that it wasn't right to go through somebody else's stuff. He wasn't the law. Didn't have a search warrant.

"Is this how you act under pressure?" Lon asks.

After a few stabs, I manage to insert the key into my locked desk drawer. My blonde wig, creepy as a shrunken head, sits on top. Below it lie the Yurman and the Rolex. Beneath them, my fake IDs and ATM cards, a page of copied credit card numbers, an envelope of cash, the court order for my name change, my new state photo identification card, the protective order against my mother, a Valentine from Lon. I produce the boxes containing the necklace and the watch; my hands shake so much that the contents rattle inside.

"Just give those to me," says Lon yanking them away. "You *are* in trouble, aren't you?" His eyes narrow with accusation.

I squint back at him. "What are you talking about? I can stop doing this if I want to." Like a knock upside the head, it hits me that Lon would rat me out to save himself. He'd say I drew him into this, that I had the soul of a thief. I can see him with a high-priced criminal attorney at a polished mahogany table working out a plea bargain.

Lon throws the Yurman and the Rolex into a plastic bag. "I'm out of here," he says, not meeting my eyes. And just like that, with the click of the dorm room door, we're over.

Expecting to be expunged from the Moresmith University system any minute and vibrating with fear, I print out all my grade reports for all my years. A survival instinct has cleared the haze from my brain and sharpened my faculties. Every few seconds I glance outside to see if Big News and Gretchen are coming. Each set of footsteps down the hall sends a new wave of panic.

Into my big backpack, I stuff my laptop, parka, shoes, underwear, the navy interview suit, toiletries, Polly Pockets. Into a plastic manuscript pouch, I slide the court order for the name change, the protective order, my copy of my thesis. I push that way down into my backpack. Nostalgic for my books, I add one Sexton and one Olds to the big backpack. Then I take them out. Travel light, I think. New life. Flee on your donkey.

I pull the Natalie Vest student ID from my wallet and replace it with my Mary Jones Maryland picture ID. I slide all the other cards into another holder. How much cash to carry? How much to withdraw? I can see my daypack crammed with cash like a bag of salad. My first thought is to close all the accounts, take all the cash. Then I remember what Dad said about showing people your money. A couple thousand dollars, then, I tell myself. Not everything. I'll just use ATMs along the way. I frown considering how I hate paying the foreign ATM fees. Then I think, idiot, that's not your money.

With trembling hands, I manage to tear the cheat sheet of credit card numbers—some used and crossed out, some not yet used—into confetti. In the women's bathroom, I flush the bits down the toilet. A swirl of water sucks the evidence away. The water returns clear.

My cell phone buzzes like a hornet. It's a call from Gretchen, and I'm about to answer when through the window I spy the two of them. Gretch is pressing her phone to her ear.

Big News is looking impatient, striding double-time. I think of answering to stall her, but that would give Big News a chance to call security or the cops. I throw my big pack on my back, sling my daypack on front-wise. I stuff my phone in my pocket, sprint from the room, and bolt out the back door of the dorm. I look guilty. Or just plain nuts. A student sees me and shakes his head as if to say: How sad is that? Someone going berserk at the end of the semester. I am thankful that he does not practice Moresmith ethics: he does not intervene.

Back home on Scott Street, I sleep in my bed. I sleep like the dead, and when I get up I tell Grandma and Pete that Lon has broken up with me. Then I lie that I have a job interview in Oklahoma and can't go to graduation.

"I've never heard of an employer saying a person couldn't go to their own graduation," says Grandma. She casts me the kind of look that asks if there's something I want to talk about.

"Corporate America," I shrug, my soul a moldy puffball of lies. I wonder if my breath comes out in a dark cloud of spores.

"Nat, what's wrong? Are you sick?" asks Pete. Instead of answering, I embrace him. He hugs me back. I can be dry-eyed when the threat level is high, but when someone is loving and kind, the sob fountain goes on full force. I leave my little brother's shirt damp with my tears.

The next morning the skies are clear. I ride away on a Peter Pan bus headed west, and after a few states I switch to a Greyhound. The bus suits me. I have nowhere to go, and the road trip prolongs the in-betweenness.

I get off the bus in Dallas because I sat with a cheerful girl through Tennessee who said she used to live in Dallas and that a college girl like me could find work there. The YWCA helps me find a temporary place to stay. My fall is quick. One day I'm an English major at Moresmith University, surrounded by heady people and velvety campus lawns; a few days later I'm homeless, wearing out my shoe leather on the streets of a strange city. But the streets can teach you a lot of things, such as where the undocumented workers go to buy their documents. Newly purchased social security card in hand, I start to fill out job applications. I start to make my way in the world.

I find a room to rent in a widow lady's house. Kitchen and laundry privileges. Near a bus line. I land a job in online customer service for a small chain of retail stores. If there's one thing I know, it's online shopping. Things are not so bad. In fact, things are very simple for this Mary Jones.

I spend only what I earn. I open up a checking account, but mostly I pay in cash. Every Sunday after I've finished my laundry and grocery shopping, I call home, or what used to be home, using a phone card or a prepaid cell. I talk to Pete about school and girls, and I tell Grandma Vest about my job, but never the real name of the company. I'll be home for Thanksgiving, I say … just five … just four … just three more months. But I doubt that my promise will turn out to be true.

When people ask what brought me here, I tell them that I moved because of a bad break with a man. They offer soulful glances, understanding nods; their niceness feels almost like friendship. But should questions of my family arise, I fib. I say that my father sold vinyl siding, my mom was a part-time nurse, but an ice storm sent their Saturn under a semi-trailer truck. Then people recoil from the terribleness. I thank them for their sympathy. "I've been dealt a bad hand," I say, "but I'm getting by—one day at a time, one foot after the other." Reassuring clichés come to my assistance, and under their cover I make my new life. I will be who I decide to be, and I decide to be Mary Jones.

# Evermay Blair

It was close to midnight on Saturday, and I was driving home from a visit with Sandra, the two-lane country road wet from a November rain and spattered with leaves, when a girl came running out of the woods and dashed straight for my car. If only she could have been snatched up on invisible strings. Instead, we collided, her eyes in my headlights, white with panic. You don't forget the eyes.

Slamming on the brakes, I scarred the road with my skid. But for nothing. Everything happened at once. We met with a sickening squashy thump with wood in it. My airbag fired out. The child went down by the front of my car. A storm of black birds banged inside my head.

What had I done? Shaking, hyperventilating, a cold sweat slicking my skin, I managed to back up a little so as not to do her more harm. Somehow, I put the car in park. I didn't mean to hit her, but I had hit her. Intent meant nothing.

Get a grip, man, I commanded myself. Inhale. Exhale. Exit the car. The girl lay, bleeding and gasping, by my right front tire. I knelt by her, and I held her hand. She was twelve or so, the age of my middle-school students. Though it was cold, she wore only a T-shirt and underpants, all now soaked scarlet with her blood.

"I'm sorry, little girl. Little girl, oh God," I sobbed,

barely able to choke out my words. I stayed by her side as she died.

Why did I not dial 911? How is it that a decent man might, in an instant, fail himself and all that is right? It was the imp of shame in my soul. I could not bear to be called to account. I knew what this deed would mean for the rest of my life. It would follow me like a tagline: Kenneth Watson was the respected vice principal of Shady Hill Middle School, but—did you know?—one night he accidentally killed a girl with his car. The imp promised me that the undiscovered crime was no crime at all. I had only to rip that black page from the calendar of my life and go on.

The girl's eyes were open, but there was no one in there anymore. I looked away from their awful upward stare, knelt by her body and, with trembling hands, picked up the shards of my shattered headlight. Then, my heart nearly bursting from my chest, the black birds banging in my head, I drove off. Let the world believe that someone else had met her flying leap. I would tell people that I hit a deer.

Get out of there, I told myself. Make it up to humanity in other ways: do good works for the rest of your life.

Collins Road was empty: one piece of good fortune, I thought in miserable self-regard. My hands kept slipping on the steering wheel. An unusual body odor seeped from my pits. The inside of my arm itched, and I let go of the steering wheel for a few seconds to scratch the troublesome spot. For about a mile, I tried to be angry with my victim. Stupid kid. Flew into the street. Did she think of the lifelong guilt she laid on the driver who hit her? And why me, why me?

Driving with caution, looking right and left for deer and runaways, I turned my agitations from myself. A girl in the woods in the middle of the night. Dressed like that. Dashing toward a stranger, any stranger, for help. Whatever risk she ran toward terrorized her less than the one she fled. Like a person who jumps from a burning building. Like a virgin who hurls herself over a cliff: death before defilement.

Was she being chased? If so, her pursuer might have glimpsed my car, made some note of my license plate. Again, the black birds banged. Struggling with the steering wheel to keep the car straight, I managed to drive home and parked in my garage, a felon. I could still call the police. Blame my delay on confusion and panic. Admit that the power of conscience came at last to guide me. But I did not do that. I spent a sleepless night, tending now and then to that itch.

Around noon, Sandra phoned to tell me

there'd been a hit-and-run on Collins Road right about the time I was traveling it.

Had I seen anything unusual? Was I okay?

I was fine. Hadn't seen a thing. I felt my neck and back stiffening with post-collision pain. After the call, I took a couple of Motrin. I didn't phone a doctor for fear my complaints would start an incriminating chain of inquiry. My itch had reddened to a rash.

I went online and searched for information about hit-and-runs. I learned that if the driver isn't found several hours after the crash, chances are he never will be. I deleted the hit-and-run search from my browser history. As each hour passed, I felt more confident that I never would be caught. In all likelihood, I would remain the respected vice principal of Shady Hill Middle School. I would never be defined by the worst thing I did.

My deed made the front page of the Monday *Intelligencer.* The girl's name was Evermay Blair. Police were searching for whoever hit her. There was an anonymous tip line. A thousand-dollar reward. If anyone noticed a white car with front-end damage, they were to call the police. On the TV news, her uncle raged from the front door of his shack in the woods, "We'll find that scum, that dirt bag. We'll hunt him down." Then he buried his face in his hands and bawled. He called to mind a guilty husband freaking out in grief to hide the fact that he had chopped up his wife or a homicidal mom hysterically claiming that someone had kidnapped her child. You saw it on the news from time to time. Of course, Evermay was running from that uncle.

I couldn't tell you how many protection-of-minors trainings I'd given to our teachers and staff and how many trainings I'd had myself. We were obligated to report the suspicion of abuse, and the fact that I would never do so on behalf of Evermay Blair turned my guilt to quicksand. My imp went back on its promise of safe passage. There might be no discovery, but there would be no peace either. Yet, really, was there a reason to investigate now? Cause of death: vehicular homicide. A quick cremation, per the bereaved uncle's request. Then the guy comforted by the mortuary staff.

I opened my laptop, searched DIY car repair, took notes, erased that search history, then took an Uber to an automotive supply shop where I bought a dent remover, a spray gun, white paint, and ordered a new lens for the smashed headlight. Deer collision, I told the clerk. Yeah, breaks your heart, he said.

I thought of the inquest that might have been, the never-to-occur autopsy that might have turned up evidence of whatever she endured and had to flee.

So, it was Ubers to work and Ubers to the grocery store for a week until I more or less brought my car to the point that it would not attract notice. My rash intensified. I raked my skin until it bled. The pain of the torn skin stopped the itching for a while, so I welcomed the pain.

When I drove my car to the shop to get the wheel alignment fixed, the mechanic shot a dubious look at my repair work. I told him the deer story.

"What was it, a fawn?"

"Yes, a fawn."

"Looks like it. Adults do a number on a vehicle. Attack it with their hoofs. Very serious business, those deer strikes." Then he asked me if I'd reported this to the insurance company or the cops, and did I want to file with my insurance? A chill ran through me when I thought of a visit by a claims adjuster. I told the guy I'd just eat it, pay cash. Simplest way, I said. Suit yourself, he said and caught my eye. I held his glance a second then looked at my watch, suppressing the urge to scratch my skin.

The rash was already on both arms and had spread to my chest. I went to the drugstore and bought some cortisone cream. That helped for a while. I was afraid that the redness would spread to my neck and face.

Following the accident, I busied myself repaying society for my hit-and-run. To my colleagues, my self-imposed sentence of community service looked like a case of résumé boosting, a campaign for a promotion in the school district, even a run for citizen of the year. At school, I started an Interethnic League and attended every PTA meeting, every basketball game and wrestling match. I headed up our Every Day Is Earth Day club. The antiviolence program I created—I called it Highways to Harmony—got some good press in the *Intelligencer*, the same newspaper that had scourged me for the hit-and-run. I held a Highways to Harmony poster contest and, in the school cafeteria, I cooked a pancake breakfast for the winning homeroom.

"You okay?" asked a teacher when she saw me scratching myself.

"Allergies," I replied. I wore long sleeves and dark-colored shirts in case my clawing drew blood, which it often did.

Over the months, I became, in many ways, a better vice principal—more understanding, less the heavy that vice principals usually are. I handed out fewer out-of-school suspensions than I used to. More parents left my office feeling relieved and understood, less worked up. I brought some kids from troubled homes into Big Brothers Big Sisters. I had always reported suspected child abuse to our state program, but now I was even more sensitive to the issue, possibly even overly suspicious, and I called the agency much more than I ever had before. I thought that Evermay would have wanted it that way. I also thought about what Benjamin Franklin said about a person's name: "It takes many good deeds to build a good reputation and only one bad one to lose it." I hoped that my good deeds would block the world from discovering my awful truth.

In April, the school board awarded me a special commendation for promoting school peace. My service work allowed me a few moments of buoyancy, but remorse and fear of exposure would always return to weigh me down, especially at night when I was home alone and scratching my skin. The rash had spread to most of my body, but my face it left untouched. I watched a lot of TV. I slept poorly. When I closed my eyes, I saw the eyes of Evermay Blair bright in my headlights. My time off during weekends filled me with dread. Then, to my relief, I found a volunteer job driving dialysis patients to their treatments.

Had it not been for my constant interactions with the middle-school students and the dialysis patients, I would have gone mad. I shrank away from normal conversation with my colleagues, loathe to share even the most harmless personal details—what I had for dinner, what I watched on TV—for fear that I would give myself away. I avoided the faculty lounge. I brought my turkey on wheat or ham on rye and ate at my desk. I substituted courtesy for conversation and cheerful protocol for personal interaction. How was I? No complaints. How's that allergy, Kenneth? Colleagues recommended remedies and doctors. And how are you? I would ask, eager to shift focus. How's the family? Thus it was that one Kenneth Watson walked alongside the other. In passing once, I saw in the glass of a school trophy case a stilted and unsmiling man with sideburns and a tense posture. I tapped on the pane of glass to see if he would vanish.

My parents lived in Florida, and I filled my emails and phone calls to them with cheer. When I visited them over spring break, I looked with longing at my old pictures. The first Kenneth with his old girlfriends. That kid grinning in front of his birthday cake. Kenneth on family vacations. Who was that guy, who lived with a heart unburdened and calm skin white as snow? He was no genius, and far from perfect, yet he sauntered through life untested by calamity, unaware of the imp within him and the shadow-self he would one day meet.

The only way to Sandra's house was by way of Collins Road, and I could not bear to drive down Collins Road again. For this reason, I had to break up with Sandra. Two weeks after the accident, she asked about making a date. I had her meet me for dinner at a restaurant near me. She told me I looked uncomfortable, fidgety, and what was that rash on my hands?

"What's going on, Kenneth? Even my parents have been asking why you haven't been back to the house."

I went into great and unnecessary detail about the PTA meetings and all my initiatives, filling up the air any way I could with my wholesome news. I described with an eager expression the posters the kids made, their environmental projects, and my new volunteer job driving dialysis patients.

"Well, I guess I don't have kidney problems," she remarked dryly. "That must be it."

How to break it off with her? I dared not tell her I had found someone else. Too easy to get caught in that fib. I politely returned her texts and phone calls, but I initiated nothing. Along with every other thing I hated myself for, I despised myself for starving out the relationship. I missed her. Before the hit-and-run, I had seriously considered marrying her.

One night she called to confront me. I could hear her summon the courage. She said we were drifting.

Why did I not phone? Why did I never call to make plans?

"I've been meaning to talk to you about that," I said.

I made one last date with her. We met at a diner. Over chicken parmesan, I told her with tears in my eyes, real tears, that I was finding it easy to be away from her. That I didn't miss her that much. It wasn't fair to keep it going. I took a gulp of water. I felt that I was putting the best part of my life into a trash compactor.

"I can't argue with a fading heart," she said. "I don't know what more there is to say." If only she had put on a jilted-girl bandolier and ripped off a round of curses or told me that I was a cold and soulless bastard, more in love with humanity than with her. But she didn't say that. She wiped her mouth with her napkin and rose from the table. In the parking lot, we embraced one last time. I pulled away, and when I got back to my house I vomited. Then I checked my email to see if any dialysis patients needed rides.

I saw the need to hide my guilt as an opponent to be bested, so I pounded the second Kenneth with more and more good works. When no one was looking, I raked my tormented skin. That spring at Shady Hill Middle School, I formed the Anti-Vaping League. I created the Drug-Awareness Support Group. Some of my colleagues thought I was over-extending myself. They said that they understood that there was a gap with Sandra out of my life, but take a break, man. They tried to fix me up with women. I demurred until the offers ended. It reached the point where I had no friends, only coworkers, colleagues, community partners, and the company of the dialysis patients I transported. I loved my conversations with the patients. We spoke on safe common ground, mostly about the weather and sports. When my day job came up, a few of them laughed about their long-ago run-ins with their principals and vice-principals. Sometimes talk would turn to donor kidneys. Young donor kidneys were best.

I yearned to confess to the police and get it over with, yet I could not confess. I practiced my charity and good works, but I could repent only to my own conscience. And my own conscience showed me no mercy.

I needed to hide my secret, and I needed to reveal it. This inner struggle led me to do curious things.

I composed an anonymous letter to the police and planned to mail it from an out-of-state post office. I wrote it out in long hand on a yellow legal pad:

*To the Chief of Police:*

*I am the person who hit Evermay Blair this past November on a wooded section of Collins Road in Pillsbury Township, Lehigh County, Pennsylvania. Remorse eats at me every day, but the longer I put off turning myself in, the harder it is to step forward. Yes, I am a coward. For me, living with guilt is better than paying the price for my crime. Maybe I'll turn out to be one of those fugitives who's the man next door, the guy who mows his lawn, waves hello and keeps to himself.*

*I want you to know that I feel that Evermay Blair was fleeing someone who molested or abused her. Why else was she in a T-shirt and underpants running into traffic in the middle of the night? Investigate that.*

I burned the letter.

A little while after that, I invited a cop, an Officer Schmidt, to Shady Hill Middle School to address a school assembly on pedestrian and bike safety.

"And what should our middle school students know about pedestrian safety at night?" I asked during the Q&A, feeling daring and a little jazzed to tread this close to my secret.

Officer Schmidt spoke about the importance of wearing light-colored clothing. Adjusting his gun belt, he added, "There's no decent reason why our youth should be on the street after dark." Then to my surprise, he brought up the case of Evermay Blair. "Now what this young lady, a person just your age," he said, waving out to the sea of middle schoolers, "was doing out on a two-lane highway in the middle of the night, we'll never know. The whole thing's a keg of worms. But a sleaze, if you'll pardon my French, ran into her and didn't even have the decency to call 911. Left her for roadkill." Officer Schmidt's face grew dark. A hush went over the students.

I don't know what sort of look passed over my face, but a colleague standing next to me put her arm around my shoulder.

After the assembly, I approached Officer Schmidt and asked if the child had recovered. He shook his head. "She was dead when we found her. It's a sin. Just a sin," he said shaking his head. "Why do you ask?" He threw me a glance.

"It's my business to care about kids," I replied as evenly as I could. He did not, I hoped, take me for a morbidly curious goon or detect, with his practiced ear, an extra note of interest in my voice.

I tried to tell myself that Evermay's trauma was over. For a few days after Schmidt's visit, I was twitchy. My rash raged worse than ever. Yet, for some reason, my face, my public mask, continued to remain free of the stain. I started a school chapter of Students Against Drunk Drivers.

May broke out in hot pink azaleas, and the students at Shady Hill poured from the buses in shorts and T-shirts, louder than usual and eager for vacation. I would be transporting dialysis patients after school let out for the year, but I would have a lot more time on my hands, and I needed more good works to fill it. I was casting about for projects when I heard about the Patient Companions program at Mallard Pond Nursing and Rehab Center. Spread over former cornfields in the upper part of the county, Mallard Pond, from the outside at least, looked like a country club. Its residents were mostly elderly. But the center also specialized in care for those in comas and persistent vegetative states—folks who had their lights blown out by stroke, drug overdose, a car crash. Suspecting that these patients might be able to hear and think, the Mallard Pond staff worried that these imprisoned souls might be bored and lonely. So, the center put out a call for community volunteers—patient companions was the term they used—who would read to these sleepers and carry on with them some kind of a cheerful one-sided chat.

I could think of no safer *pro bono* summer project and applied at once to Mallard Pond. At last I would have someone to open up to. In all these months, I had never once spoken aloud of my crime. Perhaps I could unburden myself to someone who was unconscious or deep in a suspended state: able to listen, but not respond.

"Mr. Watson, having someone of your caliber in our pilot program is a special privilege for us," said Jeri Jankowski, the head of volunteer and social services at Mallard Pond.

"I feel like I want to give back to the community," I responded with a humble shrug. Borrowing a corner of Jeri Jankowski's desk, I filled out the Patient Companions volunteer application, which asked if I had ever been convicted of a felony. Jeri was a big woman. She wore a cranberry-red pantsuit. Her office smelled of cinnamon. A fan of motivational posters, Jeri had "It's too soon to quit" and "Never be ashamed of doing what is right" framed on her office walls. I shrank from their rectitude like a shadow fleeing the light.

In contrast to its country club exterior, Mallard Pond's patient care floors were iced over in linoleum the color of old snow, and its walls were a chilly green. The vapors of vegetable beef soup and instant mashed potatoes hung in the air, interrupted at points by the reek of urine and Lestoil. As Jeri walked me down the hall, she spoke to me of the mystery of the human brain: how some patients in comas awoke and even recalled conversations they heard while unconscious, how others never emerged from their limbo. No one knew for sure where the border between coma and brain death lay.

Jeri showed me into a room and introduced me to Joseph Snavely, aka Joey Tatts, age twenty-seven, lately of the Species. Visions of vicious bikers with brass knuckles and black leather jackets swarmed through my mind. The business of the Species was mostly crystal meth and whatever else they had to do to exact payments and enforce loyalty. Joey Tatts's rap sheet was a regular not-to-do list: rape, aggravated assault, drug dealing, terroristic threats. He'd done some prison time but was now in Mallard Pond because a girlfriend beat his head in with a tire iron. Joey, explained Jeri, was unconscious and immobile. No one knew if he'd ever wake up or how impaired he'd be if he ever did come to. His roommate was an older man in the late stages of Alzheimer's. "Joey is calm as can be, but poor Mr. Frable gets agitated. Sometimes he takes a swing at his caregivers," warned Jeri. "And don't be surprised if he calls out to family that isn't there or repeats the last thing he's heard. He's quite the parrot."

At this point, Snavely had lain three months in twilight. His face and head did not look indented at all or swollen from the beating. He had thinning black hair, a long nose, a sharp Adam's apple. Through a tube in his gut he received formula, and, to prevent bedsores, aides came in every two hours to reposition him. Joey peed through a catheter into a bedside bag. He moved his bowels in a diaper. He seemed a living sack.

I knew that bikers loved body art, but Joey was in a class by himself. His illustrated skin made real nudity impossible. Under his hospital gown, he looked clothed in multi-colored long sleeves and leggings. Green snakes encircled him, skulls grinned from his arms, on one calf was a Betty, on the other a Veronica. And this was not to mention the chains, the tombstones commemorating departed bikers, the MacDonald's golden arches, a red and blue Spider-Man, several crosses, and the name of a woman. Was she the one who'd crowned him?

Joey was motionless but for this: as if some internal clock told him it was time to wake, he occasionally opened his eyes. No awareness dawned upon his gaze, yet I guessed that in his fathoms he *might* be able to hear and think. Perhaps the flame of consciousness had not completely guttered out.

"Hi, Joey," I chirruped at my first solo visit. I felt like a moron. For all I knew I was talking to myself. I thought that Mr. Frable was asleep.

"Hi, Joey. Hi, Joey. Hi, Joey," Mr. Frable bounced the greeting back at me. Joey, on the other hand, remained somnolent. A piece of me envied his mindless calm. Ah, to be tucked between the clean white sheets of oblivion.

"I hope you aren't in any pain, Joey," I continued. It hardly seemed as though the guy could process a word. I told him my name was Kenneth Watson and that I was a middle school vice principal. I tried to make a joke about being the heavy at school and said I was a softie at heart.

"Are you my son?" Mr. Frable called over to me. "My son's coming to visit me." He kicked his covers and kept asking if I were his son. I didn't know how to reply.

I began my sessions by reading Joey issues of Spider-Man and Archie comics, then moved on to Batman and Fantastic Four. I commented on major sports and how funny the late-night comedians were as I tried to tell a few of their jokes. I vented about my problems with the cable company and my broken garbage disposal. All the personal trifles I withheld from colleagues at Shady Hill Middle School, I lavished on Joey Tatts. The staff at Mallard Pond was delighted by my dedication, especially since the number of patient companions had dwindled. I kept the required observation logs and noted Joey's reactions, which were always nil. For the first few weeks I babbled on, weirdly high on my own chatter. But at night my remorse returned with visions of Evermay in the headlights. Blood from my scratching often speckled my sheets.

My first self mocked the goodness of my second self. I wanted to confess aloud my crime to Joey Tatts and kept waiting for the right moment. Being an outlaw, I thought that he would understand.

One day when Mr. Frable appeared to be asleep, the room TV droning through a talk show, and Joey between visits from nurses and aides, I sat by the side of his bed. I spoke to him in a penitent voice. "Joey, I have done things I should not have done and left undone things I should have done." I told Joey the story of my disaster, said that I wondered if the girl's leap was a plea for rescue or an act of suicide. I told him that I suspected the uncle and of my secret restitution through good deeds. How self-serving it all sounded and far from true repentance, yet as I spoke to him I noticed that, for the first time since the accident, I felt no urge to scratch my skin. I told him that I could not bring myself to confess to the cops. Maybe I was doing the right thing in telling all this to Joey, but the more I revealed, the more ashamed I felt.

"Joey, you're the only one who knows that I hit Evermay Blair."

Just then Mr. Frable started to hyperventilate and began to kick off his covers. "You hit Evermay Blair! You hit Evermay Blair!" he shrieked. "You lousy bastard." The old man lurched out of bed, his hospital gown billowing, and came at me. I dashed from the room and called for help. Some aides hustled in and wrestled with Mr. Frable, who continued to thrash and shout Evermay's name. The aides put Mr. Frable back in bed, fixed him in restraints, administered a sedative.

"I don't know what that was all about," I said, putting my hand to my chest. Those old black birds banged in my head.

"He goes off like that sometimes," said one of the aides. "Who is Evermay Blair? He's never said that name before."

I gestured that I hadn't a clue.

"Kenneth, you look pale. Let me take your blood pressure," offered the other aide.

Jeri Jankowski hurried toward me. "Kenneth, please

accept my apologies. I feel just terrible about this!" She took my hand. "Look how upset you are." She urged me to go home, but I said I wanted to say goodbye to Joey first.

As the staff hovered around us, I reached for Joey's hand.

At my touch, Joey opened his eyes. This was no reflex, no blind awakening. Coherence sharpened on his face. He gazed up at me and silently he said: *I am sorry. I am sorry for your troubles. But you hit a kid? You didn't stay with the body? Man, even I would have done that. Turn yourself in for God's sake.*

I nodded back. For a moment I felt light, restored, and calm. I knew what I had to do. Then Joey sank back into his twilight, and the leaden doors of my second self locked tight again.

The next morning, I called Jeri and told her that I could not return to Mallard Pond. The conversation was quick. I stayed home for a few days, cleaned my garage, shredded some old papers, washed my clothes. But soon I heard the call, and once again the second Kenneth took up his charge, for there was no end of damage in the world and more than enough work to fill my darkened days with purpose.

# The French Milliner's Model

One October afternoon I found on my front porch a package, the size of a hatbox. It was addressed to me and sent by my Uncle Chuck, our relative in charge of Grandma Caroline's bequeathals. I picked up the box. Something round shifted in the packing. Fearful of the likely contents, I let the parcel fall, dashed into the house, poured myself a glass of Shiraz, and drank. I took a head of lettuce from the fridge and began to tear it to pieces for our dinner salad.

My cousin Terrie from Long Island called. She, too, had received her hatbox-sized package.

"So, did you get a French milliner's model?" I asked.

"I got Therèse, what else would I get? I guess you got Babette."

"Don't know. Haven't opened it yet."

"Oh, don't be a ninny," said Terrie. "Of course, you got Babette. If I got Therèse, you got Babette."

I glanced at the clock. Soon Mason would be bringing Jen home from drama club. I texted them to leave the package on the porch.

"What are you going to do with your head?" I asked.

"Put her in the window for Halloween. Then maybe top her with a beret and plant her on an end table. Bedroom's off limits. I'll tell you that."

We managed, in unison, a faint laugh.

The milliners' models, mannequins for hat makers, were papier mâché forms, smooth as eggs, the size and shape of women's heads. Each form had a painted face framed by painted waves or ringlets and thin eyebrows that arched like parentheses over wide-open blue or umber eyes. Under a petite nose, a pair of lips pursed in a pink or red rosebud. There followed a round chin, a thin neck and narrow nape, then a painted bodice that served as a stand. Depending on how you saw things, the forms looked like pretty ladies or enormous board game tokens or guillotined heads. Each had her name written in cursive on her nape: Edith, Marie-Christine, Therèse, and Babette, the latter two purchased in honor of Terrie and me. To make matters worse, the Babette had wavy dark brown hair and umber eyes just like I did.

Gran's models were true antiques, all in excellent condition, the pride of her collection, which was mostly bric-a-brac furred over with dust, herded onto every available surface. The French milliners' models sat on a shelf above her bedroom door where they kept a vigil over Gran and Grandpa, then Gran alone. I guess they were to her as charms against darkness. But I was a nervous girl and prone to frights; I saw the heads as malevolent dolls. The Babette, in particular, seemed to have it out for me. She locked eyes with me with a stupid and canny stare, like a person who pretended not to understand you but who understood you perfectly well. Although I hated the Babette, I found it hard to break from her gaze. My twin younger brothers knew of my vulnerability and exploited it with inspired glee whenever we stayed at Gran's. Each time Mom and Dad left Gran to babysit us, I practically clung to her skirt to avoid being alone with my devious brothers. For months after those visits to Gran's house in Lambertville, New Jersey, the Babette lived in my dark imaginings, lurked in my deepest sleep, sidled up to my waking thoughts. At times, she even snuck up behind me in a mirror.

Terrie and I caught up on each other's husbands, kids, weekend plans.

"I understand how you feel about the head," said Terrie. "I get worked up about some things, too."

"Like what?" I asked.

"Like terrorism. Like identity theft. Like my diabetes."

I was a ninny indeed, still spooked by the stupid papier mâché noggin with my name on its neck. I took another swallow of wine. The room was starting to swim.

Mason and Jen entered the house with slow steps and cautious looks.

"Not like you to drink alone," said Mason, raising his eyebrows at my nearly empty glass.

I shrugged, too consumed with my fears and predicament to return a decent reply. Terrorizing me, my brothers swelled with triumph. Talk about a weak sister, a soft target. If only the head had not rolled back to me after all these years. People and their wills. Controlling you from beyond the grave.

"I can bring the box in for you, Mom," said Jen. "If you leave it outside, someone might take it. That's a thing now, porch pirates."

"Just leave it. Okay?" My tone of voice was brusque, and I felt even worse for sounding curt. My daughter shot me a stagey look of dudgeon then disappeared upstairs.

"Sorry," I called after her. "Really, Jen, sorry."

"My bequeathal from Gran," I told Mason. "It's the French milliner's model, the one with my name on it."

Mason floated me a sympathetic look. "Maybe she forgot how you felt about the head. Memory issues and all."

"Or figured I got over it. I mean I should have by now."

"It was the most logical choice for a legacy gift. She

bought it because it had your name on it and your hair and eyes, and she loved you."

Legacies were great if you were Rhodes or Nobel, giving to all humanity. A scary artifact, not so much. Gran lived on best in my fond remembrances of her: Gran reading me a story, Gran showing me how to bake an applesauce cake, Gran and I strolling along the Delaware and Raritan Canal.

A theft from the doorstep was too much to hope for. With trembling hands, I brought the package inside and took it down to the basement. Its presence disturbed me more with each passing hour.

***

Gran passed away at ninety-two, at home on oxygen and morphine, attended by one of her nurses, surrounded by her curios and collectibles. Although she and Grandpa Woodrow had five children, none had remained in the area. Not that it was any comfort to her, but scores of us returned to Lambertville, her home of more than sixty years, for the funeral. Mom and Dad drove up from Falls Church; Mason, Jen, and I flew in from Moline; cousins, aunts, and uncles descended as a great flock. My crazy twin brothers from Pittsburgh were among the few who didn't show, which was just as well with me. I said my silent good-byes to Gran. Her life had a sad beginning and a lonely end, but the middle was filled with blessings: a good marriage, a fine home, five children, a barrel of grandkids. She did annoy us with her relentless demands for attention, but even that we understood. At the funeral, Mason put his arm around my shoulder.

We gathered at a big diner for the funeral luncheon. Over pitchers of iced tea, Uncle Chuck announced that Gran had bequeathed to each family member a specially chosen item from her collections. We were to remember Gran by our legacy gifts, and we were not to sell them or give them away. The will instructed Chuck to donate the unassigned items to museums. I don't think he had a clue how hard it would be to find a home for all that junk, nor did I suspect at that point what my gift would be.

Grandma Caroline's three-story brick house stood several blocks from the Delaware River. It had a steep roof graced by gingerbread tracery, two gables, two chimneys, two inside staircases, an attic with bats, and a dumb-waiter. It sat next to a funeral home. At least the neighbors were quiet, Dad used to joke. Every time we drove up from Falls Church for a visit, Grandma Caroline took us on a tour of her collections, pointing out new acquisitions, reintroducing us to all her old pieces.

Gran amassed objects that struck her as cultured or whimsical or patriotic. And she wasn't a Noah about it; two of a kind were never enough. On her coffee table, several bands of Mexican mariachi frogs strummed their guitars and played their coronets. On the living room mantle piece, rows of labeled bird skulls, white as the moon, stared out from their eye holes. Some shelves held plates depicting the presidents, foreign dolls in traditional dress, and more specimens from nature. In front of hardbacks and paperbacks in bookcases, she had propped up mint sets of shiny coins (as if they might be valuable one day) and framed sheets of colorful commemorative postage stamps. A family of amber-eyed taxidermied foxes prowled the den. Door snakes rolled up against drafty thresholds. In the bathrooms, cats of cut glass glittered on the lids of toilet tanks.

No wall was bare. Scherenschnitte and embroidered samplers covered the living room and dining room walls in a lacy chatter of handiwork. In other rooms and hallways, photos told the family saga: my father, his brothers and sisters from birth to every childhood birthday, years of school pictures, wedding portraits, holiday shots in multi-photo frames, the generations adding on. I loved best the old black-and-white photos: Grandpa Woodrow with his parents, Grandpa as a Boy Scout, Grandpa in cap and gown, in the army, Gran and Grandpa at their wedding, candids of them on vacation in Florida, Bermuda, out West. There were so many faces in photos. I gave up trying to remember the names of all my cousins' children.

Of Gran, there were no childhood photos. During the Depression, her destitute family had fostered her out. And the foster family, whoever they were, left her no pictures, if they ever took any at all.

***

A few days later Terrie called back. By then I had shifted the box to the garage and set it next to the yellow lawn signs that said *Mason Kessler Contracting*.

"Have you opened the package yet?" she asked.

"I'm getting there," I said trying to sound as though I were closing in on the necessary task. I glanced at myself in a mirror. I hadn't been sleeping well and looked peaked. "At least we don't have to keep up the call chain. What a pain, right?"

“The call chain,” echoed Terrie. “Feels weird now that it’s over.”

“It’s like there’s something I still have to do, but I don’t have to do it.”

“Despite everything, I miss her.”

“I miss her, too,” I said and thought of Grandma Caroline sitting by her telephone table.

The call chain was a phone schedule Terrie’s mother developed to satisfy Gran’s demand for daily family phone calls. Three of us were to call Gran nightly and each was to talk to her for fifteen minutes. You had to do your time or you’d get an earful from Gran, who had a copy of the call schedule. I had to make a list of talking points to fill my fifteen minutes: tidbits about my job at the library, Mason’s clients, Jen’s classes, our health, the movies we saw. I always fulfilled my duty, as did Terrie. As did most of us. And since there were so many of us, our turns came up only once a month. My brothers couldn’t have cared less about the call chain. After enough guilt trips from Gran for missing their turns, they stopped calling.

“Listen, Babette,” said Terrie. “Luke and Keith were lousy to you, but you can’t give them the power to make you feel this way. Just open the box already.” She took a breath. “Besides maybe you got the Edith or the Marie-Christine. Maybe it's not the Babette at all. Open the box, then get rid of it the head. I give you my permission."

***

The trouble with the Babette began one rainy afternoon at Gran's. Mom and Dad had gone to New Hope to see a play, leaving us with Gran who was out at a meeting of her ladies' club. Board games bored us. None of us felt like reading. Nothing to do but watch TV, and the only decent TV set was in Gran's bedroom. Luke and Keith coaxed me into watching *The Screaming Skull*, an old horror movie from the fifties. It was hilarious, they said.

But it wasn't hilarious at all. It was about an evil husband bent on driving his second wife insane. At one point, the wife opens a closet and finds a skull inside, the first wife's skull, planted there by the husband. The wife rips out a blood-curdling scream. Electrified with terror, I screamed right along with her. Then I spun away from the TV set only to confront the heads over Gran's bedroom door. Crying and yelling, I bolted from the room, my bony brothers in their plaid shirts blown over in gales of laughter.

Having discovered my weakness, Luke and Keith played upon it with cruel invention. On visits to Gran's, they took to hiding the Babette head in a closet or a drawer where I would discover it and predictably wail. Once they told me to take out a load of towels from the dumb-waiter, and when I opened the hatch I found the head. My brothers doubled over in glee as I bellowed, then pummeled their backs with my puny fists. Ooh, that really hurts, they'd say. Napping, I might wake to find the head nestled beside me on my pillow. The one time Gran caught Luke and Keith manhandling her milliner's model, she gave them heck and whacked them with a big wooden spoon. After that, they persisted in stealth. Mom and Dad were no help. It's only a hunk of papier mâché, they said. The boys only do it because they get a rise out of you. Ignore them, and they'll stop. The wooden spoon incident aside, Gran wasn't that much help either. During my teen years when I was learning how to speak up for myself, I told Gran that the head frightened me and asked if she might she temporarily store it away when we came to visit.

"Babette," she said, her expression wilting, "I bought the model for you because it has your name and looks like you. I wanted you to love her, like a special doll. I'm sure she loves you." How peculiar and sad that sounded; after that, I knew that no more could be said of the matter.

The call I had been loathing came; Luke and Keith phoned from their shared office. They sold life insurance and annuities, prospecting via free lunch and dinner seminars. Identical twins, they loved to prank clients by sitting at each other's desks, introducing one as the other, then bubbling with giggles when visitors registered blank confusion.

The day before they called, I had relocated the box from the garage to the backyard shed where we kept our lawnmower and snow-blower. I could see the Babette glaring in the darkness, radioactive, angry at her exclusion.

"So, what did you get, Luke?" I asked preemptively.

He chortled. Keith chortled. Then both of them started to gasp and fake scream over the phone.

"The head's come back to haunt you, and you don't want to talk about it, right?" mocked Luke.

"Where are you going to keep it? Like on a closet shelf?" laughed Keith. "Shades of *The Screaming Skull*. You can't get rid of it. Can't defy a dead woman's will."

"I asked you first," I parried. "What did you guys get?"

"One of the door snakes," groused Keith.

"I got some of those cut-glass cats from the toilet tank," replied Luke.

Good old, Gran. Just what they deserved. Sure, I told them, I got the milliner's model. Everything was fine.

"Fine? You're fine with that?" challenged Keith sarcastically enunciating the word *fine*.

I took a breath and addressed them in my best conflict-resolution voice, my tone flat as a floor. "I want you both to know that scaring me with the head when we were kids was not funny. It was mean. And it left me with nightmares." I did not let them know that the old fears had returned now that the cursed effigy was mine to keep.

"Oh, God," said Luke to Keith. "Can you believe her?"

"You are so neurotic," said Keith. "You should see a headshrinker. No wait, you and the head should both go to a headshrinker. Show him how nuts you really are."

The next day at the library, which was now in full trick-or-treat mode festooned with grinning jack-o'-lanterns, dangling cardboard skeletons, and hanging paper bats, I Googled French milliners' models. To my shock, row after row of wide-eyed painted faces popped onto the screen—some plain, some pretty, some made up like floozies, some sterner than school marms. A few of the poorly conserved ones had paper flaking from their faces. I looked away from the horrid host.

The library director, Sharon, looked over my shoulder and drew back. "What on earth are those?"

"French milliners' models," I replied, clicking out of the screen. "Some people collect them."

"Well, those are absolutely hideous."

I thought of Babette festering in the shed. Was she dreaming of revenge? What was wrong with me that I obsessed over the head, yet could not bring myself to dispose of it? As if Gran would ever know.

Later that night I told Terrie about the phone call with Luke and Keith.

"What do you expect from them? They're a couple of numbskulls. Good that you called them down on their nasty pranks." She suggested that I take the head on a long ride and dump it in a ditch. "You could call it an accident."

The day before, Mason had offered to buzz saw the thing to bits, and while he meant to give me peace and himself some peace—I fretted endlessly about the head—I couldn't let the thing be destroyed.

The following day, a Saturday, I went to the shed and retrieved the box, brushed a few dead bugs from it, carried it into the house, and sliced through the packing tape with a box cutter. Uncle Chuck had wrapped the head in strips of white cloth, then cushioned it with crushed newspaper.

Trembling, yet somehow eager—*don't be a ninny*, Terrie had said—I lifted the head and peeled away the shroud. There in my hands lay the painted face: the dark wavy hair, the parenthetical eyebrows. Undimmed by age, the umber eyes fixed me in the look that I remembered, that stupid and canny stare, the knowing blankness: I do not understand you; I understand you perfectly well.

I did not gasp or shriek.

*You again*, she almost spoke the words.

"You again," I said aloud. As if she were so powerful. Plenty of things to be frightened about in this world, but not her.

As if to see better, I blinked. I cupped her rounded chin, then ran my hand down the thin stalk of her neck. She was cool to the touch having been in the shed. She withstood my caress. Maybe she liked it. I traced my name on her nape. Voodoo dolls, amulets, effigies, idols. No immanence there, but the viewer and the artist put the spirit in them.

She could not remain with me. The comic criminality of Terrie's disposal scheme amused me, though I'd never carry it out. Mason's, though well intentioned, amounted to murder. I hatched a few strategies of my own. I could wrap the Babette in a baby blanket, put her in a basket, drop her off at a random fire station. I could entrust her to a hair salon or a wig shop. Dump her in a Goodwill drop box. Half-heartedly, I emailed curators at a few museums and costume collections. I anticipated, if I ever heard from any of them, the same turndowns that Uncle Chuck would face: no space, no record of provenance, no thanks. And then I had a vision of Uncle Chuck, having done his duty—my goodness, all that packing and shipping—giving up in exasperation and unloading twenty plastic garbage bags of Gran's doodads at a Salvation Army depot.

Although I would never sell the Babette, to profit from her would be vulgar and disloyal, I poked around on a few websites surprised to find asks and offers. In excellent condition, a French milliner's model might fetch three hundred dollars. I wondered who these collectors might be. Hat makers, doll collectors, ladies who saw in those painted faces paragons of feminine prettiness? I could not sell my legacy gift, but I could give it away to the right place, and what might happen after that would be none of my affair.

That night in bed I told Mason that I had opened the box and looked at the head.

"I knew you could do it," he said, his breath minty from toothpaste. "It wasn't as bad as you thought, was it?"

"We locked eyes for a while. I think that she and I came to an understanding. At least, I did."

I proposed to Mason that we go on a road trip to antique shops and second-hand stores with the aim of unloading the head on one of them. Not for money, just to settle her into somewhere she'd feel at home.

"No money for you, you mean. But if that's what you want to do," said Mason, "I'm game." I nestled alongside him and slept well for the first time since the head came to our home.

On Sunday, I wrapped the Babette in her white rags, cushioned her with the crushed paper, and returned her to her carton. Off we went to Quad Consignment and Vintage for You in Moline, then to Time and Again and Ye Olde Shoppe in Rock Island, Born Yesterday in Davenport. A couple stores were out of business; some were old-clothes-only, no bric-a-brac. A few wanted only furniture. One sarcastic guy joked about making a piñata with her, then suggested poking a hole in her mouth for a cigarette. Our final stop would be Jinxed in Iowa City, a place I imagined filled with retired professors' home goods.

We motored past fields of wheat, corn, soybeans, grazing cows, and apple orchards ruby with fruit. We passed tractors, tankers, and trailers of poultry and pigs. The sun was warm. We stopped for a lunch of fried chicken, cole slaw, and biscuits. In the car, we discussed politics; we considered a vacation to Myrtle Beach; we talked about Jen and drama club, her college plans.

We pressed on to Iowa City and stepped into the world of used-to-be that was Jinxed, a dimly lit memory palace that once housed printing presses. Everything there, the building included, was a derelict of a former era. Upon entering, I inhaled the smell of mildew and human scent on old upholstery and clothes. Mason sneezed a few times. The guy who owned the store called himself Jinx. He had wire-rimmed glasses and gray eyes. His rooms were the end of the line for castoffs from house cleanouts and declutterings. I told him about the milliner's model, what it was made of, and used for. I carried the box that held Babette against my chest. He said he'd take us to his vintage fashion room and led us, single file, through what seemed to be the final resting place of fifty living rooms, jammed-together groups of sofas, easy chairs, coffee tables, and lamps. Then we traipsed through a room where towers of books, the former professors' libraries, I assumed, stood like the columns of a ruined temple. We passed bin after bin of framed photographs of people's long-forgotten relatives, the portraits in color, black and white, and even sepia. The portraits made me sad. All those connections now forgotten and irrelevant. What was that about being remembered unto the fourth generation, but not beyond? In the midst of the oblivion that gathered around me, I saw something compassionate about this guy, Jinx. He took in everything, turned nothing away. He had his business niche. He also reminded me of Pluto.

We arrived in his vintage fashion department, a large room even heavier with the human scent, crowded with hall trees and racks of dresses. In one corner, I saw the special gowns, a regular cotillion of old formals, in pastels and frills. I unpacked Babette on a mirrored vanity, and I could see that my artifact was curious even by Jinx's standards. I cradled Babette's face. Her knowing stare had changed to desperation.

*Don't give me away*, she seemed to say.

But you'll have company, I told her silently.

Jinx asked me how much I wanted for the model. No money, I told him. I only wanted a place for her to rest her head. Jinx, who smelled of pipe tobacco, nodded with careful seriousness. He raised an eyebrow toward Mason.

I turned and found a wall hung with row after row of ladies' hats: felt and velvet cloches, Easter bonnets, berets, hats for church, black hats with little face veils, sun hats, palm fedoras.

"Which one do you think she'd like?" he asked, humoring me. I tried several hats on her and settled on a carmine velvet cloche. It made Babette look like a girl dressed for travel, but beneath the fetching topper her expression stiffened to the armored look of one who must accept rejection, the look of one who would be sent away. Babette was old and had had many owners: she had been sent away many times, she knew the feeling. A burst of remorse burned my brow and my stomach curdled with guilt. I began to walk away from the old dresses and the wall of hats. Then, like Orpheus, I halted and glanced back. I must have stood there for some time trying to catch the eye of my French milliner's model. But she would not meet my gaze. Something in me felt closed off to myself, but I didn't know why.

"You okay?" asked Mason. "This is what you want to do, right?"

"If it's still here, you can have it back, no charge," said Jinx, running his hand through his gray hair.

I was quiet on the ride back. My feelings floated out of reach. Home at last, I collapsed in bed. I had a dream in which the head appeared to me in the early morning gloom, and she spoke to me in my own voice in words I could not understand. Sleep held me like tar. It took an act of will to pull myself out of my dream. It was five-thirty in the morning. I threw on some clothes and grabbed my purse and phone. Mason, serene in slumber, seemed far from me.

I told the GPS to guide me back to Jinxed. My fear of driving to an unfamiliar place alone and in the darkness terrorized me less than the idea of losing my strange double. I drove as fast as I could, whizzing past semis and tankers, hoping for no cops, racing back to Jinxed, praying that the horror Gran bequeathed me still was there and that she would take me back.

A half hour into the journey, my cell phone chimed with a text from Mason.

*Where in the hell are you?*

With one eye on the highway and another on the phone, I began to text:

*Going back to…*

Suddenly, the glare of headlights and the blast of a truck's horn pounced on me from behind. In a panic, I threw the phone down and, trembling, swerved to the shoulder of the road as the trucker barreled past blaring his horn angrily.

Shaking, I picked up the phone and found Mason's response.

*WTF*

*Stop texting. I'll be back later.*

I arrived at Jinxed close to seven, and in the morning light I saw my Babette staring out the front window of the store, as if she were waiting for me in her red velvet traveling hat. As I stood before her, a sly ironic smile appeared on her face. Then her expression melted with mine into a look of profound relief.

I called the store number and Jinx answered. It turned out that he lived upstairs and came down to let me in.

"I left her out in the front window to look out for you."

"Thanks for that," I replied dryly, suspecting that he'd put her on display to attract a quick sale.

We said our goodbyes. Into her box went Babette and into the back seat. Before I started the car, I called Sharon to let her know that I might be a little late for work. A family thing. No big deal. Later that evening, I called Terrie and told her about my adventure.

"Babette, everybody has their crazy. I mean that with love."

Then I phoned my mother and father, something I hadn't done in a while. We chatted mostly about my mother's begonias, a neutral subject that, under the present circumstances, gave me pleasure and relief.

***

I settled Babette on a bookshelf. At first, I stared at her the way a medieval monk might contemplate a skull, and the more I did that, the less I feared her, the less animate she appeared, the fewer glances we exchanged, the less she seemed to speak. As time passed, she fell altogether silent. I rarely noticed her the way a person rarely notices an object that is always there and never different. Only a conscious effort would draw her into my awareness. Visitors, of course, would ask about her. New eyes would wake her up. What a loving gift, some would observe. Creepy, remarked others. How chic, said a few. Kitsch, declared one person, a comment that caused Babette and me to make a face.. After a day or so, deprived of attention, Babette would fade from notice.

Mason and I grew into middle age. Jen married and had children of her own. Who could say if my French milliner's model would remain in the family? I called to mind, maybe more often than I should, the adage about remembrance and the fourth generation. I guessed that family artifacts would hang around less than that. People moved. The old had to make way for the new. Loss and oblivion could only be deferred so long.

I have imagined, however, that my grandchildren might ask me one day about their eccentric great great grandmother. Was it true that she collected curiosities and trinkets? What became of her collections? Did she have anything of value? Looking at my grandchildren, Babette and I would smile with satisfaction. I knew that I would hold onto my French milliner's model until my very last days, and, after that, I could only hope that the dear old head would find a new double and that the two of them would live under the same roof in harmony and for a very long time.

# The Other Henry Harris

The first phone call came as Henry Harris was about to spoon into his strawberry yogurt and granola. He let the phone ring. Calls were to be expected. In the obituaries that morning, Henry Harris saw that another man with his very same name had died. The sight caught him like a patch of black ice, swooped him into a weird out-of-the-body experience and into a posthumous plane.

Rereading the notice, a fraternal sympathy misted over him. Who was this other Henry Harris? His death notice was very brief. Henry wondered if his name-twin had had a good life, a happy marriage, a satisfying job. He certainly hoped so.

The business with identical names was bound to trigger phone calls, especially since the dead Henry had been sixty-one, two years younger than the live Henry. Such an untimely death! On the other hand, Henry could hardly wait for the calls of condolence to come in. Lately, he had been sandbagged by problems at work, and things were not going well at home. He was feeling morose, unappreciated. This morbid coincidence, however, had its bright side. The more grieving friends phoned, the more Henry could learn how well he was loved, how much he'd be missed. He might even hear a few sobs, then shrieks of relief and joy when his acquaintances learned that he was still alive.

The phone rang again, and Henry let his wife, Gladys, answer it. She had just come down to breakfast and had not yet seen the newspaper. With hidden satisfaction, he saw an array of emotions jump seismically across her face. Then her expression flat lined.

"Meg, what do you mean? Is he in some kind of trouble?" Gladys's gaze darkened. "Is this your idea of a practical joke?" She looked over at Henry who offered an innocent shrug.

"Well, he's not, and that's a creepy thing to call and ask." After hanging up the phone, Gladys turned to her husband. "Apparently, Henry, word is out that you've gone down for a dirt nap."

"Better luck next time," replied Henry, a toothpick stuck like a victory cigar in his teeth. He handed her the paper and pointed to his name. The day before, Gladys actually *had* commanded him to drop dead after he'd backed out of going to the theater with her and her sister, Gayle. He'd wasted a ticket and forced the two women to drive downtown by themselves.

Henry knew he had acted like a jerk, but he was stubbornly unrepentant. His sister-in-law was driving him nuts. Now in her second week as their house guest,

Gayle, a part-time florist's assistant, was on him like a case of poison ivy. She criticized everything from his wardrobe to the way he ran his video production business. It didn't help that he'd recently lost an important account, a client he'd tried hard to please, and that his computer system just had a meltdown.

The phone rang again. This time Henry answered. Silence gaped on the other end of the line. Stunned to hear a ghost, Morty Primerano, one of Henry's competitors, managed to stumble over a greeting and choked out that he was glad to hear Henry sounding so well, then suggested that they get together for lunch one day. The vulture, thought Henry, already looking to pick over his accounts.

"Morty, rumors of my demise have been greatly exaggerated," said Henry happy to have the opportunity to quote Mark Twain, of whom he was especially fond.

As if launched by the writer's spirit, Henry's thoughts floated to a scene in *Tom Sawyer* where Tom, Huck, and Joe, assumed drowned, appeared at their own funeral just in time to hear what fine fellows they'd been. This gave Henry an idea. It would be swell to sit among the mourners, to bathe in the love and tears due a dear departed Henry Harris, everyone whispering reverently about the last time he or she had spoken to the esteemed deceased. The late Henry's funeral—actually a commemoration of life service—was scheduled for Tuesday at 6 p.m. at Deeley and Block, a mortuary not far away. The path to better spirits appeared clear to Henry. He would attend the funeral of the other man and, hearing the good name of Henry Harris invoked with honor and praise, would have his mood lifted and his self-confidence restored. He knew this was completely absurd, but that did not bother him in the least.

The strong aroma of honeysuckle corkscrewed up Henry's nose. It was Gayle spraying herself with scent before descending the stairs in the manner of Norma Desmond. Twain still on his mind, Henry recalled that the writer was blessed with a kind and generous sister-in-law and wondered why he was saddled with an ogress like Gayle. Henry was at the computer in the den and tried to emit calming beta waves—beta, beta, cool, calm beta—before his sister-in-law's first carping of the day. His attempt at tranquility was only partially successful. The minute she opened her mouth, his brain waves crashed upon the rough coast of her peculiar speech. Not only did Gayle antagonize him with her criticism and perfume, she also drove Henry wild with her relentless mispronunciation of words. It was "inbitation" for invitation, "hambag" for handbag, "pepperica" for "paprika." Her articulations hit Henry like shots from a nail gun. Gladys, who was a speech therapist, had given up trying to correct her sister's speech. To form words differently would somehow draw her away from herself, and Gayle couldn't or wouldn't do that.

Henry winced as he overheard Gayle ask Gladys for "cimmammom" toast and then caught a more pointed question.

"Suppose he really did keel over one day, Glad. Maybe it would be a blessing in disguise."

Gladys mumbled something that Henry could not make out. Then one of them turned on the TV, and Henry could hear no more of their talk. He wondered if Gladys was sorry that she told him to drop dead. In the early years of their marriage, she had often told him that she wanted to die first: life without him would be unbearable. It was pure romantic Krazy Glue, a kooky and morbid way to say *I love you*. The younger Henry was always a little troubled by the death-wish thing, but he guessed it was something a man should like to hear as it spoke of need and devotion. After thirty years, however, different interests, disgruntlements, and lack of tending had eroded their romance. When calm did not prevail, each orbited the other resentfully or sailed off to do his or her own thing. Children would have provided them with a center, but they were childless, though not by choice.

Now Gayle had come to nest like a cowbird, and Henry was feeling very trespassed. She sat in his favorite chair. She commanded the TV remote. They ate only the foods she preferred. And there was the way she usurped the bits of attention that Gladys might dole out to him. The separate spheres that surrounded husband and wife grew as hard and fragile as blown-glass ornaments.

Except for their anagrammatic names and the fact that the sisters were both blue-eyed blondes with dainty hands and feet, the women were opposite in nature. Where Gladys was serious, steady, and careful, Gayle was helter-skelter, theatrical, a regular Calamity Jane. Her last marriage had ended a year ago when the husband, her fourth, ran off with another woman.

It was a Sunday, and Henry had plenty of time to prepare for the funeral of the man he now thought of as his parallel self. Research was needed. He couldn't very well go to a viewing ignorant of the late Henry Harris. No stranger to ego surfing, Henry Googled their shared name. Up came the website for his own outfit, Harris Sound and Video, links to news items about his company's business—would those days of prosperity and glamorous PR ever return?—a blurb about the girls' soccer team he sponsored, and the scholarship contributions Henry and Gladys had made to benefit local youth. They found that giving to other people's children helped fill that gap in their lives. On the Google pages, Henry found hits for Henry Harris the physician, the famed organist, the horse trader, the ardent stamp collector, the teacher, the sci-fi fan, and the guy sought for his high school reunion. But about the deceased Henry, there was nothing more than the same short obituary he had seen in the paper with an added link to the funeral home. This thwarted his research. It also made him rather sad.

"I thought you were pushing up daisies," said Gayle as she interrupted him at the computer. A red lipstick grin was wiped across her face. "I read the obituary. It was heart rendering. Would you like me to make you a funeral arrangement? Something with yellow and white chrysanthemummies?"

Properly stung by her harassments, annoyed by her diction, and overwhelmed by her honeysuckle scent, Henry expelled a mighty sneeze but made no other reply. At no time did he reveal to Gladys, and certainly not to Gayle, his plans to attend the funeral of the other Henry Harris.

Work the next day provided more than the usual turmoil. Scattered through the office voice mail and email were messages from perplexed clients and vendors asking if things were okay at Harris Sound and Video, if Henry had been under the weather, if this was a bad time to ask about alterations to a commercial. On top of that, following the crash of their computer system, only about three-quarters of their work could be restored from back-ups; many files were lost forever. Like dead souls, thought Henry, gone to nowhere. Why hadn't he backed up the system more frequently?

Henry rallied himself and shot a cheerful email to his corporate list to let everyone know that Harris Sound and Video treasured its working relationships, that service and quality were job one, and please call for a free consultation. Shuffling through some manila folders on his desk, Henry came across a past-due bill from a client named Hobart and a résumé from a job-seeker named Riley. He decided that he would attend the funeral as Hobart Riley and liked the idea of a pseudonym. It felt like protective coloring. Anyhow, he couldn't very well sign the guest book as Henry Harris.

Henry chose a tobacco-brown suit to wear to the late Henry's commemoration of life service. In the office restroom, he made sure that his tie was straight and that no remains of his lunchtime spinach salad were lodged in his teeth. Behind his glasses, his eyes looked attentive and aware. But this was also the year that age had fallen down on Henry Harris like a gray curtain, pulling at his jowls, leaching his color, leaving his person as rumpled as slept-in clothes. His tennis game had started to go downhill. And his knees hurt. How few good years a man had, he mused, how little time to make a name for oneself. In the gelid lavatory light, he practiced saying Hobart Riley, then worried about being caught in a lie or recognized by one of the mourners.

On the way to the funeral home, Henry received a cell phone call from Gayle—why should she be calling him?—and though he did not answer it, the sight of her name on the display flustered him so much that he nearly ran a red light. Shaken by the close call and nervous about the funeral, Henry Harris pulled up to Deeley and Block. The parlor was a modest establishment in a neighborhood of row homes with cracked concrete sidewalks and scarce parking. It was April and, although the weather was pleasant, the street could barely muster the look of spring. Here and there a few overgrown forsythias hung out like big heads of unruly blond hair. Discarded soda cans and garbage from fast food restaurants littered the gutters and grass strips along the sidewalks.

Upon entering the funeral parlor, Henry was prepared

to be assaulted by the smell of air freshener, which he'd known funeral directors to spray during viewings. Henry was pleased to find the air at Deeley and Block clear and odorless. He was even more surprised to see a big tray of Tastykakes set out on a hall table. Henry passed on the Yodels, Yankee Doodles, and Peanut Butter Kandy Kakes, then signed the guest book as Hobart Riley, the pen slightly shaky in his hand. Many of the mourners were munching the Tastykakes and milling around; others were lined up to comfort Mrs. Harris, their two adult children, and two seniors who must have been the late Henry's parents. No pastor was in sight.

Being Hobart Riley seemed easy enough. Other folks respected his loss, and he respected theirs. He even said, "It's a sad day" to a few mourners, and they nodded back with solemn sympathy. The room, however, was only half filled, and Henry felt somewhat conspicuous. Everyone seemed to know each other, and a few folks glanced at him as if trying to place him. Henry busied himself by watching a PowerPoint presentation on a laptop that showed Henry as a high school grad, a groom with his bride, with his poker pals, raising a mug of beer, with his children at birthdays and holidays. The other Henry Harris seemed like a cheerful guy, stout with a gummy smile. He wore his hair very short on the sides with a woodpecker ruff on top. Not to judge a man without standing in his shoes, thought Henry, but so far this chap didn't seem to be any great shakes. It idly crossed Henry's mind that if the dead Henry really had made a name for himself, the present Henry would feel jealous and outdone.

The PowerPoint was part of a shrine to the late Henry that also included a stack of navy and tan fliers that said, "We Fondly Remember Henry Harris," a family photo album, something that looked like an Aladdin's lamp, some floral arrangements (sure enough, white and yellow mums), a deck of cards, several stacks of poker chips, a six-pack of Yeungling, and a plaque from the Tastykake Baking Company commending Henry for outstanding service. So that was it. He'd worked for Tastykake. But what did he do there? And where was the body?

Henry realized that the guy had been cremated and packed into that Aladdin's lamp. Henry had always favored cremation, but the sight of a man's life, all sixty-one years of it, burned down and packed into a receptacle caused him a pang of grief. He saw himself dead, a cup of dust, his consciousness unplugged, no more to this world or any other world as far as he was concerned.

A man in a plaid shirt walked up to Henry and reminisced with him about the family's famous barbeques. "It's what memories are made of," said Henry, at ease as Hobart Riley. The man in the plaid shirt responded with a dim smile, turning away he angled a suspicious look at Henry.

An informal service began, and friends and relatives spoke up to offer their remembrances.

"Salt of the earth," declared someone. "He doted on his Clarita."

"He came over to our house last year when Fred was sick and mowed the lawn," said a woman.

"Save a spot at that big poker table up there for me, Hank," said a man reverently. "He was a real Tastykake man. Could tell you how much sugar they used each day at the plant. And how many Tastykakes you'd have to line up to make a mile."

"You weren't perfect, but we loved you," said a male voice, and a chuckle rose from the crowd.

Henry chuckled along with everyone, but he felt disappointed. He gained no vicarious boost from the love. Nothing anyone said made his heart swell with borrowed pride. Although he did take away that he ought to be more helpful to others and nicer to Gladys, this adventure was pretty much a dud. And why should he feel better hearing the late man's tributes? The other Henry Harris was a total stranger. The two of them had nothing in common but a name, a meaningless name. Henry decided to quietly make his exit.

"I see we have a new friend here," said the man in the plaid shirt. "What's your name?"

"Hobart. Hobart Riley," Henry choked out. The name tasted funny in his mouth. The congregation turned to Henry, who felt hot under the spotlight and saw that he was quite overdressed. Most of the men were in windbreakers and shirtsleeves. Be vague. Be a man of few words, Henry counseled himself. Now, more than ever, he wished to flee.

"And how did you know Hank?"

"Through work. He was a great guy. Always so cheerful." Henry smiled bravely and nodded expecting everyone to nod back. Instead, the eyes of the dead man's co-workers and kin rolled toward him like animated billiard balls massing for attack. The room grew silent. Henry's heart rate speeded up.

A rough-looking type with dirty fingernails, fixed him with a sidelong stare. "I worked with Hank for thirty years, and we never knew a Hobart Riley."

Henry's underarms grew damp. Sweat beaded up on his brow. "Actually, I worked for one of the suppliers. I didn't see Henry all that often, but when I was there he made me feel welcome."

"Hank was a janitor, mister. Just like me. On the night shift. Just who the hell are you?"

Mrs. Harris wobbled in her chair. Chatter began to simmer in the room, then boiled harder.

Henry stood up. "I guess I'll be going," he said and began to sidle down the aisle of metal folding chairs, bumping other people's knees.

"You just hang on there, Riley," said the man in the plaid shirt. "I want to see some ID."

"Is this about money?" snarled the janitor coworker. He shoved his face so close to Henry's that Henry could smell his breath, which reeked of spoiled milk. He grabbed Henry by the lapel and jerked him toward the door. Henry felt a sharp object in his back. Was it a finger jabbing him? A knife? He didn't want his good suit ripped or blood drawn, but who knew what might happen. These people were ruffians, thugs.

"You're not welcome here, mister," said the funeral director, a pallid man with a very tiny nose.

Henry Harris half slid, half flew as the friends of the other Henry Harris bounced him from Deeley and Block like a drunk from a bar. He was up in the air for a moment, then crashed on the concrete steps. He managed to break his fall a little with his hands, then fell down again close to the curb. Pain splintered through him, swiping his breath away. Through his daze, he heard the sound of clucking. Smirking, reddish faces looked down on him from the door of the funeral parlor, and then the door shut.

Unable to rise at first, he rolled to his side. My knees, Henry thought in panic. He could not bend them. He could see his bloody knees and shins through his ripped trousers. The heels of his hands were scraped and sticky with blood and street grit. A passerby stepped around him as if he were a bum or an addict. Then a couple came by and helped him up. A bad slip and fall, he told them. "Sheesh," said the woman, "You could sue or something." They offered to call 911. Henry said it wasn't necessary.

His tobacco-brown suit was ruined, the armholes ripped at the seams, the jacket cuffs and pant legs in shreds. With the couple's help, Henry managed to walk stiff legged to his car. Thanking the strangers and trying not to weep in front of them (it was kindness, not meanness that threatened his composure), he slowly swiveled into the driver's seat and managed to drive home. It was hard to grip the steering wheel, which was smeared with his blood. How destructible he was. And how brought low. What would he think if a stranger appeared at his wife's funeral pretending to know her? Well, he certainly wouldn't heave the person out the door. He thought about getting some paper towels and Lysol to wipe off the steering wheel.

Gladys inhaled with alarm as Henry propelled himself into the living room, limbs wired with pain. "My God, what happened?" she cried rushing toward her husband. She embraced him gingerly, careful not to touch any hurt parts.

Gayle sauntered into the room. Seeing Henry, she burst into laughter as if entertained by a slapstick character. "Who kunk food you?" she chortled, chopping the air karate style. "What'd you do, fight over a parking space?"

Gladys whirled around and glared at her sister. Gayle retreated to the guest bedroom.

Henry's wife helped him off with his clothes. She had to use a kitchen shears to cut off his pant legs.

"I fell down some stairs," said Henry. "I can't believe what a klutz, I was."

"That was one doozy of a fall," said Gladys.

She gave him a sponge bath. Her tenderness was still there. He trembled in her hands, grateful and vulnerable, wanting more than anything to restore their couplehood. He looked at his wounds and thought of those who did him harm. Was he going to be okay? His face contorted like a rubber mask. He covered it with his hurt hands. Henry didn't want Gladys to see him cry.

He thanked Gladys for taking care of him. She put her hand gently on his shoulder and said, "I'm your wife. That's what I do."

Henry spent the night on the couch with ice packs on his knees (it was impossible for him to make it up the stairs), and in the morning he saw to his extreme and silent joy that Gayle's two suitcases were packed and standing by the door. He pretended to sleep as the sisters ate a wordless breakfast. Then they left the house.

In the morning light, he shifted his bruised knees and thought of how those hooligans had nearly crippled him and what an idiot he'd been to think he could have his self-esteem vamped up by way of another man's praise. And as for what he meant to the world, as for remembrance, legacies, Aladdin's lamps: who would recall him or any other person for very long? You blow in, you make the grass wave a little, then you pass like a breeze. So be it, mused Henry. He gazed at the clock. It was the old-fashioned kind with black hands that shuffled, now so slowly, around the dial. Henry Harris could hardly wait for his wife to come home.

# Monkey Island

The battle of the junior-class science trip to Puerto Rico began at home. Self-conscious about her weight, certain that she'd be snubbed by the glamour girls on the trip roster, sad that none of her friends could afford the pricey journey, Chessie Partrell refused to go.

"Science and Spanish are your favorite subjects," said her father. "You'll be the star."

"Maybe during activities, Dad, but what about all the other hours of the day?"

"Act friendly to others, and they'll act friendly to you," encouraged her mother. Then sensing her daughter's still-sunken spirits, she ventured, "If it's about the weight issue, go on a diet."

Like Chessie could melt off forty pounds in six weeks.

"Or take up swimming again," her mom added. "You looked great when you used to swim."

Not exactly a quick fix, thought Chessie.

Still, what her mother said about swimming reminded Chessie of how at ease she used to feel in the water, light and free as a mermaid.

"Chessie," leveled her father, "You have to go. Mom and I booked a getaway to Montreal for those days. Pity us freezing up north while you're soaking up the Caribbean sun." Caught in their net, Chessie gave her parents the fish eye.

The next day Chessie's mother took her to the mall where they managed to find a black swimsuit with a loose-fitting top and matching cover shorts. Following their shopping success, they ate diet vanilla frozen yogurt and lingered before a pet store aquarium where neon tetras flickered, weightless and carefree. A little mechanical mermaid sat in the tank and waved at them.

***

As soon as the students and their teacher-chaperones landed in San Juan, the glamour girls split into two tribes, one led by Jaina Bricker, the other by Samantha LeMieux. They looked like rainbow ice pops in their tight tank tops. They wore blue jeans cropped to the crotch and spent most of their time giggling, texting, and sometimes disappearing with the boys on the trip. They acted like Chessie was a potted plant.

Aching for someone to talk to, Chessie tried to make herself useful to the girls by offering to translate for them at a tourist shop. "Everyone's bilingual here," said Jaina dismissively, looking up from a display of painted seashells. "Listen, I'm really kind of busy. Okay?"

Chessie blushed in embarrassment. When Sherry Maas flashed Chessie a big smile and asked to borrow a Kleenex, Chessie cheerfully offered her several thinking she'd made a possible pal. But it turned out that Sherry's friendliness lasted only as long as she needed a Kleenex.

The Puerto Ricans turned out to be way nicer than the kids from school. The housekeeping ladies at the hotel always had a cheerful *¿cómo estás?* for her. And island food was good, especially the *tostones* and the fruit-juice drinks. But most of the time it seemed that only the little frogs, the *coquís*, spoke to her, incessantly repeating their name.

Resigned to the fact that she was either going to be ignored or insulted, Chessie decided that she would lose herself in nature studies. During the class hike through El Yunque rainforest, she sampled the intoxicating aroma of the ylang-ylang perfume flowers and found herself hypnotized by the waterfalls, each one prettier than the next. At the Arecibo Observatory, she took careful notes during the astronomy lecture and was amazed by the giant radio telescope that hung over the land like a humongous white spider. Days were filled with field trips followed by free time at the hotel pool. In a lounge chair, all covered up in loose white trousers and a big pink tee shirt, Chessie perspired and tried to read the newspaper *El Nuevo Día* as the other girls in their bikinis cooled off in the beautiful blue-green pool, shrieking with laughter and, she assumed from the sometimes conspiratorial tone of their voices, dishing about classmates. Every so often, boys gave some of the girls rides on their shoulders or pushed them into the pool.

At night, the teachers, Mr. Heyde and Ms. Lee, vanished, and the ice-pop girls roamed Old San Juan with the boys. For the first two nights, Chessie stayed in her hotel room looking at American and Puerto Rican TV with her roommate, Drucie Matthews, the other misfit, a weird girl who was always twisting her finger in her ear. Chessie went on Facebook and posted about the trip, but she could only do so much of that, and anyhow, Puerto Rico was out there. No sense in being cooped up in the hotel room. On the third night, Chessie asked the people at the front desk about evening activities.

"*¿Solita?*" the man at the desk asked a little concerned.

"I might go with my roommate," Chessie said with a shrug. The man told her how to take a taxi to the Fine Arts Cinema. Very safe for young women, he said. Drucie, no surprise, was too chicken to go, even in a cab. So Chessie took a shower, washed her long mocha mane, applied the new coconut-scented conditioner she had bought at a *farmacía,* dressed in a pair of flowered trousers, a big top, and went off to the movies. *Solita. No problema.* She chose a Spanish-language comedy that, thankfully, had plenty of sight gags, and she even picked up a few new trendy phrases from the dialogue.

Chessie returned to the hotel just as a group of tipsy classmates stumbled into the lobby.

"Where were you?" asked Samantha, apparently dumbfounded to see Chessie out and about.

"At the movies," replied Chessie.

"Who'd you go with?" interrogated Samantha, her face scrunched into an incredulous sneer.

Chessie chose not to dignify that with an answer and, instead, marched into the elevator. She felt so empowered by her solo adventure that she momentarily forgot that the next day was the excursion to Monkey Island, the dreaded bathing-suit day.

When the time came to report to the tour bus, Chessie left her hotel room wearing her new plus-size black suit with the loose blousy top, the black cover shorts, and her oversized black tee. She packed her sun block and towel and tucked two energy bars in her waterproof belt bag just in case they got stranded. As usual, everyone was saving a place on the tour bus for someone else, even that loser Drucie waved her off. The good feelings from last night's adventure went out like the tide. Chessie finally plopped down next to Jason Otis, the class clown, who poked her gut and called her the Michelin tire woman, then Miche for short. The name stuck and soon everyone was calling her Miche: *Hi, Miche. How's it going, Miche*?

"Oh, come on, Miche, lighten up," cajoled Jason when he saw her looking glum. Then he started humming the Raffi song, "Baby Beluga in the Deep Blue Sea." Chessie looked out the bus window and tried to ignore him. Tears stung her eyes, but she would not let herself cry. She had to suffer through this day, then one more, and the trip would be over.

Jason never managed to date the hot girls, but he always tried to flirt with them. On the bus, he waved around a brochure for a parasailing company called the Frayed Knot and poked Jaina Bricker on the arm. "Hey, Jaina, these people asked me if I wanted to go parasailing, but you know what I said?"

"Ask me if I care," said Jaina.

"I said 'fraid not. 'Fraid not!"

"You are so immature," said Jaina. She slicked her lips with some paint-on gloss then drew her hand through her highlighted hair so that people could see the two purple hickeys that tattooed her neck.

On the excursion boat, named *La Ninfa Marina*, the ice-pop girls peeled down to their teeny bikinis. Chessie stayed in her black cover shorts and black oversize tee. She knew she looked like a manatee in a lineup of Miss Americas. Everybody slim. Not a spare tire or a rumple of cellulite among them, not even on Drucie, in her blue, polka-dotted, boyleg one-piecer. All the boys ogled all the girls. Chessie tried to tent her giant tee over her knees. Then, thankfully, the captain made everyone don puffy life vests.

As usual, Mr. Heyde and Ms. Lee were spending a lot of time with their heads together and not doing a very good job of supervising. A couple of kids were hooking up in a corner of the boat, and some of the guys boasted loudly about how many *piña coladas* and *cervezas* they had ordered with their borrowed IDs. Captain Sánchez, the skipper, finally blew a conch shell to get everyone's attention. Chessie imagined the ancient Taino people calling to each other, but most of the kids just snickered.

The captain announced that the trip to Monkey Island and the snorkel stop at the shipwreck would take three hours. Jason burst into the *Gilligan's Island* theme song about a three-hour tour, and all the kids, even Chessie, joined in looking pointedly at the teachers when the "professor and Mary Ann" part came up.

Ms. Lee turned toward them, red in the face. "Okay, people, you are officially in school right now," she said. "I can and will be taking names of students who fail to pay attention or who show a lack of respect."

Mr. Heyde nodded in approval.

The captain, a spry old guy who kept bragging that he was seventy-three years young, explained that Monkey Island was a breeding colony for rhesus monkeys. Only scientists were allowed to set foot on the island, but tourists could view the monkeys from a distance. That was strictly for the monkeys' safety, said Sánchez, but when they approached the island, lush with foliage and shaggy palms, everyone saw a sign posted in a clump of trees:

| | |
|---|---|
| *Attention* | *Atención* |
| *Danger* | *Peligro* |
| *These monkeys attack.* | *Estos monos atacan.* |

"Don't get too close or they'll rip you to rhesus pieces! Rhesus pieces!" guffawed Jason as he made monkey sounds and a bite face. Everyone laughed. Even the teachers. Even Chessie. She liked seeing Jason make himself look silly.

"No, they are not aggressive at all," said the captain. "Do you know what the most aggressive animal is?" One kid suggested tigers. Another sharks. Killer bees, offered Mr. Heyde. "No, it's man," said Sánchez with a solemn note in his voice.

Chessie cast a barbed glance at Jason and the ice-pop girls.

Captain Sánchez was a regular PR guy for the monkeys. He explained that the scientists mostly kept the rhesus monkeys there to observe their social behavior. "They are closest in behavior to humans. They divide themselves into two tribes. Just like the Democrats and the Republicans. The rulers are females, and the females remain in their tribes, but sometimes the males travel across borders to mate. And then they come back to their tribes."

Mr. Heyde lifted his eyebrows. Ms. Lee focused on a distant seagull.

As they boated around the island, the girls smoothed sun block on each other, and everyone snapped pictures with their cell phones.

Chessie trained her sights on the island and was the first to spy a monkey in the trees. Then more and more appeared. Some ran along the beach. They were much bigger than she expected and looked like cougars, tawny and amazingly fast. They shimmied effortlessly up the palm trees. Captain Sánchez said they could even swim. Chessie saw a troop sprint across a spit of sand that separated one part of the island from another. From time to time, said the captain, researchers would remove a monkey for experiments, but then that monkey would be contaminated, and it was never returned to the island.

Chessie liked watching the monkeys doing their monkey business, but she also felt very sorry for them. In her psych class, she'd read of those terrible experiments in which baby monkeys were put in solitary confinement. She couldn't forget that photograph of the wizened little baby monkey pathetically clinging to his robot-faced surrogate mom. Of course, the monkeys went mental. Treated like that who wouldn't? At least here the monkeys had the run of the island with their monkey families and monkey friends.

For snorkeling at the wreck, everyone had to go in pairs. Chessie looked the other way so that Drucie wouldn't choose her, and soon she was the odd one out. Mr. Heyde announced that Chessie would have to team with Aisha Moore and Samantha LeMieux. Samantha, the worst buddy possible! Hearing the order, Samantha made a face like a Greek tragedy mask and drew her hands through her hair in mock woe. As soon as the captain anchored, Aisha and Samantha sprang from the boat into the shallow water, slipped on their flippers, donned their diving masks, and took off without Chessie.

"Hey, wait up!" cried Chessie. Still wearing her cover shorts and her belt bag, she splashed into the warm Caribbean water and swam after the two girls. They didn't stop or turn around. She rationalized that as long as she could see them she'd be okay.

Chessie felt light in the ocean, good in her skin. The water befriended her, made her one with its waves. The sea vegetation tickled her ankles. The grasses swayed in the current like meadow grass in a breeze, and, just like birds in the air, a few fish swam over the sea lawn. Chessie found swimming with the flippers nearly effortless. She got used to mouth-breathing through the snorkel tube in no time. She swished through the water with new-found grace, at home in the peace and silence of the aquatic world.

Chessie followed Sam and Aisha to the shipwreck. Her hair floated around her like a dusky cloud. Looking down at the ocean floor on her way to the wreck, she spied a lost anchor stuck in the sand. Fuzzy with brownish algae, it made her think of human remains. She shivered and hastily flippered away from it.

The captain had explained that the ship, which had been carrying sugar, had sunk in the nineteen-forties in a storm, and its remains lay completely submerged in only eight feet of water. No one had died in the wreck, but it was spooky enough. The blackened ribs of the ship looked like a charred human skeleton. But pink and white coral colonies had formed on the rusted metal, and Chessie liked the way life and beauty had resumed in the ruins. Yellow-and-black striped fish, aquamarine fish with eyespots on their tails, little orange fish, and others threaded in and out of the ship's black bones. So mesmerized was Chessie that she had to remind herself to look about her in order not to collide with the jutting metal bars of the ship. All was tranquil and blissful. She even found a starfish, picked it up, examined it, and, with much care, returned it to the ocean floor.

Where were Samantha and Aisha? Chessie swirled around, looking in all directions. The girls had vanished. Surfacing and treading water, she could make out *La Ninfa Marina* maybe a quarter mile away. A hot shock of panic seared her nerves. Frantically she waved her arms and called out, "Over here! Don't leave me!"

Crowned with palms and cavelike with thickets of

lower-growth trees, Monkey Island loomed before her. Chessie was on the oceanside of the island, mainland nowhere in sight. Badly in need of rest, fearful of the monkeys, and furious at Samantha and Aisha—near tears in fact—Chessie swam toward the island, which was no more than twenty yards away. She reached walkable water and waded ashore.

The first thing that greeted her was a hideous iguana. It gave her a stupid dead-eyed look. She pushed her mask with its snorkel tube up over her forehead like a headband, cast off her life vest, removed her flippers and tucked them under her arm. She heard no human sounds, and that was eerie. On the other hand, with no one around, she wasn't self-conscious about her shape. She felt free.

Also, she was famished. Good thing she had packed those energy bars. Chessie unwrapped a peanut butter, granola, and chocolate treat and took a bite. It was delicious. She finished the bar and, not one to litter, carefully tucked the wrapper back into her belt bag, then gasped when a rhesus monkey emerged from a patch of trees. It moseyed up to her and sat down on its haunches.

He—or was it she?—had a pinkish-red hairless face, light-colored eyes, and appeared to be the size of a fox.

The hair on its head made it look like it was wearing a brush cut. A few more monkeys approached, looking at her quizzically. They were all tawny gray with long tails and white hair on their chests. None of the monkeys looked cheerful, but Chessie guessed that was just the way nature tugged down their mouths. At least they weren't making comments about her weight or giving her the cold shoulder. And what funny little hands they had and long fingerlike toes. One of the monkeys had a ragged ear, and he stayed to the edge of the group. A mother monkey appeared cuddling a baby. The baby had an older-looking face than the mom, and the mom had flat saggy breasts with long red nipples. More and more monkeys gathered around Chessie. Soon, she was the center of attention. She had companionship. Companionship of a sort.

"I'm not a scientist," she told the group. "So you don't have to worry. I won't hurt you. In fact, I think what you've gone through for science has been awful." The primates looked at her intently as if trying to understand. She wondered what they'd evolve into in a couple million years. A few more appeared. They certainly did not seem to be an endangered species. And they didn't look ferocious. *Not aggressive at all.* That's what Captain Sánchez had said.

Watching her remove the other energy bar, a few of them made a low warbling sound. They looked hungry. She broke off a piece of the bar and tossed it to the mom and child couple. The baby monkey was cute. The mother monkey snatched up the treat, gobbled it, and warbled. More monkeys approached. One little fellow tugged at one of Chessie's flippers and looked up at her with a sad face. She gave it a morsel. Then she doled out bits to several other monkeys until she had no food left. But the monkeys didn't know that; they gathered closer. She found herself in the company of about two dozen animals.

"So what's it like having the run of the island?" she asked, growing nervous. She recalled the warning sign in English and Spanish. Should she believe Captain Sánchez or the sign? Instinct told her that greater safety lay in keeping herself away from this crowd. But it was too late for that.

A couple of the animals grunted or purred. She reached out to pet the child monkey with the sad face. The mother monkey shot her arm out like a bolt of hairy lightning and took a swipe at Chessie. Chessie jumped back, screamed, and dropped her flippers. The mother threatened Chessie with a silent open-mouthed stare, ridged teeth and sharp canines in full display. Furious, Chessie glared back at her and, as she would to a dog, shouted, "No! No!" But these were wild animals, and Chessie's response only incited them. They began to gang up on her. She backed away and snatched her fallen flippers from the rocky beach.

But when she looked up, she saw a big male, maybe an alpha, menacing her with his own open-mouthed stare, his fangs thicker and sharper than the female's. His eyes, the color of tea, appeared steeped in intelligence. He reached for Chessie's belt bag. She smacked him with a flipper. He hit her back then pounced and bit her on the arm. Chessie shrieked. Blood oozed from the two punctures left by his teeth. Trembling, she unclipped her belt bag and threw it as far as she could over the gang. They dashed over to it in search of food. One found her hotel key card and held it up like booty.

The alpha gave out a shrill chitter-chatter sound. A few others picked up the chitter-chatter. Then, without warning, a monkey jumped up and bit Chessie's thigh. It sprang up again and bit her on the cheek. Hard. So close to her eye! Then, like a horde of superballs, other monkeys bounced up, biting her arms, neck, and legs. Blood ran from the puncture points. As if it couldn't get worse, one nasty monkey pulled her cover shorts down to her ankles. Another climbed her like a palm tree and rummaged through her coconut-scented hair. Chessie violently flung her head to dislodge it. Finally, she grabbed its arm and tore the creature from her hair, smashing it onto the rocks. It lay still. *Rhesus pieces*. Jason's joke came back to her. Then she lost her footing and fell. In the seconds she was down, the monkeys swarmed on her, biting, drawing more blood. One animal sank its fangs into her collarbone area and sheared through the shoulder strap of her swimsuit. One boob fell out.

She would not die like this. *She would not*. Scrambling up Chessie roared, "Raaahh!" She hurled rocks at the monkeys as hard as she could. Enraged, she aimed for their heads. They ducked, but she pegged a few, and when she did she felt deep triumph. Yet as before, her barrage only aggravated the gang. Again, they advanced. Flight. That was the thing. She ran to the shore and jammed on her flippers. Abandoning the mask and snorkel, she plunged clumsily into the surf and fell flat on her face in the shallows before she finally made it into swimmable water.

At first, a few of the monkeys swam after her. Run, jump, climb, bite, swim—was there anything they couldn't do? Miraculously, after a few moments, the monkeys fell back and returned to shore.

Kicking her legs, churning arm over arm through the water, Chessie powered herself out to sea. Her pulse surged way over its speed limit. She feared that her heart would pound its way out of her chest. It would not have been far to the mainland, but she was on the oceanside of the island. She noticed thin streams of blood curlicuing in the water from her many wounds and thought of sharks. Surely a rescuer would come. Then, with a gulp of air, she realized a rescuer might never come. In that case, would her death be fast or slow? How much would it hurt? Chessie imagined her parents, their faces numb with grief. She tried to see Samantha and Aisha haunted by a lifetime of guilt. That vision, at least, offered her some satisfaction.

In the far distance Chessie could see pleasure craft. A parasailer tethered to a boat soared high in the sky. She cried out, but her tiny human voice meant nothing in the vastness.

Chessie knew that she had to regain her strength in order to swim some more, so she decided to take a break. She turned over and floated on her back. She gazed at the sky, so deep and blue. No help to be found there. She realized she'd been swimming with one breast out. She felt okay about that. She felt elemental. About sharks there was nothing she could do, though she did hear of divers punching them in the nose as a last resort. Rest. If nothing else, she could rest. Chessie almost dozed off. The sun grew larger and more orange in the west.

The sound of a motorboat, the first human sound she'd heard in hours, buzzed at the edges of her hearing. It was the most beautiful sound, better than the best symphony. She scanned the waters then found the source, a little white open boat with one man in it, a fisherman, hoping for an evening catch. "Help! *¡Auxilio!*" she shrieked and waved her arms in the air. Somehow the fisherman saw or heard her. When she saw that he was heading her way, she nearly levitated with joy.

But it was hard to haul her into the boat. Chessie removed her flippers and tossed them aboard, but the little craft nearly capsized as the man, a skinny sinewy guy managed to pull and drag Chessie to a point where, beyond all modesty, she threw one leg over a gunwale and dumped herself safely inside. Her suit was askew and her naked breast stared out. Chessie did her best to cover it with her arms and long hair.

The fisherman threw off his shirt and helped her put it on. Shaking uncontrollably, Chessie clamped her hands from arm to chest to neck to cheek to thigh over her many wounds trying to stanch the oozing blood.

And now, given its chance, the pain had started to stab her.

"*Díos mio. Díos mio,*" he kept saying, plus some other stuff that Chessie couldn't understand. She sat in the boat looking at the fisherman and at the endless water and sky and began to cry in huge, choking, convulsive sobs. The fisherman put his hand on an unbitten part of her shoulder and called her *hija.* His kindness made her cry more. She kept thanking the man and felt bad that he had to go home without his fish for dinner.

The fisherman, his name was Jorge, took Chessie back to his little house where his wife, a big woman, washed her wounds with soap and water and made some bandages with towels. She gave Chessie a shift and even some underpants. The towels helped slow the bleeding, but the wounds still throbbed. Chessie asked the woman to please write down their name and address. "*Para agradecerles luego,*" she said, hoping she got the *por* and *para* thing right. They stroked her hair and told her she was a good person who didn't deserve to suffer. Or at least that's what she thought they said. Then some police arrived and rushed her to a hospital.

The ER doctor gave her an antibiotic, a tetanus shot, and a painkiller. He cleaned her wounds and bandaged them. Then he told her that she'd need a series of rabies shots and an antiviral for herpes in case the monkeys carried it, which they sometimes did. "Just precautions," he said as wrote the prescriptions. Chessie started to cry. Herpes? Rabies? All this because the girls and the teachers had left her behind. "All will be well," the doctor assured her. "You'll heal. Señorita, you are one tough gal."

A flurry of phone calls followed. To her parents, still in Montreal. To the hotel in San Juan. The teachers. The airline.

"How could this have happened?" demanded Mr. Heyde with a scold in his voice. Chessie was incensed. How dare he try to flip the blame to her?

"Just get my handbag out of the room safe, pack my bag, and bring them to the hospital," she ordered, sounding very grown up, very much in charge, and in no mood to account to him. Two hours later, her things arrived, and a cab stood waiting to take her to the *aeropuerto*.

Standing with her wheelie bag, ready to board the plane, gazing at her many wounds, Chessie could hardly believe that she had been attacked by wild animals, battled them, swum out to sea, been rescued by a fisherman. And yet she had.

***

A week later, Chessie was back at school choosing to wear tank tops and low-cut sundresses that revealed her combat wounds. To Chessie, the scabs and scars gleamed like garnets surrounded by orchids of bruises. Her first errand was to shop for a suitable replacement shirt for Jorge and a dress for his wife, which she promptly mailed to her saviors in Puerto Rico. At first, when neighbors and store clerks eyed the gruesome array upon her skin and asked what happened, Chessie would recount the whole saga. But she soon found that she loathed repeating the shocking events to every questioner. So she took to simply saying, "The monkeys did it." Then she would look at her interrogators mildly as her bedizened skin stared back. Sometimes people's faces froze with sad or startled looks as if she'd been attacked at the zoo or by vicious pets. But others looked at her as if she were a smart-aleck, a lunatic, maybe even a self-cutter.

In the principal's office for a mediation session, Chessie's eyes were dry. Her parents had wanted to come along for support, but Chessie said she preferred to go it alone. After all, she'd fought off the monkeys by herself and practically swam her heart out. She could deal with this.

When asked to tell their side of the story, Samantha and Aisha claimed that it was really Chessie's fault for going off on her own.

Thrusting a monkey-bitten arm at them, Chessie sprang up. "I wasn't going off by myself. I was looking at the fish in the wreck. You're the ones who abandoned me." Her voice was hot and harsh. "What do you think a buddy system means?" Sam and Aisha rolled their painted eyes.

She glared at Mr. Heyde and Ms. Lee and shook her head, "Some leaders you were." The bite marks on her neck flared redder. "Didn't you even think to take a head count on the boat?"

"We figured she was picked up by some of the researchers," Mr. Heyde said to the principal, his voice thick with self-justification. He avoided eye contact with Chessie.

The next day Mr. Heyde and Ms. Lee were gone, replaced with substitutes. A few of the kids who had been on the trip to Puerto Rico waved to Chessie in the hallways. But it was a big high school, and, for the most part, the students from the trip diffused into the many crowds.

Surprisingly, the kids on the swim team seemed to hold her in high esteem. They said stuff to her like *way to go* and gave her the thumbs up sign.

For a while, rumors of what happened to Chessie Partrell flowed through the student body. Some kids whispered that researchers had put Chessie in a cage and experimented on her. According to others, she had sex with the monkeys. Theories about her escape involved pirates, a millionaire on a yacht, and a helicopter search operation. But in all versions this image emerged: that of a girl alone in the sea with clouds of long dark hair, a sort of chubby mermaid pulling through the water: Chessie Partrell, monkey fighter.

# A Visit to the Old House

On the rare occasions that my sister Alice and I traveled back to St. Louis—usually for a wedding or funeral—we had a ritual: a burger and fries at Steak 'n Shake followed by a visit to our old house. It was a two-story built in the 1930s. Its red brick reminded me of an itchy tweed jacket I used to have. With its arched Tudor door and windows eyebrowed with rays of white stone trim, the front of the house looked like a face mildly surprised to see us.

Over thirty-five years had passed since we lived there, and yet we yearned to see the inside once again. We would park in front, sit in our rental car intending to knock, chickening out at the last moment. The aftermath of our childhood was nothing that a fortune in therapy and a commitment to letting go couldn't fix, but Alice and I were junkies for bad memories. We popped them like pills. Hepped up on the bygones, we would gaze at the curtained picture window and relive the old Punch-and-Judy show. It didn't make us feel good, but it made us feel real. What sort of family lived there now? A happy one we hoped. We imagined cheerful moms and dads who raised their kids according to the most enlightened theories of child psychology. Never on any of our stakeouts did we catch a glimpse of the residents, not even through a lamp-lit window at night.

***

Our stepmother, Elsa, had called us in a panic. Dad, now eighty-five, was in the hospital, and Elsa feared the worst. We flew in at once, Alice from San Diego, I from Boston. Little movies of good-bye scenes—confession and forgiveness, tearful embraces, the damages of the past blown away in apologies and sighs—played in my mind.

I was surprised to see that Alice, two years my junior, had grown so gray. Bleary-eyed and rumpled, she met me, as planned, at the rental car desk at Lambert-St. Louis. We were both suited up in oversized tops: she in ochre and I in plum, the right hues for fall, and black elastic-waistbanded slacks. I noticed that we still dressed alike. As I drove to Missouri Baptist Hospital, Alice treated me to a call-by-call of her scramble to find three different neighbors to care for her three dogs, and she kept phoning and texting those neighbors to see if the dogs were okay. It was easier for me. My cat had died a few months ago. Some condolences from Alice about my loss would have been nice.

An infected gall bladder, said Dad's charge nurse, and caught in the nick of time. Dad's quick improvement, the physical side of it at least, astounded everyone. We found him in the bed, Gulliver-style, pegged down by leads and tubes. A bag of darkish urine hung by the side of his bed. He turned to us with a friendly but vacant half-smile. Several days of white whiskers (couldn't someone shave him?) put a frost on his cheeks and chin. Elsa was absent, but I spied two bags from Neiman Marcus on the floor by the window. I assumed that Dad had yelled at her. She was a revenge shopper with excellent taste in clothes and a big stack of store credit cards. Dad had not been so generous with Mom during their marriage, but he got off easy in the divorce. Only ten years of alimony, and then she died.

"Hi, Dad," we chimed. We embraced him with quick fluttering touches. Birds landing, birds taking off. We weren't big on hugs.

"Well, I guess I'm someone's dad," he said in a sociable tone. Alice and I caught each other's eye. Elsa had said nothing of dementia. "Do I know you?"

Best to try to take it in stride. "We're Alice and Deborah, your daughters." I said, my throat catching for a second. "Elsa said you were in the hospital, so we came to see you." I told him he looked pretty good for a guy who just had surgery.

"I guess they thought I was a goner. They call in the daughters when they think you're a goner."

“Oh come on, Dad. You’re not a goner,” Alice said. “You want some juice?” She brought a little plastic cup of apple juice with a straw up to Dad’s mouth. He shook his head. Alice flashed him a big smile. He mirrored back a sort of watch-the-birdie grin. Dad asked where Elsa was and when she was coming back.

We embarked on upbeat monologues about our jobs. Alice, who worked in the produce department at an Albertson’s, filled Dad in about all the new fall squash. When my turn came to update him about my routine in the mailroom at Boston University, he faded into sleep. The sight of my father ebbing made me not want to let him go.

We hung around for a half hour while Dad snoozed. The humid odor of hospital chow smudged the air. None of it was for him. No solid food for at least another day. Alice kept calling and texting her dog sitters. Channel surfing on the staticky hospital TV, I came upon a program about a young Kenyan filmmaker who’d made a movie about reconciliation workshops in Rwanda after the genocide. Perpetrators and survivors got together and talked. Crimes were confessed. There was weeping. Terrible weeping. Following the interview show, a program came on about decluttering your home. Dad continued to sleep, so we left.

Steak 'n Shake with its familiar red walls and black-and-white tiled floor, its odor of steakburgers, onions, and fries, tried to trick me into thinking it was still old times. A polite teenager in a paper cap took our order. The skinny matchstick fries arrived piled on the white plate like a little heap of straw. The right mix of crunchy, salty, and hot. As good as ever. I squirted on some ketchup.

"Elsa and Dad have side-by-side plots all picked out," I said.

"I don't think the old man's checking out yet," replied Alice. "And I like this dementia thing. It's smoothed him out some." She took a long slurp of her milkshake. It had two flavors, strawberry next to chocolate, in one glass. They called it a side-by-side shake. "I wonder how I'll feel when he's dead," she said, her voice flat as a sidewalk. She checked her cell phone for news of her dogs. As a kid, Alice got the worst of Dad. He hit her more. He liked to let her know how disappointed he was in her. Sometimes she couldn't take it and back-talked. On the day of her eighth birthday, she said she didn't have to pick up her toys because it was her birthday, and just like that Dad cancelled her party. Sent the little girls home in their party dresses with their wrapped and ribboned gifts. Then he punched the cake Mom had baked and threw it into the garbage. We didn't plan any birthday parties after that.

Images from the Rwanda program hovered in my mind. I told Alice that I kind of wanted Dad to admit he had some regrets about his parenting. That would be enough for me.

"Fat chance, that'll happen. At least he's got a new personality now. We should just try to enjoy it. The new, refreshing, harmless Elbert Ridley."

"I don't know. Mean then. Nice now. The old crimes still stand. But before he kicks the bucket maybe some admission, some regret." I thought of Elsa's shopping bags in the hospital room. Maybe he didn't yell at her. Maybe it was retail therapy to help herself cheer up.

"It's not like he's a war criminal, Deborah. Suppose he did have his mind. Do you think he'd apologize for anything? If you're so concerned about it, why don't you just forgive him? Unilaterally."

"Why don't you?"

Alice's face tightened up. She picked up her phone and started to scroll through her contacts, I guess to call one of her dog people.

"Okay, sorry," I said

"Okay, sorry," said Alice

***

It was early October, and the huge maple that shaded the old house shed its leaves in the breeze. As usual, we parked in front. The people who lived there had hung a pineapple flag, the sign of welcome, over the door. I had been taking an American architecture course at BU and now saw that our old house was a textbook example of Depression-era St. Louis brickwork. They didn't build middle-class houses like this anymore. Symmetries and arch shapes abounded, same and different. A zigzag line of brick demarcated the first story from the second. A checkerboard band of raised and recessed brick wainscoted the front wall just above the foundation. Why had I never noticed that before? I had always admired the white stone rays over the windows, but now I saw that a separate set of rays sunshined over the front door and another set of white stone trim fanned out over the arched, many-mullioned picture window. On the window seat inside, we used to wait long hours for Mom to come home. In junior high, we sentried there on the lookout for Dad. The maple leaves were thick on the lawn.

"Deb, do you remember the time that Dad made us

rake the leaves, and we got really sore arms and didn't finish the job?"

"And you tried to put a book in your pants so the spanking wouldn't hurt?"

"But then he figured it out and slapped me silly."

"He slapped me silly, too, don't forget." A young mom was pushing her baby along in a stroller. "Alice, do you remember when Dad got mad and threw a knife across the table, and it stuck in the milk carton? And it made a white fountain."

"That was a good one," she said. "Deb, do you remember when Dad hit me so hard he broke his hand?"

"And I pulled him off of you?"

"Then he started beating on you."

"Well, I did save you."

"Yes, you saved me."

"Then he went around with a cast on his hand, and, when anyone asked what happened, he chortled like a big kidder that he broke his hand beating the kids."

"That may have been the all-time best one," said Alice.

"I wonder if anyone believed him."

Rating Dad's outbursts was one of our pastimes, but the sob sister thing was starting to bore me. Always the same lousy stories. Not that our Mom was any Shirley

Partridge. She screamed at us each morning before we left for school. We miss her anyway. We could cry to her, and she'd understand. She used to make chicken pot pie and decoupaged pictures of the Monkees onto key chains for us. When we were in high school, our parents divorced and sold the old house. Dad moved to Kirkwood, and we went to live with Mom in a bland modern condo in Creve Coeur. By the time Mom got ovarian cancer, we were already living on separate coasts. She donated her body to science, so no grave.

The young mom with the stroller disappeared down the block. The pineapple flag beckoned.

"I'm going in," I announced, marched up the front path, and banged the brass door knocker. Our old horseshoe-shaped door knocker, but polished now. I rang the ding-dong. No answer. Relief started to wash over me. Emboldened by the owners' absence, I ventured to the back of the house and immediately found myself in an alternate universe. Not because things were so different, but because they were so the same. The detached wooden one-car garage, repainted in the same brown and beige, still stood at the end of the driveway. The old screened-in porch remained as well. Odd that no one had removed or renovated it. It held a few wicker chairs and end tables. On the floor I spied some brightly colored plastic toddler toys. I remembered how we played there on hot humid summer days. Then I climbed the old cement stairs, guarded by the same pipe railing, and tapped at the back door. Again, no answer. The amber stained-glass fleur-de-lys still emblazoned the kitchen window. Walking back to the car along the concrete driveway, I squatted down to peek through one of the basement windows. Unable to see anything in the gloom, I recalled the rathskeller's knotty pine paneling and musty odor, the built-in bench seats with lift-off tops and scary underneath storage compartments, also very musty. In those compartments, we stored broken toys and games with missing parts.

I reported my findings to Alice. She declared that we would have to return when the owners were there. Then we went for manicures.

***

Dad and Elsa were watching a dance show on TV when we came back to the hospital. Like Dad and Mom in their better days, Dad and Elsa were ballroom dancers. Elsa, looking attractive as always, wore a light-blue pantsuit with silver jewelry. She was trying to act extra chipper. Dad recognized us this time. After the greetings, I told them that Alice and I had been by the old house.

"Those were the good old days," Dad said.

Alice and I registered no expression.

"We were hoping that a happy family lived there," I said.

"We were happy there," said Dad sounding nostalgic and light-hearted, not at all like himself. The historical revisionist thing ran against my principles. And Alice's.

"We were not..." began Alice, but Elsa cut her off by making the "sounds like" sign from charades and then a shadow boxing move, by which she meant *sounds like fighting*. Instead of speaking, Elsa sometimes pantomimed. It was kind of pathetic, but it kept the peace. Elsa said something about the TV personality who was trying to do the two-step. Dad tilted his head as if he didn't understand. Then he stared at the TV.

I patted her hand. She was a young senior, only in her seventies. She would be able to care for Dad or at least arrange for attendants who could. It wasn't like we'd have to change the paternal diapers or anything. Dad and Elsa had plenty of money. Our father had made a good living at Weber Land Development.

"He seems a little, uh, jovial," said Alice.

"Not the same Elbert," I said.

"They have him on Celexa and Wellbutrin," whispered Elsa. "Makes a difference."

"You're serious?"

"You mean that's all it took?" said Alice. She looked at Dad this way and that as if to make sure she knew him. Elsa shrugged. She, too, was in awe at Dad's transformation, though she was used to it. He'd been on those pills for a year.

We invited Elsa to go to the movies, but she wanted to stay by Dad's bedside. They'd been one another's habit for thirty years, married way longer than Mom and Dad.

"We should go back to the old house," said Alice as we walked to our car. "That family should be home by now."

***

The curtains of the old house were open. The glow of lamplight warmed the windows. The pineapple flag ruffled in the evening breeze. Parked in the driveway was a Mazda, an SUV stood out front. We saw a man walk across the living room. Alice strode to the door and knocked. I stayed a few paces behind.

The man, a good-looking guy with dark wavy hair, answered the door. Weirdly he was wearing a Weber

Land Development sweatshirt. It was that alternate universe thing again. He looked at us like we were about to hand him copies of *The Watchtower*.

Blushing and stumbling over her words, Alice got it out that we'd lived in the house as kids and wanted to see it one last time. She added a little bit about Dad in the hospital and us in from out of town. And what a coincidence: our Dad had worked at Weber, too.

"Had you ever heard of him?" I asked, giving Dad's name. "Used to be comptroller. Was a good dancer?"

"Way before my time," said the man who introduced himself as Mitch. He shook our hands. His hand was warm. "Hey, Mama," he called to his wife who was sitting on the sofa, reading a book to a little boy and a little girl. "That okay with you? These ladies used to live here." The wife, Beth, was all for it. She said she was eager to know more about the biography of the house.

Mitch led us into the living room. None of the inside architecture had changed. The shape of the space felt so familiar that it was like being inside my own head. Now I wanted to confront the memories, both good and bad—even if they were memories that wouldn't have been made had Celexa and Wellbutrin been around. Maybe. And if our father had agreed to go to a shrink and take the medication, another maybe.

There in the time warp, I felt right at home. I knew my way around. I gazed at the living room fireplace. Its cement mantelpiece now sported a line of neatly angled family photos. I recognized the arch between the living room and dining room and the French doors to the screened porch. I was very impressed with the arch motif. All the previous residents had respected the inside spaces of the house. Never knocked out any walls.

"Look how small the window seat is," I remarked to Alice.

"It seemed so big when we were kids."

"Remember when we used to sit there and play 'the next one' waiting for Mom to come home?" The young couple exchanged a glance. Beth adjusted her tortoise shell headband. Alice shot me a corrective frown. I worried that Beth, at first so interested in the house's biography, now took us for a jinx.

In the tiny kitchen—new fridge, new stove, of course—the original wood paneled cabinetry remained. I smiled as I looked at the amber fleur-de-lys in the lattice-patterned window above the sink. I always loved the stained glass. On the tour, Mitch carried the little girl, who hugged her dad's neck and looked at us with big eyes. Beth acted as tour guide. The boy, who seemed to be about six, followed us clutching a plastic T. Rex.

I could tell that Beth wanted to contain the tour to the first floor, but I asked her if we could see our old bedrooms. Her sense of hospitality won out over her reluctance, and she led us up the stairs, which were very out of code by today's standards, too steep, too shallow. How often we tumbled down them to the landing where the telephone niche was, the niche that held our heavy, black, cloth-corded phone. Now the niche held the couple's wedding photo. And there was a baby gate at the top of the stairs.

I stepped into my old bedroom. I wanted to get the feeling back. I expected excitement, fear, maybe anger. Instead, I stood in a mist of regret and sorrow. "That's where we had curtains with animal eyes," I said pointing to my old window.

"Don't tell me the place is haunted," said Beth.

"Nah, I had a weird imagination."

We followed Alice as she wandered into her old room. She asked if she could open the closet door. I knew why she had to see it. After Dad had punished her, she would go to the closet to sob. As we grew older, Dad still hit, and hit with words as well: what was to become of you? who would ever marry you? and so on and so forth. But then there was the time Alice got bitten by a dog, and Dad carried her to the car and took her to the emergency room. Sometimes, we'd get through a day with no trauma at all. Not that we could trust the peace.

"I used to think that closet was so big," Alice said.

"That was our toy closet," I told Mitch and Beth. "Happy times there." Alice hung back a little as we descended the treacherous stairs.

I asked one last favor: permission to see the rathskeller. Opening the basement door—it was the same planked basement door—I sensed a new openness and lightness. The walls now wore a coat of jonquil. The storage benches with the dead doll compartments had been removed. The musty smell was gone.

"Where's the knotty pine?" I asked.

"It was too dark down there. I had to freshen things up," said Mitch. "I painted over the paneling. See? And put in these overhead lights."

I couldn't recognize the rathskeller. It was so bright. So new. So not Ridley.

"It's lovely," I said, only half meaning it. I regretted that he'd painted over the knotty pine.

Alice and I thanked the couple. They were old enough to be my children, had I ever had children. I wanted to tell them that the house was happy now, but I didn't say that. Instead, I wished them many joyful years there. As we walked to our car, the mix of strange and familiar fizzed in my head. I turned to have one last look at the old house. With its open door and bright windows, it looked pleased and comfortable with itself. I'm doing just fine, it seemed to say, and you should, too. Mitch and Beth waved to us, and we waved back.

***

Although the doctors and nurses kept shaking their heads in awe at the miracle of Elbert Ridley's recovery, we knew that our father had embarked upon his long slow decline. Mild as milk, he busied himself with word-search puzzles and TV. He grinned a lot, spoke agreeably about everything, took his pills without complaint. Alice, who was still calling her dog sitters three times a day, kept maintaining that we should just enjoy our harmless new old man. But was the past not real? I asked her. Had we not worn it all our years?

We extended our visit a few more days, but our leave time was running out. When it came to say good-bye, I held my father's papery hand then bent my face to his neck. I started to shake and weep. I wept because I was afraid of death, because I felt light and free and not quite myself, because I had a new dad, though not for long.

"There, there," he said. "Don't cry. It will be all right. Elsa, Elsa, help this lady. Ask her what is wrong."

# One beneath the Other

Zach set up his easel in the bathroom as his fiancée Beth slid into the tub. She was a tall solid woman with broad shoulders, and for the sitting she tied her dark red hair up with a ribbon. The lavender scent of her bath salts tickled Zach's nose.

Beth turned to Zach with a playful look. Her eyes were moss green. Nice to look into. Not like his ex-wife's eyes. During the final years of their marriage, he seldom met Martha's gaze, fearful of catching a warning glare. At his peril did he suggest that she not leave the water running or that she recycle the junk mail. And when his mother died, Martha did not console him. People came to pay sympathy calls, but she stayed upstairs, claiming a migraine. Friends told Zach that he should ask for a divorce. Martha spared him the task.

It was partly with relief, partly with regret, that Zach applied two layers of gesso over the nude he painted of Martha ten years ago. That work was also a bath painting and technically superb. A petite woman, Martha had a sharp nose and high forehead. She took up less room in the tub. When she moved out, she neglected to take her bath portrait. From time to time, Zach wondered if she would come banging on the door, demanding the painting. He had considered consigning the work at a gallery in town. Would have been funny if Martha spied herself on the wall, naked and for sale.

For reasons not entirely clear to him, Zach held onto the portrait. He stored it in the attic, covered by a white sheet, half afraid to confront it. Until now.

Over the course of several sittings, Zach sketched the basic outline of Beth in the tub, established the shadows and highlights, began to work on the colors. During these live sessions, the two played games of twenty questions, choosing as their subjects famous people and places. Beth's secret answers were the swimmer Michael Phelps, Hawaii, and the North Pole. For one of his secret answers, Zach chose Leonardo da Vinci. Zach was fascinated that art researchers had discovered the image of another woman beneath the *Mona Lisa.* As he painted over Martha, he wondered why Leonardo had covered over the first woman. Zach glanced at his reflection in the bathroom mirror, surprised to see how worried he looked. What if his portrait of Beth were not as expert as the portrait of Martha?

Beth did not know that the white surface on which she was taking shape concealed Martha's image. Zach was not sure what she would make of that. Would she see it as a gift, a triumph? Would she be upset to know that the shadow of the other woman lay beneath her?

Was she not deserving of a virgin canvas? Well, he liked the idea of obliterating Martha and replacing her with sweet Beth. Still, he envisioned his ex-wife materializing one day, harrying him for the canvas. If that happened, he knew what he would do. He would tell Martha that her portrait had vanished. And he would say that with the blankest look he could paint on his face.

# Sendings

After dark, cloaked by the red-and-yellow plaid curtains of her bedroom, Betsy Baines peered through her binoculars into the Eastman's house. The amber-lit rooms glowed like dioramas of the ideal life. From the big living room picture window—rarely did the Eastmans draw their blinds and draperies—Betsy watched the family talking, reading, and watching TV. The teenage daughter had decorated her room with posters of what Betsy assumed were the latest pop stars. She often lounged with her cell phone on a fluffy bed surrounded by stuffed animals. Star maps covered the back wall of the boy's room. A small telescope on a tripod was perched in front of his window, and some evenings he gazed through it. Betsy wondered if the kid ever peeked into neighbors' houses. You could see a lot with a telescope like that, much more than with binoculars, even high-powered ones like hers.

This evening, when the children were up in their rooms, she focused on the family's living room and spied stuck-up Cathy Eastman gesturing in an agitated manner toward her husband, Doug. In her hand were two white envelopes. He examined the envelopes then said something to his wife. Cathy's posture relaxed. The couple cozied up to each other on the couch and turned on the television.

Rosy satisfaction bloomed in Betsy's heart. Her second letter had arrived, and now things would get interesting.

***

Cathy Eastman found the first letter that arrived in the mail rather curious. The envelope bore no return address and contained nothing but a blank sheet of paper. The letter seemed so odd that she kept it. A few days later, Cathy received a second mailing identical to the first: a plain white business-sized envelope, her name and address exactly correct and computer-printed, first-class stamp affixed, return address omitted, and nothing enclosed but a blank sheet of paper. What was she supposed to receive? An invitation, an invoice, a notice about her daughter's cheerleading practice or her son's astronomy club? A precise and punctilious person, Cathy paged through her calendars, scrolled through her emails and financial accounts, read and reread the papers in the pigeonholes of her desk in search of something she ought to be expecting. She found no clue. Yet something had been intended for her.

The more she thought about the letters, the more they pecked at her composure. That evening after the kids were in bed, Cathy showed her husband the two envelopes. She could understand one strange letter, but two? This was no big deal, Doug assured her. It only meant that a lettershop was screwing up, wasting some marketer's money. Soon someone would discover the error, and the annoyance would end.

A feeling of relief slid though Cathy. "For a while there, I thought that someone was doing it on purpose."

"Not a chance. Too senseless, no point to it. Come over here." Cathy sat down next to her husband on the couch. She was wearing a skirt. He stroked her thigh. His touch distracted her most pleasantly.

Doug and Cathy watched a movie together several times a week. They favored horror flicks and spy movies, films with lots of twists, turns, secret intelligence, and thrilling car chases. That evening, they watched *The Bourne Identity,* a story about an assassin with amnesia whose old colleagues were hunting him down.

***

Betsy Baines of Parkside Drive bore no great animus, merely a glancing sort of animus, toward her pretty neighbor who lived a few doors down from her on Parkside. The Eastman home stood on the cul de sac, and due to the way the street curved and the houses sat at angles, Betsy could see into the Eastman's front-facing windows, a situation that made for convenient and discreet observation. As for the blank letters, Betsy was not messing with Cathy as much as she was testing her. The woman's sheer normality—she seemed a paper doll of the typical suburban wife and mother—made her a prime subject for Betsy's experiment, a project much more serious and determined than a practical joke, but if you wanted to call it a cosmic joke you could. If only Mrs. McPerfect, jogging by in her shorty shorts, had deigned to return a smile or a wave a few weeks ago when Betsy had gathered the courage to greet her with a quick "hi" and a wave. The snub struck a gong of resentment in Betsy that reverberated brassily with all the other clanging memories of all the other times she had been excluded or rebuffed by this schoolmate, or that prospective date, or those coworkers. She'd had enough, and now it was time to give someone their due. Hence the secret recruitment of this snotty airhead into her experiment, and, really, the invention of the experiment itself. Her plan gave her a jolt of pleasure, the way she felt when she savored the chocolates she snitched from her mother's stash and got away with it, at least until her mother discovered the theft and yelled at her.

With her experiment, there was that sense of gratification, but there was also the higher road, the pursuit of knowledge. Like the psychologists and sociologists whose studies she proofread for social science journals, Betsy wanted to discover something about human behavior: in this case, how a normal person would react if she received a steady stream of meaningless mail, messages as unparseable as white-on-white paintings, silent whispers that said nothing, but said it with persistence. Therefore, Betsy undertook to mail Cathy Eastman a series of envelopes each with a blank sheet of paper inside. The missives were admittedly silly stimuli, harmless little stressors, blank waves from the universe. Well, maybe not the universe, but from no detectible sender. Her subject might ignore the absurdity or grow mildly perturbed by it, maybe even go crazy asking herself wherefrom, wherefore, and why me?

Perhaps she was overdoing the philosophical bit, getting ahead of herself in the heady department. Cathy Eastman, who appeared to be forty or so, about the same age as Betsy, looked too fresh-faced, fit, and well-adjusted to be very deep. Not as deep as Betsy, for sure. And envy her? No way did Betsy want to be a wife and mother. Being a daughter was more than enough for her. It was just that Cathy had it all, all except the common courtesy to return a greeting to a neighbor who was trying to reach out for the slightest, lightest, feather-touch of connection.

It was a bright April day. Betsy, masked by her red-and-yellow plaid curtains, refocused her binoculars as Cathy opened her mailbox, thumbed through the contents, then stood as though seized. The third white letter had arrived. The woman's shocked response set off a bottle rocket of triumph in Betsy. This was reportable, a solid data point for her study. Cathy, ponytail bobbing, tried to run after the mail truck, but the truck was already too far down the street. Betsy watched her neighbor trudge back, shaking her head, clearly perturbed. She gathered the mail from the sidewalk and disappeared into her house on the cul de sac, a two-story with light-blue siding and a well-tended box hedge under the living room picture window.

Betsy knew that her study had flaws: limited opportunities for observation, only one subject, no specific hypothesis, and so on. But as far as ethics were concerned, heck, she was literally shooting with blanks, so what harm could she do? She went to the kitchen and fixed herself a plate of tortilla chips with melted cheese. Then she cadged a chocolate from her mother's newest hiding place. Then it was back to proofreading scientific papers in her home office, which was also her bedroom. She had an excellent reputation for accuracy—hawk-eye her editors called her—and, as a freelancer, she never lacked for work. She could only imagine the dumb stuff Cathy read, if she read at all, probably bodice-buster romances. Betsy had had it with those. They only left her hot and bothered. And for what? And for whom?

For crying out loud, her mother had *Days of Our Lives* on full blast. She had to yell down for the second time that day to tell her to turn down the TV. How could a person concentrate with all that racket?

"Get yourself some ear plugs," her mother hollered.

"Get yourself some hearing aids," Betsy shouted back.

"Why don't you get yourself a life?"

Good one, Mom, thought Betsy, glad that she had sneaked a chocolate.

***

Trembling, Cathy set the mail on the kitchen counter and stared at the third anonymous envelope with a mix of fear and anger. Why was she being targeted like this? What sort of mind concocted such a scheme? She was about to slice open the envelope with a steak knife when it occurred to her that it was dangerous to open the envelope inside the house—it might contain anthrax or one of those Russian nerve poisons—so she donned an N95 mask and safety goggles, took the blasted thing into the garage, slit it open with a box cutter, and shook it out over the black garbage can lid. No white powder. That was good, but dumb to operate without gloves. Cathy slid the envelope in a clear plastic bag and wrote the date on the bag. She bagged the two previous letters in separate bags. Then she showered thoroughly.

At the podiatrists' office, where she worked part-time in billing and insurance, Cathy could barely keep her mind on claim forms, procedure codes, and dates of service. Getting the anonymous envelopes was worse than getting a legal notice. At least you knew where one of those came from.

Dr. Sanders asked if she were okay; she looked shaky.

"Just one of those days," Cathy replied.

"Husband malfunction?" ventured Dr. Freiberg, the other podiatrist.

"Oh gosh, nothing like that."

Well, at least it wasn't *that*. She told herself to consider the torments she was not facing, how good and steady her life was—except for the fact that she was being harassed by a nameless force. Despite her husband's reassurance, Cathy concluded that the persistence of the mailings, their very precision, really did mean that someone was out to get her. Maybe that's what she got for watching spy movies and horror flicks. As much as they pleased with their emotional jolts, they also whetted her sense of suspicion. She had a natural tendency toward fearfulness—a reasonable attitude, considering all the bad things that could happen to you nowadays from attackers both seen and unseen. But now there was this, her own life, and she was being menaced.

Caught in the web of threat and uncertainty, she was, as Dr. Sanders observed, jumpy. But she was also on guard, her awareness tuned way up as she tried to find clues or, at least, intuit them. So little to go on. No return address, and the letters blank.

Perhaps they were not blank. Maybe her inscrutable foe had written them in invisible ink. Yes! She felt proud of herself for the surmise. Instead of filing insurance claims, she looked up invisible ink on her cell phone and came upon a kids' activities site that showed how to write secret messages with lemon juice. Pat, the office manager, floated by to ask her a question. Cathy quickly turned her cell phone face down. Then, at her first opportunity, she furtively continued her search. Another website offered that vinegar and, in desperate situations, urine could serve the purpose.

As soon as she got home, Cathy retrieved the letters from the garage, turned on a table lamp, and placed each white sheet over the bulb. No writing emerged. Then she tried holding one of the sheets over a candle, but that made the paper catch fire. She hastily clapped out the flames. Fine thing, burning down her house searching for clues. Her daughter Jenny asked what was burning. Cathy said that she was trying out a new candle. She felt foolish about the fire but smart about the invisible ink notion.

Doug now agreed this was officially irregular, no longer a matter of a lame lettershop. Probably not a case of poison and evidently not hate mail penned in invisible ink, but Cathy was wise to take precautions and think of possibilities, good to keep the remaining evidence in labeled plastic bags in the garage. Maybe good to keep a log of the envelopes' dates and postmarks. The postmarks were strictly local from their town of Middlehampton or adjacent Billington. Cathy found a small spiral notebook and dedicated it to her record keeping. She wasn't sure if Doug were humoring her, but the evidence collection appealed to her diligent nature, made her feel as if she were on the hunt.

That night, they watched the horror movie *The Invisible Man*. In the story, a vengeful genius makes himself invisible and terrorizes a young woman who broke up with him. Everyone thinks she is psychotic, responsible for crimes committed by the invisible man, but then she sleuths it out, gets the guy to resolidify himself, and cuts his throat.

"Did you have words with someone? A spat with a neighbor or anyone?" Doug squinted as if to tease some truth out of her.

Cathy shot him a look.

"I'm only trying to come up with ideas. You never know what motivates people."

Unable to sleep, she shuffled through her recent past in search of offenses she might have given.

The next day, Cathy called up Rochelle Mills, whose daughter did not make the cheerleading squad, leading perhaps to hard feelings against Jenny Eastman, and, by extension, Cathy. She waded into an awkward conversation with Rochelle, praising her daughter Vanessa's cheerleading talent. Definitely Vanessa should have been picked for the squad. Both Vanessa and Jenny should be on the squad together. Cathy said that she felt bad about it.

"Huh?" said Rochelle. "That's not on you. Why are you even calling me about this?"

"I was just thinking of your and Vanessa's feelings." Cathy felt her words dribbling down her chin.

Rochelle said that Cathy should not take things so seriously.

Cathy then called her next-door-neighbor Mr. Traxler and apologized for asking him to pick up the poop his Collie made on her lawn.

"It's no trouble for me to pick it up," said Cathy. "Please accept my apologies. Sissy's such a dear. She's welcome anytime."

"Kind of you to call. A man and his dog and all that. But no hard feelings. We shouldn't sweat the small stuff."

Maybe Mr. Traxler was the secret sender, and now that she'd made amends the letters would end. But they kept coming, now faster than before. Cathy stowed each one in its own labeled plastic bag, logging everything in her small spiral notebook. She could not call to mind any other person she might have miffed or outright offended, though you never knew what flutter of a butterfly's wing might lead to a hurricane.

She and Doug agreed the letters, she now called

them sendings, were clearly a campaign. Worried that this might be a sign of dark web activity, Doug, who was the branch manager of a bank, did a credit report on Cathy, froze her credit, put alerts on her bank and credit card accounts, signed her up for identity theft monitoring, and looked her up on a background-check website. Super creepy to see how much info was out there. They found no active threats, yet still the envelopes kept coming. Ten of them by now. They made Cathy slam the mailbox shut. Sometimes they made her cry. Sometimes she saw them as a form of passive aggression, other times as aggressive aggression. Who was doing this and why did they keep doing it?

One evening, she looked up stalking and harassment by U. S. Mail. This fit the definition all right: repeated conduct for no legitimate purpose, directed at a specific person—herself!—to annoy, alarm, and distress. She spent so much time on the computer reading up on the topic that she forgot to pick up Kyle from astronomy club.

She sought advice from the mailman who said that he could only deliver the mail and that those letters were all correctly stamped and addressed. He had to deliver them.

"You could refuse them," he said. "They'd go to the dead mail center."

"But what good what that do?" asked Cathy. "It won't stop them from coming."

"Seems like shenanigans, but you could take it up with the postmaster."

***

The sight of Cathy consulting with the mailman sent a hot zap through Betsy. She did not like the idea that she might somehow be found out, her experiment crashing into trouble with the law. On the other hand, she was pleased to see how terrible Cathy looked, as if some fizzing boiling bottled potion were trapped in her. No doubt, that look on her face meant that one of the white letters had arrived, giving Betsy something more to type into the Excel file in which she tracked her observations. But as soon as Cathy retreated into her house, Betsy's opportunities for scientific observation ended. It wasn't like she could affix electrodes to the woman's head and read her brainwaves like the psychologists did. She would have to find a way to interview Cathy Eastman.

A couple days later, Betsy, hidden by her red-and-yellow plaid curtains, trained her binoculars on Cathy as she left for one of her frequent jogs. The time was right for an interception. Having prepared another mailing, Betsy stowed it, along with the surgical gloves she used to handle the envelopes, stamps, and paper in a drawer. She pulled on a pink sweat outfit that read "Get Fit." If it worked out, she'd be able to add interview notes to her visual observations. A breakthrough for sure, but what to say to her subject? She had no trouble talking mechanics and style with editors and production managers but fumbled with social chat. Not that she had anyone to be social with. How she wished the publishing staff would include her in the occasional lunch or happy hour. At home, she squabbled with her mother or talked to herself. She was a good conversationalist at her imaginary dinner parties, voicing her opinions on different types of creativity, positive psychology, and learned helplessness.

"It's about time you went out for some exercise," said Betsy's mother, who was about to leave for her quilting circle. "Sitting on your duff and eating doughnuts isn't doing your diabetes any favors."

"Watching soap operas all day isn't doing your brain a lot of good."

She ducked out of the house before her mother could

swat another remark her way. Pounding heavy footed around the bend—how long had it been since she tried to run?—she met up with her neighbor.

"Nice day for a run," Betsy panted. So smooth, just the right thing to say on a chance encounter.

Cathy, sweating, her face set in exertion or distress—Betsy couldn't tell which—waved back in acknowledgment.

How about that? Betsy felt noticed, and it made her feel good. Maybe Mrs. McPerfect wasn't so stuck up after all. Perhaps she was on the road, not to friendship, but to friendliness with Cathy, which would be great although that would wreck the experiment. It would certainly change the parameters. Science was like that. Expectations overturned. The act of observing something changed it. The uncertainty principle at work.

Betsy reported the encounter in her Excel file. She was going to treat herself to a doughnut, then thought better of it. She even started to wonder if she should stop mailing the blank sheets of paper.

***

The next day, Cathy, unsure of what fright awaited her, went out to get her mail. Lucky this time. Only bills, a lawn-care flier, and an ad for a self-help book. The bold print on the envelope teased, "Find more peace than you've ever had before!" A spring storm was gathering. She wouldn't run today. Despite the threatening weather, the heavy-set lady in pink sweats ambled by.

"Out here trying to get some exercise," said the lady in pink. She had thinning light brown hair and an eager tone of voice. They appeared to be close in age. "You're quite the runner. Do you do a mile a day?"

Cathy found the question a little specific for small talk between strangers, but maybe exercise newbies asked things like that. "Give or take," she replied with a shrug pretending to be very interested in the lawn-care flier. She hoped the neighbor lady—she assumed that the woman was a neighbor lady—would pick up on the social cue and be on her way. But that did not happen. The woman gazed up and down at Cathy, inspecting her right there out in the open as if she were a specimen. So skeevy. Cathy's expression curdled. It wasn't a nice face. It would offend. She looked down at her mail to collect herself, to give her unpleasant expression a chance to melt away. "Got to get going. Have a good one," she said excusing herself. Blessedly, a rumble of thunder shooed her inside.

Three days later, one of those blasted sendings arrived. As usual, she logged in the evidence and bagged it in its own plastic bag. To try to escape from the anxiety, she lit out for a run—she was running more and more these days, as much to clear her head as for the cardio—and had not gone a block when an idea flew into her head—the letters might be intended for another Cathy Eastman. She wasn't the only person with that name, a fact she discovered when she'd idly Googled herself. Someone was out to get one of the other Cathy Eastmans—poor her—and had selected the wrong address. She felt protective of the good name of Cathy Eastman. The gals should look out for each other or certainly get to the bottom of a troublesome or dangerous identity mix-up. And why that other Cathy Eastman anyway? Had she jilted some creep she met online?

Cathy raced back to her house. Keen with purpose, she Googled her name. There were a dozen other Cathy Eastmans, young and old, Black and white. One lived in Canton, Ohio, another in Eugene, Oregon, one in Cape Girardeau, Missouri. None, however, resided near Middlehampton, Pennsylvania. She searched other possible spellings of Eastman and Cathy with a *K*. While she entertained the possibility that another local Cathy Eastman with no web presence might be the intended target, reasoning told her that the awful letters were meant for no other Cathy Eastman but her. Not only that, but all the computer searching made her lose track of the time. She arrived late for work looking preoccupied and frazzled. The doctors asked her if she wanted to take a personal day, a spa day perhaps.

Doug offered to take her to the doctor to get something to help her sleep or help smooth out her moods.

"Pills are not going to help. It's not in my head." She sounded snappy, and that made her feel worse. He was only trying to help.

They were watching Hitchcock's *The Birds*. Doug had suggested a comedy, but Cathy had chosen *The Birds*.

"It's not like we lost our jobs or the kids got hurt," said Doug.

"Yes, I should look on the bright side."

"Some person without a life, that's what I think, is playing a prank."

"I should let them have their fun."

"Until it peters out."

"What if it doesn't peter out? It might take on a life of its own. Some nasty stuff lasts forever."

It was weird, almost funny, that the sendings could chase her like the killer crows and gulls in the movie. She hatched the idea that the sendings were rooted in some kind of prejudice someone had against her. What was it about her? Maybe if she changed herself in some way the persecution would stop. But change in what way? And why change at all? Would the family have to move? Oh, come now, she told herself. Let's not exaggerate.

And why couldn't she go for her morning run without that pink neighbor lady intercepting her?

Discovering the fifteenth sending, Cathy banged the mailbox shut so hard she almost knocked it off its post. She drove to the post office with her log and one of the bagged letters. The postmaster couldn't get his head around the fact that there was nothing written on the sheets of paper: no threats, no extortion.

"Blank mail, not blackmail," he said, trying to joke. "No harm, no foul, you could say." His face reminded her of drywall. She knew the type: the type who found six ways to do nothing. "Has anyone else received these mailings?"

"How would I know what other people get in their mail?

"I am being stalked and harassed. It involves the U.S. Mail. That's a federal offense. Federal offense means prison time and fines. I can show you the statute." She took out her cell phone to pull up the website.

"You don't have to school me, lady," grumbled the

postmaster. "How are we supposed to track that letter? There's no return address."

"Fingerprints. DNA." Was he a simpleton?

He exhaled an impatient snort and said she could report it to the police. If it had to go to the Postal Inspection Service, it could go there. But postal inspectors took on serious matters like fraud and terrorism. Fingerprints and DNA were a whole other level. As if she were not, in her own way, being terrorized by this squadron of ghosts. She was angry at the secret sender and now at the postmaster who thought that she was worked up about a whole bunch of nothing.

She drove to the police station and spoke to a cop, a big guy with a rosy face who had a silver badge and a name tag that read Randell. On his sleeves were the insignia of the Middlehampton Township police, and on his big black belt hung his pistol, handcuffs, nightstick, radio and what she assumed was a taser. Protective or oppressive, depending on what side of the array you were on. Cathy repeated her story, showed Randell one piece of bagged and labeled evidence and her log in the small spiral notebook.

"Impressive. You ought to come work for us."

She shrugged with modest pride. She worked her

face into a half smile, then worry drew down her expression.

"Sorry you're getting pranked," Randell said as he took notes. She didn't much like that he called it a prank, but that's how Doug had seen it, too. Had she had words with a neighbor? A breakup with, er, an admirer? He eyed her wedding ring. A problem with a coworker? She shook her head. Not serious enough to be sent for fingerprint and chemical analysis, he said, and told her to continue collecting the evidence, to keep an eye out, to document as much as she could. He gave her his card. She felt deputized, hopeful, and empowered.

Back at home, she dug into last night's mooshu beef and fried rice. She looked at her kitchen table, her walls, and doors. All the solidity around her. She peered out the window at the wide blue sky, the space that eleven-year-old Kyle said was not as empty as you'd think. Who was out there making trouble for her?

She was also mildly worried to learn, via Jenny, that Kyle not only enjoyed looking at the moon, the stars, and planets with his telescope but that he had recently been using it to look through neighbors' windows. He'd watched, according to Jenny, people eating, sitting at their computers, sometimes even walking around naked. While Cathy did not hit the roof, she told Kyle very firmly not to spy on the neighbors and threatened to take his telescope away if the peeping continued. After this, the Eastmans closed all their blinds and draperies after dark.

***

Betsy, in her pink "Get Fit" sweats, sauntered up to Cathy as she paged through her mail.

"Good grief, what is it?" Betsy said as she saw Cathy's expression tighten.

"Something in the mail," replied Cathy. Betsy recognized this as the voice of few words, the voice people used when they wanted to avoid a conversation with her. But this was no time to back off. It was time to press.

"Looks like it bugs you. Like it *really* bugs you. Do you want to talk about it?"

"Listen, I don't really know you."

"We keep running into each other. Well, I mean you're running. I'm walking. I'm Tiffany, by the way."

Cathy said her name was Cathy then mumbled that she had to go. She didn't tell her to have a good one.

Rejected, pissed off actually, Betsy had to remind herself of science, the need for objectivity and professional distance. The high path. But now she was extra glad she'd picked Cathy as her subject. What a bitch!

Two days later, Betsy dashed out of the house as she saw Cathy rounding the bend. They were on a first-name basis now. She wasn't sure what runner protocol was, but she opened a conversation with Cathy, which caused her to stop running.

"Get one of those letters today?"

Cathy stood catching her breath and regarded Betsy with a focused eye. "Tiffany, what do you mean? What letters?"

"The letters that bug you."

"Did I tell you something about letters?"

"The other day." Betsy gulped. Had she misremembered?

"I don't believe I told you what I got in my mail." Her eyes darted around as if she were trying to recall the previous conversation.

"I've been getting some strange letters myself," said Betsy.

"Oh, what kind?" asked Cathy. The attention made Betsy want to share and confide, but it also made her fearful of scattering lies that were too hard to keep track of.

"They're about nothing. They're blank."

"Who are they from?" Cathy looked at Betsy with a keen eye.

"They're from nobody," said Betsy her face flushing. "No return address." Boy, this was dumb, she thought. Deeper and deeper into dumb.

"Did you inform the post office? The police? Maybe we should go together to report this. Bring all our letters. Show the evidence. Maybe there's more to this than we know."

Betsy loved the sound of "we" and the imagined common ground.

"Only I threw my letters away." Betsy could feel sweat beading on her upper lip. Then she glanced at her watch and said she had to be somewhere. "Have a good one," she said.

Cathy gave her a sober look then nodded in acknowledgment.

Betsy shuffled back to her house. Her mother greeted her with a harangue about leaving the dishes in the sink, the coffeepot on, her towels on the bathroom floor, and not taking out the trash.

"Quit nagging."

"You know what nagging is? It's reminding someone to do something they should have done in the first place."

"So, I'm worthless. Why don't I just get a knife and stab myself?" said Betsy.

"If it'll make you happy, go right ahead."

A vision of her mother as a warty toad formed in her mind. Still, her mother owned the house, and her social security funded the taxes and utilities. Betsy financed the rest of their needs with her freelance pay. Neither could get by without the other. So hostile symbiosis it had to be.

Now she had her new friend to think of and their shared plight. Maybe it was time to start sending herself blank letters and keeping them for evidence in case the two gals made an afternoon of it, had coffee together, then drove over to the post office or the police station to talk about the anonymous letters. Suppose the cops gave her a polygraph test. Or put her in an airless room to interrogate her. It was time to close down the experiment.

***

There was a woman, Cathy told Doug, an unpleasant woman in the neighborhood who crossed her path, what maybe seven times now? She was the nosy type and particularly interested in what Cathy got in her mail. They had settled on the couch and were about to watch *Goldfinger*.

"Fleming has this part in the novel," said Doug, "where Bond runs into Goldfinger one time too many. And Goldfinger says, 'Mr. Bond, they have a saying in Chicago: Once is happenstance. Twice is coincidence. The third time it's enemy action.'" Doug nodded to Cathy with a meaningful look. "The way that woman materializes before you, it can't be accidental."

Cathy's expression lifted with sudden insight. She sprang from the couch and ran to the garage to note, as well as she could recall, the dates of Tiffany's magical appearances. Often they were on days or close to the days she found those sendings in the mail. Yet, Tiffany said that she, too, received the mysterious mail.

Then they watched *Goldfinger*.

For the next two days, instead of going out for her morning run, Cathy peeked through the miniblinds of Kyle's bedroom window. And on the second day, Tiffany in her pink sweats strolled to the Eastman home, paused and looked around. With Cathy nowhere in sight, the other woman shielded her eyes from the morning sun and tried to look through the picture window. Disappointed, she turned back down Parkside Drive.

Cathy quickly sighted Tiffany in Kyle's telescope and stared in awe as she walked in the front door of 4562 Parkside. Cathy had passed the house many times but had not really looked at it closely until now. Its tan siding was faded and in need of repairs. One gutter was partially detached. The garage roof sagged. A scraggly shrub stood in front. Searching the address online, she found that the residents were Estelle Baines, sixty-seven, and Betsy Baines, forty-one. There was no Tiffany. If Betsy lied and said her name was Tiffany, maybe she also lied about receiving the blank letters. Maybe she was the secret sender, methodically destroying her peace, making her chase after clues, taking up all her mental and emotional energy. Then trying to be her girlfriend. It was sad, pathetic, absurd, and nuts. God save her from a life like that.

Cathy could have paid one of the search sites for the residents' phone number and email. Instead, she paid a visit to Officer Randell. He was even more impressed with her than before. She had mild qualms about her sneakiness, as sneakiness was nothing to brag about. But her sneakiness was nothing compared to the pink lady's sneakiness. Singling her out, and for what?

***

Betsy was finishing her pancakes when the doorbell rang. "Middlehampton Police. Open up, please," announced a stern male voice. She was shocked to find two police officers each with his pistol, handcuffs, nightstick, radio, taser, and who knows what else hanging off their big black belts. Betsy's heart began to race. Would they bend her head down when they put her in a cop car? Would they search the house? Take her computer?

"Are you Betsy Baines?" said the one whose name tag read Randell.

Betsy's mother, still in her housecoat, hovered behind her daughter. "Give us a moment please, ma'am," Curtis said to her.

Randell asked Betsy to step outside, took down her full name and date of birth. He asked if she went by any other names. She frowned at him as if to say *who would ever do that?* Randell and Curtis looked her straight in the eye.

"We have had reports of mailings being sent to a specific individual in the neighborhood, in plain white envelopes with no return address, blank sheets of paper inside."

Curtis looked like he was trying to keep a straight face.

"Are you responsible for this?" asked Randell. His expression looked like cement.

"No," she replied in voice she feared sounded false bottomed. The weird idea floated before her that some other person was living her life. You could never be sure what other people were up to.

"Well, that's fine, Ms. Baines, but if for some reason you are the person sending the anonymous mail, please stop. And if you know who is doing it, get them to stop because it is bothering your neighbor. No one wants this to get any more serious than it is now…involving the U. S. Mail and all."

Betsy nodded. She had a lump in her throat. The cops drove off. Her mind slid through all the possible repercussions. She could be arrested. She would have a criminal record. She'd fail background checks. She'd be unable to get work. Her mother might kick her out. She might go to jail. Was she a criminal?

"Yesterday afternoon, that duo came to see me. Are you going around telling people your name is Tiffany?" Her mother's eyes widened until the whites showed all around.

"Why don't you just turn on the TV, Mom?"

"Why don't you just act normal?"

"Why don't I just punch you in the face?"

"Why don't I just throw you out of this house?"

Betsy deleted the Excel file of her mailings, observations, and interviews with Cathy Eastman, even though she knew that a computer forensics expert could dig the file out anyway. She buried her surgical gloves in trash. How did the cops know to come to her door? Her mailings were completely untraceable. She put the lens caps on her binoculars and stowed them next to her dictionary, style manual, a ceramic pot she made in grade school, and her old teddy bear. She felt sick to her stomach. She cleaned the bathroom, picked up her clothes, and took out the trash without being asked.

***

Cathy Eastman looked through her son's telescope as the cops questioned Betsy Baines. She did not exult in the scene. She reflected on how much precious time and peace those sendings had stolen from her life. They were intentional and relentless. Not a big bunch of nothing at all. Like a false rumor, they accumulated power, avalanched her with fear and anxiety. Why had Betsy Baines campaigned against her like that? Against a perfect stranger? Well, they would ghost each other from now on if they happened to cross each other's path. Unless a confession and apology were forthcoming. Doubtful, but you never knew. In that case, she supposed that she would be honor bound to accept the apology. Deep down, she felt sorry for Betsy Baines. She seemed to be home all the time. Did she work? She appeared to be very lonely. Did she have friends? It was so hard to make friends.

Truly amazing, how much you could see at close range with a telescope. Cathy spied a fine red-shouldered hawk on the Baines's roof, the hawk's handsome black-and-white-banded tail clearly visible. The sharp-eyed creature scanned the terrain looking for prey. For a second, she thought she saw the raptor turn its gaze to her.

# House Parties

Jess and Rand Morrow, she in the Kia with the children and he in his silver Porsche, left the Philadelphia townhouse they had just sold and drove to their new home in the Poconos. Rand nosed through traffic and zipped out of sight. It made Jess think of those algebra problems she could never solve, the ones with two trains traveling at different speeds, where you had to figure out how far apart they'd be by noon. Only the Morrows were headed to the same place and for the same reason, so why the race? Or maybe it was a good sign, Rand all excited to start their new life. She tucked her hair behind her ear and adjusted her glasses.

They had made a pact. Their new home in Edgewood Village, a development carved out of forest and field, was to be their fresh start, a haven where they would collaborate on the art of their marriage, a work Jess hoped would come to resemble a Peaceable Kingdom painting, not the abstract Jackson Pollock mess it was turning out to be.

Before they decided to replant themselves, faithlessness had nearly sawed down their relationship. As soon as covid let up, Rand, who just as easily could have continued to work from home, began commuting full-time back to work, often returning late smelling of his office wife. Jess, needing someone to talk to about the anger and hurt, went into therapy. But that devolved into necking sessions with her shrink, who charged her his usual hourly fee and, after a month or so, tried to sell her on intercourse. Why have half the pleasure when you can have all the pleasure? he would importune, condom packet in hand. He was a very good kisser, but she had her limits, and her guilty conscience wasn't exactly helping matters. So, she broke it off.

Jess and Rand met in college in a class on the love poems of Pablo Neruda. Attracted to each other, inspired by Neruda's lyrics, yearning to give themselves over to love as the poet had, they plunged into the maelstrom and thought of nothing and no one but one another. They married a few years after college in a sustainable wedding: invitations on recycled paper, an all-organic dinner, a gift registry option to donate to the Arbor Day Foundation. For a while, all was sweet as a honeymoon. Whenever the relationship ran off course, sex would always bring them back. But now that they were in their early thirties and seven years into wedlock, parents of Kimmie six and Mikey four, they were off-roading. Really in the weeds. In the living room, in the kitchen, in the car, even while they were out at a restaurant, Rand texted constantly with his office wife, chortling at this, grinning at that. When Jess protested, he'd snap that he was looking something up. Well, then why don't you look up at me? Jess would say, embarrassed by her plaintiveness.

Rejected in favor of the office wife, Jess left Rand to go to bed alone while she stayed up late, sitting at the kitchen table, sketching parts of lions, goats, rabbits, horses, and wolves. She devoted herself to her wonderland of vignettes, scattering the charcoaled heads and hind-ends of beasts on sheets of paper. That she could not finish a figure or arrange the parts into a composition irked Rand far more than it should. He questioned her ability, he from whom she sought shelter in her solitary craft.

The Morrows knew that all this was very bad.

Somehow a ray of grace found its way through the glowering clouds, and the two, being willing enemies and game, agreed to try to reconstitute their union in a new environment. This disappointed their drama-loving friends for whom divorce was a spectator sport and worried their other friends who said that, unless they sought couples counseling, they'd pack their problems along with their dishes and books. Counseling. She hadn't been able to persuade Rand to try counseling with her, so she'd gone alone. Then look what happened.

Location, Jess countered to those doubtful friends,

mattered a great deal when it came to quality of life. Think of immigrants, Rand said. Think of the American spirit, everyone always on the move to a better place.

Therefore, the Morrows left their gentrified section of Philadelphia, which had its own share of threats—carjackings, shootings, street-corner drug deals—and bought a four-bedroom Colonial in a new upscale development in the Pocono Mountains. The purchase made them extra glad that some of their wedding guests had donated to the Arbor Day Foundation, as many acres of woodland had to be cleared to make way for Edgewood Village. And speaking of location, if the plague had taught people one thing it was this: if you could work from home during the lockdown, you could work from home almost anywhere. For Jess, a freelance copywriter always based at home, nothing much changed. Rand, who worked for a digital security firm, had work-from-home privileges all along. How the office wife felt about his decision to return to telecommuting was another matter. Jess overheard a few tense phone conversations, and after that his constant texting ceased. Jess and Rand began to rediscover each other.

As radical as their relocation plan was, the Morrows knew it was genius the moment they set foot in Edgewood Village. No sooner had the sales agent left them to wander around on their own than Trey and Bettina Smith, an attractive Black couple, sauntered up to them and invited them over for a glass of wine, thoughtfully providing juice boxes for the kids. He was an actuary. She made soaps and candles. Ed Lake-Sanders and Jane Lake-Sanders materialized with a bag of chips. They worked for a learning management company.

"Anytime you need anything," said Bettina, "we're here for you."

"Ditto," said Ed. He had pale hair and plump rosy cheeks.

"We love getting new neighbors," said Jane. She wore pink lipstick and had a pillowy figure.

Everyone in Edgewood Village, explained Bettina, was an exile from Philadelphia, New Jersey, or New York, and almost everyone worked at home in tech, finance, marketing, digital this or database that. Since all had left their original communities to live in this new place, the residents were eager to forge new ties. Indeed, they were mad for parties. Not a weekend went by, said Trey, without a gathering, large or small, at someone's house.

Yes, what a very good idea this move was, mused Jess as she drove along the turnpike. Peace, fresh air, safety, a new start. Rand's divorce from the office wife. A break-up with the shrink. New friends.

An exceptionally large committee of turkey vultures appeared in the distance. Like debris from a slow-motion tornado, the birds swirled in the air.

The rumble strips on the highway shook her to attention. Heart thumping, she swerved back into her lane. Drivers honked at her. The jerk of the car and the commotion woke the kids. Kimmie looked bewildered. Mikey started to cry.

"Don't cry, baby," she comforted him. "Mommy's here." Shaken, she continued with keen attention and forty minutes later pulled up to their new home.

Rand, looking sporty in his Hawaiian shirt, slightly sweating in the July heat, was talking to Scott and Charlotte McGillan, their next-door neighbors. The McGillan's toddler sat in a stroller protected by a sunshade. Rand waved merrily at Jess as she struggled the children out of their car seats.

Charlotte angled an expectant look at Rand.

"Hey, Dad," said Scott nudging Rand, who saw that he ought to hustle over to help with the kids.

Every second, Jess loved Edgewood Village more and more.

After the Morrows settled into their home, the Mc-

Gillans hosted a welcome party. Jess wore a yellow sundress and a silvery headband that complemented the light-blue frames of her glasses. Rand came in Bermuda shorts and a bold striped shirt. The Morrows got a crash course in the neighbors, and the neighbors got a crash course on them. Yes, they'd moved here to flee the city. Working from home was the best, the one good thing to come of the covid shutdown. Of course, they were nature lovers. That was half the reason they'd come here. The rush of introductions took place amid the clinking of ice in highballs, the uncorking of wine bottles, the uncapping of bottles of beer. The Morrows brought finger sandwiches. Trey and Bettina came with canapés of lox and cream cheese on little squares of party rye. Stan Goldberg, who developed immersive geographic software, and Mimi Goldberg, a social media marketing consultant, brought pigs in a blanket.

Jane Lake-Sanders, swaddled in a pink bandeau top, went around saying *voulez-vous* to everyone as she offered her saltines topped with squirts of canned cheese.

"I'll take one of those," said Stan.

"I'll bet you would," said Mimi.

Frank Stunkard, an annuity salesman, also helped himself to Jane's saltines. He wore a white polo shirt unbuttoned to show his hairy chest. His wife, Sophie, who taught Zumba at a local gym, was absent. Jess began to see who *voulezed* who.

People started to talk about the January 6 riot at the Capitol and the attempt to overturn the election. Frank said his wife believed that the 2020 presidential election was rigged.

"Well, Biden won fair and square, and I don't go for the Big Lie," said Mimi.

"Neither do I," said Frank. "I'm just saying that's what Sophie thinks."

"That's Sophie for you," said Ed. "She has her own ways. By the way, do you ski?" he pivoted the conversation to Jess and Rand. "Jane and I ski." He ushered the Morrows through the crowd and introduced John Somersby, a financial advisor, and then Ken Dobbs and Ray Hernandez, a gay couple. Ken was a computer systems engineer, and Ray specialized in face recognition software. Funny the way all these tech professionals were living in the woods, thought Jess. It turned out that Ken and Ray were hunters and also loved to barbeque.

"We have the Audi of grills," said Ken. "Not the Mercedes of grills."

"He wanted the Mercedes of grills," said Ray.

"But I didn't buy the Mercedes of grills. I wanted my husband to be happy, so I economized."

Impressed at their good example, Jess left Rand to soak up more marriage tips from Ken and Ray and wandered off to check on the kids who were playing with the other guests' children in the McGillan's playroom. Jess couldn't decide who was the most cutting-edge tech professional in Edgewood Village. Was it Ray Hernandez? Or Scott McGillan? Scott was an industrial designer who consulted with international clients in a virtual workspace. His avatar talked to his clients' avatars or something like that.

"You should see him," said Charlotte. "He looks like he's in a science fiction movie with his headset on." A part-time church secretary, Charlotte was one of the few residents of Edgewood Village who didn't work from home. "And the church has a daycare center in case you need that."

"The answer to my prayers," replied Jess. Really, could there be a better place than Edgewood Village?

The Morrows walked home carrying the children as coyotes howled in the darkness.

They had expected to encounter deer, foxes, and the usual assortment of small mammals, but the wolfish canines came as a surprise.

"What do you think of Jane?" Jess asked Rand as the two undressed for bed.

"Kind of hot to trot. What do you think of Stan?"

"Same."

"Maybe it's just party behavior. Acting like it's college, mixing things up for fun." Rand nestled his genitals against Jess's back.

"Party behavior," echoed Jess.

She learned more about the coyotes. They were shy and usually trotted off into the cover of trees as soon as they sensed you. They were very smart but very bad if you kept chickens. When Ken and Ray's cat went missing, the neighbors debated whether it had gone feral or if a hooter dog had snatched it.

Jess began to sketch coyotes, parts of them at least, from photographs. She did some research and learned that male coyotes sniffed out female dogs in heat, so you had to spay or keep your dog indoors during estrus. The two species could mate, and then you'd get coydogs. Coyotes paired for life. Only if the female died, did the male seek another mate, and sometimes the widowers stayed single.

On a Saturday afternoon, some of the men gathered to shoot hoops at the home of John Somersby. The women kept an eye on the children who romped on John's well-tended lawn and cheered on the guys. Mimi sidled up to Jess. She revealed that John's wife had died of breast cancer a year ago. They'd had no kids. The Stunkards were childless too. Frank had had a health scare last winter. He'd called the ambulance himself. His wife didn't trust the medical establishment and wanted to treat him with herbs and vitamins she bought online. She was an anti-vaxxer and anti-masker, and she liked guns. No surprise there, considering her politics. But she had a dog she adored, a German Shepherd, and loved her so much that she wanted to breed her. Maybe because of the no-kid thing. You never knew.

Bettina and Charlotte tried to redirect the conversation to TV shows, cocktail recipes, the local outlets, and summer festivals, but Mimi carried on. They edged away. The Stunkards and the Lake-Sanders, neither of whom were at basketball, were only mildly married, she whispered to Jess. "A certain amount of mixing and matching goes on here. Not with everyone, of course." She cast a righteous glance at Bettina and Charlotte. "Just the free thinkers." John liked to talk to the girls, she explained, but you could totally understand that, the poor guy. He was trying online dating. Mimi said nothing about her and her husband Stan. Jess wondered how Mimi sized up the Morrows. The gossip was a heaping helping of everything you wanted to know or maybe didn't want to know, but clearly couldn't ask. It also made Jess's ears feel dirty. Not many secrets in Edgewood Village. Social media marketing was a perfect career choice for Mimi. She saw all the connections and intersections, or appeared to.

Jess's parents drove up from Elkins Park, and Rand barbequed steaks on his new grill, which Jess noted proudly was a highly rated reliable grill but not a luxury grill.

"The one that our neighbors, Ken and Ray, have is the Audi of grills. Ours is more like the Toyota of grills. But I wanted Jess to be happy, so I didn't buy high-end."

"Best steak I've ever had," said Jess's dad.

"Ken and Ray are husband and husband," said Rand. "They host a fair number of barbeques. We have a lot of parties here. Almost one a week."

The parents looked surprised.

"That's all well and good," Jess's mom said. "You need allies to watch your house when you're away, pick up your packages and such. But oughtn't you keep a little distance?" She warned about yentas, knowing too much about one another's business, and mentioned, off hand, something about thy neighbor's wife. The memory of the conversation with Mimi buzzed in Jess's head. She cut her steak. Rand helped himself to more potato salad.

"I'm taking online drawing classes now," Jess broke in. She was pursuing her artwork with happier ambition these days and had bought herself new charcoals, graphite pencils, and high-quality drawing paper. She no longer stayed up late at night working at the kitchen table after Rand had gone to bed.

"Online? How do you do that?" asked her father.

"You upload images of your work to a web platform. It goes into the cloud and the teacher critiques your work."

Jess's dad shook his head. "Everything is in the cloud. Everything is disappearing into thin air."

"We call it the post-physical environment," said Rand. This did not cheer up his father-in-law.

"You're still here, Zvi," said Jess's mom, patting her husband's arm. She opened the box of rugelach she'd brought from Lipkin's Bakery and asked if Jess were still drawing animal parts and what the teacher said about her work.

"She said that I should go beyond the studies and try to put things together in a composition, like one animal chasing another animal or attacking it or eating it."

"That would be interesting," said Rand.

"Sounds violent," said Jess's mom.

"It's nature. Red in tooth and claw," said Jess. "I told her I'd think about it."

On one of their weekend drives, the Morrows had visited a local museum and came upon one of Edward Hicks's *Peaceable Kingdom* paintings. The Quaker artist had lived in the area. Jess's heart rushed when she saw the work, which she had learned of in an American art class in college. As in the prophesy of Isaiah, the wolf dwelled with the lamb, the leopard lay with the kid. An ox with great U-shaped horns stood by a bear and a lion. Hicks's lion stared at the viewer with wide-open eyes. Jess couldn't decide if that was a look of accusation or expectancy: as in when are you humans going to learn to live together in peace? She thought of trying to group her animals together that way, in a pose unreal and ideal.

That night, as the Morrows walked Jess's parents past the bear-proof trash can containers to their car, they saw a dark form trot into the woods.

"It's only a coyote, Mom," Jess assured her. "Not a wolf."

"What a relief," replied her mom.

"At least it's not a bear," said her dad.

Trey and Bettina Smith gave an early fall party. Everyone was drinking rum punch, Bettina's specialty. Trey presented an array of chopped salads and humus and tahina with pitas. Jess brought chopped liver. She and Trey got into a big chopped liver discussion. Should you use schmaltz or go healthier with light mayo? Caramelize the onions? Add thyme?

The Smiths had a rec room and the Disney channel. The neighborhood children settled down in front of the TV with their toy trucks, stuffed animals, and snacks.

Stan Goldberg came up to Jess with a tray of honeydew cubes on toothpicks.

"Honey do?" He punned with a wink or was it a leer. "Honey do?"

Jess took a piece of fruit with what she hoped was a festive smile. Stan moved on to Jane Lake-Sanders with the same line.

"Honey, do," she giggled, opened her mouth wide, and let Stan feed her pieces of melon. Later Jess found them canoodling in the walk-in pantry.

"Viewer discretion advised," commented Bettina as she floated by, took Jess by the elbow, and guided her to the safe harbor of Scott and Charlotte.

"I Wanna Dance with Somebody" played on the sound system. Rand took Bettina for a whirl. Ken and Ray did waves and dips. Stan and Jane went at it disco style. Mimi knocked back rum punch. John Somersby was dancing with Sophie Stunkard. She was a sinewy redhead. She gyrated, twirled, and moon walked, showing off her body skills. John eyed Jess for the next dance. A cha-cha came on, a dance that always made her smile. John held out his hand in invitation. He was a very good dancer and led with finesse.

When "Fireball" started up, Sophie snaked her way over to Rand. He tried to shimmy and mirror her fancy footwork, but he could not match Sophie's Zumba-instructor skill. No one could. She moved closer to Rand thrusting her hips. Jess gave Rand the side-eye. Frank Stunkard danced with the McGillans. The Stunkards liked to dance, just not with each other. Hits by Rihanna came on, then "Shake It Off" by Taylor Swift. Finally, a slow dance brought Jess and Rand together. John Somersby wanted to cut in, but Rand declined.

The Morrows walked home carrying their children. A great horned owl hooted from someone's rooftop. In the woods, the coyotes called to their kind. Once the children were in bed, Jess and Rand had their usual post-mortem about the party.

"I saw you dancing with Sophie. Really going at it, you two."

"Seriously? I couldn't keep up with her. Anyway, she asked me to dance. I didn't ask her."

"Frank told me that she went to Washington on January 6 to cheer on the insurrectionists. He couldn't talk her out of going."

"That was two years ago. Maybe her politics have died down."

"Does a leopard change its spots?"

"Maybe the spots fade," Rand said wishfully. "John Somersby likes you. He looks at you a lot."

"He's a very good dancer. He needs someone to dance with."

"No. He likes you."

"Well, I like you better," said Jess.

A few weeks later, when Rand was in New York consulting with a client and the kids were at daycare, John Somersby appeared unannounced at the Morrow's door. He presented Jess with some freshly baked oatmeal raisin cookies on a green ceramic plate. The cookies smelled divine. John was an investment advisor, but he hadn't come to her house to talk about stocks and bonds. She couldn't very well take his offering and send him on his way, so she poured him a cup of coffee. He asked how she liked the neighborhood and inquired about her job. Most people found her corporate communications work boring, but John listened with respect as she talked about brochures, press releases, and newsletters. He even asked relevant questions. Jess tried to stick to business. How long had he been in finance? How did he like working from home? Did he often visit clients?

John was a tall man with handsome slender features. They were alone together in her house. A moment which, of course, he had planned, and it felt vaguely like entrapment. Jess fibbed and said she had a scheduled phone call with a client, then rose to clear their plates. John stood up with her, and, after she placed the dishes in the dishwasher, he turned her toward him and looked into her eyes. Then he put his hand on the back of her neck and kissed her. At first softly, then his mouth began to search. She felt herself being taken. She liked it and she did not like it. She stepped back from him.

"I was just..." he managed. "I don't know what got into me. I thought we had a connection. It's okay around here as long as we're discreet. A lot of people here are free thinkers." There was that phrase again. The one Mimi had used, like it was a local shibboleth.

"I'm sorry, but we can't do this." She felt sad rejecting a lonely widower and a little tiny bit sad denying herself John Somersby. She gave him back his green ceramic plate with the leftover cookies. How to explain the plate and the cookies to Rand? Or how to return the plate to John later without making it look like a next step on her part? Everyone in Edgewood Village was home almost all the time. How could someone not have seen him walking up to her front door? Or worse, if he had walked up to her back door. A backdoor man. Either way, people would assume things, and what if Mimi had spied them?

Jess said she hoped that they'd remain friends. Then she let him out the front door, mindful of the old superstition Rand had taught her: you go out the door you came in. It had something to do with good luck and bad luck.

One November afternoon as Jess was watching Mikey on his tricycle and Kimmie on her two-wheeler, Sophie Stunkard strolled by with Penny, her purebred German Shepherd. The kids wanted to pet the dog, but Sophie pulled back on the leash. The dog was not as well trained as she could be, Sophie explained.

"If all goes well, we'll have puppies," she told the children. "And you can play with the puppies." She explained to Jess that Penny had a stud date with an AKC sire. It was all lined up for early February when Penny would be in estrus. Jess recalled what Mimi had told her about Sophie and Penny, that the woman felt an inordinate amount of love for her dog and wanted more little Pennys.

"Penny's a good girl. Aren't you, Penny?" cooed Sophie. She caressed the dog behind its ears, then knelt and buried her face in the dog's strong neck. Then the two continued on their walk.

It touched Jess and sorrowed her to see how extravagantly this strange woman adored her dog. On the other hand, German Shepherds always made Jess nervous. The breed had a bad political history. Jess wondered where Frank Stunkard fit into all the parts of Sophie's life. The man was no prince. Jess caught wind of something between Frank and Jane Lake-Sanders. Well, that Jane got around. One of the free thinkers. Jess supposed that if all parties in the marriage were free thinkers it was okay, but what if only one of them was a free thinker? Or if one of them used to be then stopped seeing things that way? Frank made Jess feel squirmy. He often fixed her with a probing look.

The air had a bite in it. As Jess led the children home, she spied a papery gray hornet's nest dangling from a leafless sycamore. It made her think of a piñata filled with bad things.

The months passed with an assortment of small gatherings and bigger parties. Jess and Rand hosted a potluck supper. Ken and Ray held a barbeque. They used their outdoor grill in all weathers. No one threw any more dance parties. At least none that she knew of. The Morrows spent Chanukah at the home of Jess's parents. They celebrated Christmas with Rand's family. One morning in January, Jess saw John Somersby wave good-bye to a woman who pulled out of his driveway. She surmised that she would receive no more of his courtly attentions.

The Stunkards announced that they were hosting a party. It was to be a doggie bridal shower for Penny to celebrate her scheduled date with the AKC stud. Jess and Rand lined up a babysitter. Everyone was to bring a dog treat for Penny and dress fancy, or as fancy as you cared to, Sophie amended. And there would be dancing.

"She certainly dotes on that dog," Rand said.

"It makes me sad," said Jess.

"But then there will be puppies and more little things for her to love."

Jess bought a Busy Bone at the grocery store. She made spicy cheese dip for the snack table. She dressed for the party in a pink sweater and a swingy black skirt. The moon was out, and the snow reflected the lunar light, which brightened up the night. John Somersby approached the Stunkards' house accompanied by a woman. Maybe the same woman who'd driven off that one morning from his house.

"Looks like you've got competition," said Rand.

"Maybe that online dating has paid off for him."

The Stunkards, well, presumably Sophie, had taped bridal shower decorations to their windows and tied helium balloons to their mailbox. It was the first time the Morrows had been in the Stunkards' house. It smelled of dog and woodsmoke. Frank greeted the guests and took their coats. Sophie played DJ and tended bar. Jess looked around. In a hutch stood several of Frank's framed sales awards, Sophie's Zumba commendations, her framed NRA marksman certificates, a photo of Sophie and Penny, a red Make America Great Again hat, and a handgun. A fire crackled in the fireplace. Over the mantlepiece hung what looked like a high-powered rifle. Lots of people in the Poconos hunted, but Jess didn't know if they did it with high-powered rifles. She wasn't sure if the display of firearms should bother her, but it did.

"I'd like you to meet my girlfriend Maggie," said John as he introduced a pleasant-faced woman to Jess and the rest of the neighbors. The two women shook hands.

Rand went to mingle with the Smiths and the McGillans. Jess wandered around the living room and den.

The Stunkards had a sliding glass door that let out onto their patio, and beyond that lay their lawn, then the woods. You could see quite a way out thanks to the light of the moonlit snow. Unlike the Morrows and most of the neighbors, the Stunkards had not fenced their backyard. Despite her qualms about the rifle over the mantlepiece, Jess settled on the sofa by the fireplace.

Frank sat down next to her. He made small talk about the weather and her spicy cheese dip.

"Looks like your friend has an official girlfriend," he said with a tilt of his head

"She seems like a lovely person. So nice of you guys to host a party. I'm sure Sophie is looking forward to those puppies."

"Perfectly okay to change the subject," he said. Frank stared at her breasts then moved his gaze up to her eyes. "Let me see how you look without your glasses."

Shocked and embarrassed, Jess blushed. What a thing to say. It was like asking her to take off her clothes. Very old-school sexist. A Dorothy Parker poem came to mind, the one about men seldom making passes at girls who wear glasses. All the more reason to keep the glasses on.

"I like seeing," said Jess with a shrug. "Gotta keep them on to see."

Frank's expression dropped.

"Where's the guest of honor?"

"We put her in the basement. She's irritable because she's in heat. Barking, snapping, being a bitch. Hence the phrase, right?"

Frank was such a dick. Jess thought of Penny, the poor thing. Not that she wanted to have the dog around, but she could hear her constant barking, scratching, and banging. The guests edged away from that angry racket as they passed by the basement door.

"We brought Penny a Busy Bone for her bridal shower. I bet she'd like that Busy Bone now," said Jess. "Good luck with the breeding." She got up to freshen her drink.

Sophie was playing Zumba music, a mix of Latin dance styles. Rand asked Jess to cha-cha. John and Maggie were on the dance floor. He nodded to Jess in acknowledgment, then returned, smitten, to Maggie.

Penny, riled up and neglected, barked and banged relentlessly. Sophie ran down to the basement to soothe the bride-to-be then returned to invite Rand to a merengue. She was slinked into a short tight red dress with rows of fringe that swayed when she shook. Their merengue went well as long as Sophie was stepping solo, Rand attempting to mirror her steps. But he got bolixed up when she reached for his hands. The Latin dancing was beyond the skill of most of the guests, who were happy enough to sway and step free form. Everyone gathered in a circle to watch Ken and Ray go into a hot bachata. The couple beckoned Frank to join them. The three turned, separated, twirled, joined hands. People applauded. But nothing could drown out the dog noise. Frank went down to the basement, brought Penny up on a tight leash, opened the sliding glass door, and led her outside. Peace settled over the party.

All was fun and festive until Sophie charged up from the basement with a stricken look.

"Where's Penny?" she shrieked. Jess knew that voice. A frantic mother's voice, the kind you use when you can't find your child.

Somebody turned off the sound system, and everyone froze.

"I put her on the tie-out. Her barking was driving everyone nuts," said Frank. "We can watch her through the patio door."

"But you're not watching her!" Sophie shouted. "She's out in the open!"

"Relax. Everyone's dog is in their house."

"The coyotes! The coyotes!" screamed Sophie. She flicked on the backyard lights. Everyone ran to the sliding glass door and gasped. A coyote had mounted Sophie's chained-up pure-bred German Shepherd. Penny's rump was up, her tail angled to one side. The two canines were locked. A feral wail escaped from Sophie's throat.

She yanked open the sliding glass door, her face contorted with rage. She picked up a lawn chair, charged at the wild animal, then dashed back into the house. Mimi Goldberg ran to the snack table, grabbed her casserole and threw it at the coyote.

"Turn on the garden hose!" yelled Jane Lake-Sanders, but, of course, the Stunkards had shut off the outside water for the winter.

Jess joined the guests in hazing the wild animal, "Shoo! Scram! Get out of here!" They began to toss wine bottles, beer cans, and snowballs. Some of the projectiles hit Penny. A few landed on the coyote. Red fringe swinging, Sophie barreled through the crowd, pointing her handgun.

She pumped shot after shot into coyote. It fell away from Penny with a *woomph* and lay on the snow in agony. Penny turned to her mate, sniffed at him, confused or curious, then backed away. Jess, Rand, and all the guests stared in horror at the scene, which looked like a terrible movie that had turned into real life. Jane vomited. Jess tried not to. The coyote was spasming and panting. Frothy blood flowed from its mouth. Though paralyzed, it was alert enough to see Sophie approach. He looked at her with his yellow eyes. She took the kill shot. His animal soul fled, fled somewhere.

Sophie was shaking, but she had a gun, and everyone kept their distance from her save Ken Dobbs, who held out his hand for the weapon. He told her it was over now. She could give him the gun. Carefully pointing the pistol away from the people, Ken removed the rest of the bullets. Sophie knelt in the snow and broke down before Penny, but she did not dare touch her beloved dog, who was now somehow a different dog.

Frank was standing by himself. People looked at him, then looked away from him.

"You'll take her to the vet," said Bettina. "He'll check her out. Maybe she didn't…" Her voice trailed off before she could say something like "conceive" or "get pregnant."

"Frank, unhook Penny from the tie-out and take her inside," said Rand.

Frank did as he was told.

Rand walked Sophie inside. He and Scott McGillan sat on either side of her on the couch in front of the fireplace.

"I…I wanted a bridal shower for Penny," she sobbed. "My girl, my Penny," she said over and over.

"She'll be okay. She's fine. She just…" Rand tried to console her.

"…had her first experience," said Scott.

The two men stayed with Sophie while Jess and a group of guests went about collecting glasses and plates, putting them in the dishwasher, packing up leftovers, wiping down the countertops. Through the sliding glass door, Jess saw others cleaning up the backyard, stepping around the bloody corpse of the coyote.

When they had restored the house to order, the guests filed out into the cold February night and walked to their homes in ceremonious silence. No owl hooted. No coyote howled. The snow still glowed in the moonlight, but it was no longer beautiful and seemed to Jess like a cold grave blanket. Was Penny Sophie's one true friend? None of the women in the neighborhood had much to do with her. They didn't like the way she flirted with their husbands. Then there were her politics and weird beliefs. But, oh God, how lonely that strange woman must be. The loneliest people had the deepest bonds with their pets. She gave that dog a good life, that was for sure. What if Penny did conceive? Would Sophie let her give birth to coydogs, try again with a pure-bred sire? Or would she do a spay and abort? In that case, no precious little puppies for Sophie to love, at least not from Penny. What would happen to the Stunkards? Hard to consider what was going on in that house now. She wouldn't be surprised if she heard more gunfire from their house. But she heard no more shots.

Jess expected to find their house a chaos of cookie crumbs and scattered toys, but the babysitter had neatened up the place and even posed the children's stuffed animals into a little friendship circle.

"Did you hear gunfire?" asked the babysitter.

"No. We were at a party," said Rand. "Loud music, lots of talking, you know."

The Morrows did not hold their usual party post-mortem. The whole night was one post-mortem. How quickly, thought Jess, could long-laid plans fall to ruin and mirth turn to grief. The couple did not make love, nor did they speak. They embraced in tender silence and stayed that way until slumber made them separate, and each slid away into the wilds of sleep.

## Acknowledgments


I gratefully acknowledge the following publications in which these stories, sometimes in earlier versions, first appeared.

*Amarillo Bay*: "Evermay Blair"
*Department of Language and Literature.* Bucks County Community College: "Tell Us about Your Experience"
*The Broadkill Review*: "The Path to Halfway Falls"
*Cleaver*: "The Ask Sandwich" and "The Dirty Martini" (under the title "The Birthday Present")
*ELJ/Elm Leaves Journal*: "One beneath the Other"
*Evening Street Review*: "The French Milliner's Model"
*Green Hills Literary Lantern*: "Little Secrets"
*Jewish Fiction.net*: "Frieda and Her Golem"
*The Monarch Review*: "Baby and Gorilla"
*Per Contra*: "The Husband and the Gypsy"
*Press 1*: "The Other Henry Harris"
*The Rag*: "You Take Care Now, Mary Jones"
*Rathalla Review*: "A Visit to the Old House"
*The Satirist*: "Student Rebellion"
*The Saturday Evening Post*: "The Lady with a Hundred Pockets"
*Valparaiso Fiction Review*: "Mothers and Daughters"
*Young Adult Review Network/YARN*: "Monkey Island"

"Tell Us about Your Experience" won first prize in the 2021 Bucks County Short Fiction Contest, judged by Megan Angelo.

The following stories were reprinted in various issues of *The 33rd*, an annual anthology series published by the Drexel Publishing Group for the use of Drexel University students in first-year writing courses: "The Ask Sandwich," "The Lady with a Hundred Pockets," "Monkey Island," "Student Rebellion," and "One beneath the Other."

"The Ask Sandwich" was reprinted in *The Schuylkill Valley Journal* and *Shale: Extreme Fiction for Extreme Times* (Texture Press).

I give deepest thanks to the above-listed publications and their editors and especially to my publisher Tod Thilleman and Aurelia Lavallee of Spuyten Duyvil. This collection would not be possible without the help of many readers and dear friends who read these stories in earlier versions and offered encouragement, edits, and guidance. Thank you, Joy Stocke, Deb Burnham, Michelle Moore, Steve Almond and the workshoppers in the VCFA Post-Graduate workshop, Kathy Volk Miller, Cassandra Hirsch, Jill Moses, Gail Rosen, Valerie Fox, Ellen Foos of Ragged Sky Press, Bill Bayer, Roger Kurtz, Abioseh Porter, Fred Siegel, Miriam Kotzin, and Barbara Levin.

Melina Meshako

LYNN LEVIN is a poet and writer. *House Parties* is her debut collection of short fiction. Levin's previous books include the poetry collections *The Minor Virtues* (Ragged Sky, 2020) and *Miss Plastique* (Ragged Sky, 2013). The co-author of *Poems for the Writing: Prompts for Poets* (Texture, 2019, 2013), Levin is also the translator from the Spanish of the poetry collection *Birds on the Kiswar Tree* by Odi Gonzales (2Leaf/U of Chicago P, 2014). Her poems, short stories, essays, and translations have appeared in *Boulevard*, *The Hopkins Review*, *Southwest Review*, *Michigan Quarterly Review*, *Valparaiso Fiction Review*, *The Broadkill Review*, *Cleaver*, *Mandorla*, *Solstice*, and many other places. Lynn Levin was born in St. Louis, Missouri and lives in Bucks County, Pennsylvania. She teaches writing and literature at Drexel University, and, for many years, she taught creative writing at the University of Pennsylvania. Her website is lynnlevinpoet.com.